Scavengers

Scavengers

A Novel

———

Kathleen Boland

VIKING

VIKING
An imprint of Penguin Random House LLC
1745 Broadway, New York, NY 10019
penguinrandomhouse.com

Grateful acknowledgment is made to Don Congdon Associates, Inc. and
Counterpoint Press for permission to reprint an excerpt from "A Sonnet for
Everett Ruess" by Edward Abbey from *The Best of Edward Abbey*. Copyright
© 1983 by Edward Abbey and copyright © 1994 by Clarke C. Abbey. Reprinted
with the permission of Don Congdon Associates, Inc. and The Permissions
Company, LLC on behalf of Counterpoint Press, counterpointpress.com.

Designed by Nerylsa Dijol

LIBRARY OF CONGRESS CATALOGING-IN-PUBLICATION DATA
Names: Boland, Kathleen (Novelist) author
Title: Scavengers : a novel / Kathleen Boland.
Description: New York, NY : Viking, 2026.
Identifiers: LCCN 2025002120 (print) | LCCN 2025002121 (ebook) |
ISBN 9780593834480 hardcover | ISBN 9780593834497 ebook |
ISBN 9798217061976 international edition
Subjects: LCSH: Mothers and daughters—Fiction |
Treasure hunting—Fiction | LCGFT: Fiction | Novels
Classification: LCC PS3602.O647 S27 2026 (print) | LCC PS3602.O647
(ebook) | DDC 813/.6—dc23/eng/20250620
LC record available at https://lccn.loc.gov/2025002120
LC ebook record available at https://lccn.loc.gov/2025002121

Printed in the United States of America
1st Printing

The authorized representative in the EU for product safety and compliance
is Penguin Random House Ireland, Morrison Chambers, 32 Nassau
Street, Dublin D02 YH68, Ireland, https://eu-contact.penguin.ie.

To my family

We're all bums on a scavenger hunt.

—JOY WILLIAMS

Look, people make shit up all the time. We're all a bunch of filthy liars. White lies, big lies, anonymous sources, self-checkout, dating profiles, cover letters, orgasms, calories, taxes. We can lie about everything and we do. Gold is valuable, diamonds are precious, growth is guaranteed. The most likely to succeed. The best coffee in the city. The greatest country in the world.

Phil preferred a Quarter Pounder with Cheese before going to box seats at the opera. He was calm whenever his preferred football team lost, which was the Browns, so that was all the time. He liked to run half marathons and never got visibly drunk. We were pretty sure he never cheated on his wife, which seemed to impress the guys on the trading desk the most, at least by how often they mentioned it. Inclined to argyle sweaters and tall in a soft-boned, hunched-over kind of way, he was the quiet cousin to whom you could confess your worst secrets because you knew he'd never say a thing. He was steady and he was a pushover. People liked him, people trusted him, and people mostly forgot he was there. Phil was our weather guy.

Other junior analysts considered working for Phil a demotion. Better to be on natural gas or FX where you could create a solid base for an eventual move into securities, where the parties and paychecks were bigger. But Phil was the calmest analyst on the desk, never once hurling a stapler or screaming at an intern. He'd drink exactly one cup of coffee in the morning and scoot in his chair anytime someone walked behind him. He made it seem like you could be in the business for a long time and maybe not turn into an adrenaline-addled asshole. He seemed nice.

But like most nice people, he was weird. He was famous for finding ways to mention how the *Farmers' Almanac* never revealed its methodologies, how its lead researcher published their predictions under a pseudonym because of safety concerns. Phil gave his kid the same fake name, Caleb, but no one was sure if that was on purpose. Like the almanac, Phil hid his methodologies. He was adamantly tight-lipped about the math and data behind his models. Despite being his junior analyst, the closest you got to his research process were the first drafts of his reports, which only revealed a deep aversion to commas. Your career trucked along like this for years, despite rain, snow, sleet, or hail: Phil doing all the heavy-hitting forecasts, while you were left with only the most basic administrative reports.

People loved to come up to your desk and ask, "Want to talk about the weather?" like it was funny. Weather forecasts are the definition of making shit up. In ten days it'll be sixty-five degrees and partly sunny. The hurricane will make landfall. There'll be frost by October. Bullshit. Modern-day weather forecasting was developed by the same guy who founded chaos theory, which makes sense, because we still aren't entirely sure how clouds are formed. Sure, algorithms and satellites mean we have a fairly good idea when there'll be snow, but we can't guarantee how much, or how long it'll stick around. The longer you churn out basic weather analyses, the more obvious it becomes that all those people in front of green screens are gesturing to overeducated guesses. Any kid who's ever woken up at the crack of dawn hoping for a promised six to eight inches and canceled school to find slush and running buses could tell you weathermen were full of shit. But somehow, stumbling into adulthood, we forget that. We worry about rain right up until the bride walks down the aisle, and yet every other day we trust the forecasts despite all indications otherwise.

The bank was no exception. People considered Phil reliable. If he told you what was up with evapotranspiration rates in central Nebraska, you believed him, and nine times out of ten, he was in the ballpark. Phil knew when hurricanes could form, knew the prime conditions for tornadoes, knew which temperatures made a cyclone likely. But he couldn't know what happened next. No one could.

Phil had a stroke. His wife found him on a Saturday night slumped over in his home office, monitors buzzing with Bloomberg chats, cheek against the keyboard as his brain went to jelly. The next week, she called the desk to thank everyone for the gift basket and flowers, said his doctors were shocked at how well he was rebounding, can't keep Phil away from his forecasts for long, ha ha ha. But who could say it wouldn't happen again? After years of toiling away as a glorified research assistant, regurgitating information for a respectable salary plus year-end bonus, now was the chance for you to do—and be—more. Your beloved grandmother just died, and your maybe-boyfriend wasn't answering your texts, but maybe, finally, life was giving you a break. It wasn't like life was getting cheaper; if anything, it was getting more expensive. Your mother's rent, your student loans, your rent. But Phil's position and the mid-six-figure salary that came with it? Up for grabs.

The market is a bunch of people trying to convince you something is really important, trying to get you to buy in, so they can sell out. However, compared to everyone else at the bank, the commodities desk bought and sold things that were actually real. The milk in your latte, your grandmother's wedding ring, a tank of gas, everyone's electric bill. And weather is the fundamental determinant, the factor that impacts every crop, plane, cow, and wire. You need to know the weather if you want to know the price. With Phil gone, you needed something big. Hurricanes were everyone's favorite prom date, analyzed and forecasted so much their names made the news. Earthquakes and tornadoes were glorious but anyone's guess, blizzards too banal.

A memory: Eleven years old, driving with your mother across Iowa. A vast, furious shelf of black clouds carving over the horizon. The sudden gale-force winds made the Chrysler fishtail, your mother pulling over, hazards blinking, cars and trucks barreling past. Within minutes, maybe seconds, pale afternoon daylight gave way to a thundering darkness, wind roaring and rocking the car. At first the two of you were silent, watching as highway signs were ripped from their posts, green sheets for DES MOINES fluttering out across the surrounding fields like lint; in the distance, a radio tower shuddered and tipped over, as if tripped; a corncob whipped out of the murk, missile-fast, and smashed the Chrysler's headlight in an explosion of glass and kernel. You and your mother clutched each other as a swirling spout descended a dozen yards ahead, its pointed wisp touching down in the grassy highway median, and for a frozen, hellish second, the entire world rotated around its skinny axis, until it lunged toward the fields and raged out of view. The car windows burped with pressure changes, the lightning paparazzi, everything and everyone screaming. And then, like a shade snapping up, it was over. The wind died and the light bloomed. Clouds thinned into harmless smears. Gingerly, you opened the car doors. Outside was a different world: the asphalt blanketed in leaves and mud, the surrounding cornfields flattened as if by some giant hand, the silence. Your mother pulled you into her belly and you let her. She wept; you wept. Eventually, a truck pulled up and a grizzled man leaned out the window and asked if everyone was all right. Your mother sputtered, *What the fuck was that.*

Derecho. Understudied. Most common in the breadbasket states, spring through fall. Hulked-out thunderstorms so regional and infrequent most people on the coasts had never heard of them. You didn't know it at the time, but now, researching at your desk, you see how utilities were out for a month, ruining the delivery of various local agricultural reports, and no one realized how many crops were lost until weeks later. Vast swaths of corn and soybeans destroyed. Farms crippled by obliterated silos, collapsed barns, mangled irrigation pipes. Prices exploded, and though they calmed down after a month or so, there was a window. An opportunity.

There were indications of a low-pressure front building in the Rockies, forecasted to sweep out over Iowa and Missouri and into the Midwest. Soybean and corn prices had been shaky all year, regular hedging against farmer debt combined with late frosts. For the next week, increased likelihood of severe thunderstorms with gale-force winds from the Dakotas to Ohio. It was mid-June. Crops were at 40 percent maturity. Phil had started calling the desk, telling traders—not you—his theory on why they should feel bullish about upcoming snowmelts in the Arctic Circle, all good stuff usually, but people couldn't help but notice his slurred words. That's from the stroke, right? they'd ask you nervously. He never really drank, right?

Lightning strikes once, maybe twice.

It was supposed to be a casual thing, a quick mention that there might be a rare severe weather event jeopardizing huge swaths of US farmland, an offhanded comment that would give someone enough pause to ask for more intel, in which case you'd deliver a report that was so succinct, so insightful, it would lead them to wonder whether maybe it shouldn't just be Phil doing this full time; maybe someone else's analyses could be useful, maybe. The derecho may not happen, but it wouldn't matter—what mattered was taking the shot. The credo of the trading desk: Make the play, become a player. You're either up or you're down.

Matt had been down, like everyone else that quarter, but no one knew just how far. Marriage on the rocks, overmortgaged North Shore McMansion, three kids in private school, and clients demanding returns. He was desperate, so when he heard about a possible derecho from you while you shared the elevator that morning, he demanded details. There were the algorithms and models, forecasts and historic trends, but dig deeper: no actual proof. Which, at first, seemed fine to both of you. When a mining company or car manufacturer publishes their earnings report, they always include a fair amount of fudging. Profit can be based on pure speculation and usually is. The entire financial industry runs on gut instinct and probability. When Matt heard you say a weird storm should be monitored because there's a chance of agricultural chaos, he went all in. It shouldn't have surprised you.

When Matt made the trade, a fund in Singapore noticed the order level and hedged, and then a Chicago desk called in a trade, and then another, and then another, and then another. There was soon a frenzy, prices skyrocketing beyond any reasonable level, eye-watering for everyone from Nebraska pension fund holders to Swiss shipping merchants. For the next few hours, the desk was a circus, the Weather Channel blaring from the TVs, the traders—Matt most of all—glued to radar maps, dissecting wind and temperature changes in the Midwest. No one thought to follow up with the person who'd pitched the derecho possibility, despite your having a very public panic attack in the office kitchen, until Phil showed up.

"Show me," he said, still dressed in argyle, though now haggard and hunched in a wheelchair. Matt had called him to explain the situation and Phil demanded to come in. His wife wheeled him up to your desk. He could only use his left hand to scroll through your spreadsheets, the mouse awkward and limp under his palm. The cursor lingered on each data point. Matt stood behind you, loudly snapping gum. Other analysts huddled around, arms crossed and waiting. You chugged a Diet Coke and tasted nothing. After a small eternity, Phil folded his hands into his lap and looked directly at you. "If a storm hits, it hits tomorrow," he slurred softly. "But it won't be big enough for these kinds of positions." The analysts snorted and headed back to their computers. Matt disappeared, supposedly on a smoke break but rumored for the bar around the block. Phil's wife pushed his wheelchair to the elevator, greeting everyone she passed, while Phil fell asleep. You sat at your desk and stayed there, wide-eyed and manic, clicking and refreshing, leaving only to get another can of Diet Coke, for the next eight hours, hyped up on caffeine and pure terror.

Strong winds, reports of a toppled silo in Sioux City, some lightning, and nothing else. Through the phone you could hear Phil shake his head. "Bea, this is so unlike you. Why didn't you consult me first? I could've prevented all of this." But the damage was done. The positions were drawn back, the market stabilized, and soon enough compliance became involved. A meeting with HR, a conference call with the feds. A hold on any research until the situation was fully assessed. After a few days, Matt still hadn't come back from his smoke break. Within a week, a freshly cut Ivy math major is interviewing in the conference room. Within a month, you're in the conference room and they're handing you papers.

People make shit up all the time, but sooner or later, the storm comes. It always does.

PART ONE

Meet Me in the Beehive

A map, it is said, organizes wonder.

—ELLEN MELOY

It was a bland, too-bright afternoon typical of mid-August and Bea Macon had forgotten her sunglasses. Standing at the curb of the Salt Lake City airport, she squinted, trying to decipher the oncoming license plates against the glare, and nearly missed the car. She apologized to the driver as she climbed into the back seat, pulling her small duffel bag in behind her, and made the mistake of telling him she didn't realize it was this sunny in Utah. Of course it is, the driver said, young and cleanly shaven. He pulled out into traffic and began to quiz her. Was this her first time here? Does she ski? Does she hike? Did she bring a water bottle? Bea said yes hoping to get him to shut up, but he wouldn't. The altitude! The inversion! He yelled. Yes, she said. Yes.

Her mother, Christy, had not answered any of Bea's texts. The last response had been the night before, when Christy had sent a picture of a plastic bear of honey squeezed over a mug of tea. CANT WAIT TO SEE YOU TOMORROW HONEY. As of last night, her mother's fingernails were fluorescent blue. Christy had not offered to pick Bea up from the airport, nor had she responded to Bea's updates about how and when Bea's plane was landing, taxiing, and deboarding. A simple acknowledgment would've been appreciated, especially since this was the first time Bea had visited since her mother moved out west. Granted, she had only given her mother twenty-four hours' notice, having bought the one-way from JFK to SLC the day before. Bea sent Christy the flight information with a simple Surprise!!! She provided no other explanation. Her mother had called immediately, breathless and ecstatic, talking hiking plans and packing tips, but Bea hadn't heard from Christy since the honey bear. Perhaps Christy had a busy morning, Bea thought. But what could her mother possibly be doing? It wasn't like Christy had a job. Then again, it wasn't like Bea did, either.

The highway was a dozen lanes, teeming with cars and trucks and trailers in both directions, wider than anything Bea had seen. There was so much space here, Bea thought. Too much space. The driver seamlessly slid into a far lane, accelerated, and asked where she was from. New York, Bea said. Brooklyn. The driver pretended to puke. Have you ever been? Bea asked. The driver shook his head. I hear the people are mean, but you seem nice. Bea's phone binged. The subletter, asking if she could use Bea's towels. Bea sent a thumbs-up. She went to her conversation with her mother. On my way, she sent. She went to the apps and scrolled. No new posts from Grant or Carolyn. Recent emails were mostly bills and Bea deleted them unopened.

"Why are you here?" the driver asked.

"Sorry?" Bea looked up.

He stared at her in the rearview. "What brings you to Salt Lake?"

"My mother lives here."

"You don't sound too excited to see her," he said. They pulled off the highway.

"I'm not."

The driver chuckled. "Then why come all the way out here?"

"I don't really have a choice," Bea said, which was true. For the past month, no one had taken her up on offers to grab a coffee or a drink, not even the lowliest summer interns, and no recruiter had responded to her resume. At first, the silence from Manhattan's financial world was comedic. Sure, she thought, ignore me for a bit. Bea knew they had to pretend like what happened was a big deal. The feds had gotten involved, people had lost some money. But since when did anyone care about the SEC? Since when did a few million matter? She worked for Phil for almost ten years. Phil was a well-respected guy, but people knew he never wrote the daily reports. Hell, Matt had already landed himself a job with a new fund in Chicago. Bea knew she couldn't go back to her old job, but she assumed she'd find something else. She assumed she had more chances, more choices.

Yet here she was, severance almost gone, driving down roads so wide and suburban it was hard to imagine downtown was, as the driver kept saying, only fifteen minutes away. "This is a good neighborhood," the driver said. "No one used to want to be around here, but it's getting nicer. Still cheap, though! Cheap cheap cheap!" He wouldn't stop talking. Bea wished he would stop talking. "Your mother is smart to live out here. Does she rent or own? I bet she pays nothing."

He was wrong, it wasn't nothing. It was something, something Bea paid for but was quickly becoming unable to. She did the math. There was maybe two months left, three if she were smart about it, though doing so would require giving up her apartment and telling

Christy she was unemployed, both of which Bea refused to do, because, she thought, it would be ultimately unnecessary. People who worked at the bank weren't blacklisted, not really. Bea knew too much, had been too close, had worked too hard. The hours, years at the desk: People wanted that experience. They always did. It was only a matter of time until she got another job, and then she'd go back to New York, and it'd be like none of this ever happened.

The car took a hard turn and the houses became smaller, the yards more unkept. The driver asked Bea if he could turn on the radio. Bea shrugged. There was talk of birth certificates, of the president. Bea looked through her bag for her headphones, but then the car stopped. "Nice house," the driver said, unlocking the doors. "Watch out for that juniper bush. It's too big, full of spiders. Like our government!" He began to laugh. Bea muttered a thanks and pulled herself out of the car. She could still hear him laughing as she walked up the front steps.

The house was smaller than she remembered, though Bea had only seen it pixelated on the rental website her mother had sent, and Bea had paid less attention to the photos than the rent and fees. Squat, stucco, square. An overgrown bush with, as promised, spiderwebs. Iridescent house numbers peeled back from the doorframe. She knocked. No response. She adjusted the strap of her duffel, pulled out her phone, and texted her mother. There was a chime inside. Bea knocked again and then the driver called out. "All good?" he asked. Bea nodded, waved, and tried the doorknob. Unlocked. She sighed, annoyed, and then let herself in.

The plants. She'd forgotten about the plants. The house was

filled with them, more foliage than furniture, the light inside gold-tinted and chlorophyllic. Every nook and cranny filled with a leaf or branch or both, shaggy ferns bursting from the ceiling, oxalis bobbing above the cabinets, pothos spewing in lush curtains across the windows. Bea heeled off her sneakers next to a small magnolia by the front door. She recognized the plant, remembered how she would peel open its fat, pink petals and make wishes. She loves me, she loves me not. Bea knew most of her mother's plants, had grown up with the succulents and cacti that crowded the TV stand, the olive bush next to the couch, a collection that would've been proof of a stunningly impressive green thumb if Bea didn't know every last one of them was fake. It was warm in the house, and the slant of sunlight across the room fell on an especially dense patch of bamboo. They smelled the same, the plants, a musty plastic, the smell of her childhood, and the sense memory of it stilled her. Then, a noise from a distant room. "Hello?" Bea yelled. "Christine? Mom?"

There wasn't much else aside from the plants. The house came furnished and the landlord had provided sparse, cheap furniture. A lumpy couch, a narrow coffee table. A TV. A table. Some chairs. Bea shrugged off her duffel onto the couch and made her way to the kitchen. There were a few photos taped to the fridge. One of Bea and Grandma Gertie during a county fair decades ago, Bea small and towheaded and holding blue cotton candy, Gertie rigid and unsmiling and seemingly stern until—look closer—you saw the puff of blue pinched between her fingers. The other of Bea during her college graduation, grinning with her diploma, Gertie next to her with a giant, open-mouthed smile. Both photos curled at the corners, slightly faded. There was a magnet for a local roofing service holding up a cluster of coupons, a short grocery list (eggs, mustard, rubber cement), and a postcard. Bea pulled the postcard out of the stack. It was of a desert scene, red cliffs and blue sky. Slanted, old-fashioned handwriting on the back in thin blue ink. *Let the search begin. See you soon. B.* The postage was stamped a week ago. Bea reread it, confused. Her mother didn't have friends. B? Who else was B?

"Hello, hello!" Christy sang out, appearing from the hallway in a swirl of teal and fuchsia. She held out a small potted aspen tree. "Sorry I couldn't pick you up, honey, but I was getting a surprise for you! Surprise! It's from a local artist. Hand-painted leaves and just look at these branches. See how the bark pattern changes along the stems?" Christy bent the tree toward Bea, unconcerned by the hard angle, since, as Christy explained, its trunk had a pliable steel core. "The craftsmanship is remarkable. Much better than the pictures and that never happens." Her mother rubbed the yellow leaves. "They change color in September, so it's a Virgo, like you." She put the tree down on the table, adjusted its potted base, and then wiped her hands as if there had been actual dirt involved. She pointed at Bea and then the aspen. "Beautiful and beautiful!"

"You know I prefer—"

Christy waved her hands, annoyed. "Oh, I know, I know."

Bea held up the postcard. "Who's B?"

Christy took the card without acknowledging the question, pocketing it into her flowy pants. "How was your flight? It's, what, five hours from New York? You must be tired. You look tired. Even with a two-hour difference, your circadian dysregulation is probably off the charts." Christy began to explain how important it was to sleep as soon as possible after a flight, how plane air quality impacted so much. Bea nodded absently. Her mother hadn't been on a plane since leaving Montreal, and back then, they didn't make you take off your shoes.

Bea opened the fridge and grabbed a beer. "Is it always so hot in here?"

"The AC is crap. Doesn't work half the time, but who needs it? Not me. Didn't in Montreal, don't now. You hungry? You've got to be hungry. Just wait until you see what I made for brunch."

"I'm not hungry," Bea said, even though she was.

"You know what, how about you go take a shower, it'll make you feel better. Don't give me that look, you've been scowling since the moment you walked in. Go shower. You'll do us both a favor, you smell like an airplane. Yes, you do, and when you're done, we'll eat."

"I didn't bring shampoo." Christy never cooked, ever, but maybe her mother had changed. Bea leaned against the counter. Even without AC, the house wasn't so bad. She could stay for a while. Apply for jobs, save money, prepare for what's next. She sipped the beer. Maybe she could finally get a dog. Then, as her mother took the beer out of her hand and took one long gulp, revised: a cat.

Christy belched into her fist. "You can use mine. The extra room is down the hall past the bathroom. Left towels for you on the futon. Now get out of here, I have to cook."

When Bea reemerged, toweling her wet hair, the table was set with a shaker of bacon bits, a package of tortillas, a bowl of raw spinach, and a partially sliced block of cheddar cheese. There was no hot sauce, her mother the type to think pepperoni too spicy. The only cooked food was a plate of scrambled eggs. "You loved breakfast burritos when you were little," Christy said, sitting down across from Bea. "You would insist on them for breakfast, lunch, and dinner. Remember?" Her mother then smiled in a way that was so anxious, so needy, that Bea had to go to the fridge and crack another beer.

It was the first meal they'd shared in nearly six months, ever since the house in Stamford sold. It was spring, a month or so after Gertie died, and Christy had decided to move to Utah. Her mother said she felt drawn westward and Bea didn't have the energy to ask why. Phil had just gone on medical leave. Bea was staying up until dawn covering for him, researching freight congestions and plane routes, desperate for any insights to bring the desk. Once the buyer's earnest money was deposited, mother and daughter planned a goodbye dinner at Gertie's favorite diner on the Post Road. A memorial of sorts, they decided, since there wasn't money enough for a funeral. Christy called ahead to make sure banana cream pie would be available, but then a wintery mix blew into the forecast. Christy left for Utah early to beat it, taking the trusty Chrysler and her favorite plants with her. Bea didn't know her mother had left until Christy was already in Salt Lake, calling about a lease on a small bungalow north of the airport. They still hadn't given Gertie a proper memorial.

Christy was talking about the mountains, how she wanted to go hiking. Bea wasn't listening. She picked spinach from between her molars, stared at the wall. Her phone binged. It was the subletter, asking where her extra sheets were. Bea wondered if the subletter had had sex in her bed yet. Sun crossed the room. She nodded as her mother asked if Bea knew about the lake. "It's actually salty," her mother said. "They're not lying about that." Bea drank her beer and felt her shoulders loosen. She went to her texts with Grant. Nothing from him since the last time she'd seen him, the night she was fired. She'd texted since, even sent a nude, but he never responded. She went to the app, pulled up Carolyn's profile. Nothing new. Same with Martha's profile. Bea put her phone face down on the table and finished her beer.

Christy quieted and motioned at Bea's phone. "Something wrong at work?"

"What?" Bea said quickly, too quickly.

"Work?"

Bea shoveled cold eggs into her mouth. "No," she said between bites. "Everything's fine."

"How are things going with Grant?" Christy loved to discuss Grant, ever since Bea had mentioned him offhandedly about a year ago. It was around the time he had invited Bea to a concert in Bushwick and Bea, thrilled, thought they were finally going to evolve past the late-night texts summoning her to his apartment. That was before Gertie died, before the derecho, before she found out about Carolyn. Christy had been giddy to learn about a boyfriend, which is how Christy referred to him, and Bea never corrected her. Christy brought Grant up every chance she got and Bea usually didn't mind. It had been a relief to talk to her mother about something other than Gertie or money—Bea had even started to look forward to their easy gossip about Grant's latest food delivery choice. The chats made him seem like her boyfriend, made her believe he could be. But that was before. "Aren't you going to the Hamptons or something?" her mother asked. "With all your college friends?"

"Nope," Bea said, keeping her voice casual. "You mentioned hiking? I'd love to hike. Should we go tomorrow?"

Her mother wasn't deterred. "I thought it was all planned. Rented some gigantic house, or it's probably someone's family's house, even worse, but pick your own poison. Going with college friends, right? Martha and, oh, what was her name, Linda? No, that wasn't it—"

"Carolyn," Bea said. Carolyn, her freshman year roommate. Bea stabbed a pile of spinach with her fork and exhaled slowly through her nose. Carolyn.

"Wasn't this the first your first trip together as a couple?"

"I have to work."

"Oh, honey, you sure you can't take some vacation days?"

"No," Bea snapped. She shoved the spinach into her mouth. Grant had once mentioned a Hamptons trip, something over the long weekend with all their old college friends. At the time, it had seemed like an invitation, and Christy had spent numerous calls discussing outfits and logistics with Bea. They had been thrilled, the calls lasted for hours. "I can't because I'm using all of my vacation days to come here." Bea was surprised at how honest it sounded.

Her mother seemed to believe her, too, mouth agape. "All of them?" she asked.

"Yes," Bea said firmly.

"How long are you planning to be here for?"

"Trying to get rid of me already?" Bea meant for it to be a joke, but her tone was too sharp. Christy didn't respond.

They ate quietly, Bea forcing a few more forkfuls of spinach, until Christy pulled a tablet out from a pocket. Her mother jabbed at the screen. Bea pointed at the tablet with her fork. She didn't bother adjusting her tone this time. "Where did you get that?"

Her mother ignored her.

"Do you have a receipt?" Bea demanded. "Can I see a receipt?"

Christy didn't look up. "I need some rubber cement. Want to go to the store with me? We can get green juices on the way, I'm afraid this spinach isn't going to cut it in terms of my digestion today. You still drive, right?"

"I asked you a question."

Christy sighed. "So did I."

"You almost went to jail."

"The guy wasn't even a cop."

"You said you wouldn't do it again. It was, and I quote: a one-time thrill. Presliced cantaloupe, jumper cables, and firewood. We never even used the fireplace in Connecticut."

Her mother leaned back and put her feet up on the chair next to Bea. Christy was wearing the kind of shoes where the toes were separated like fingers in a glove, each with its own individually wrapped rubber sole. "We used it all the time. Remember the solstice party, how we burned our wishes? You made me throw your paper in for you, you were too scared of the flames." Bea remembered but pretended she didn't. Christy waved her hands. "Who cares if they banned me, they're an overpriced Walmart. It was cold and snowy, and I wanted some ambiance before I handed over the keys to my childhood home, sue me."

"That's not the point. The point is you were stealing."

"You show up here and eat my food—"

"I pay for your groceries."

"—and you can't even drive your sick mother to the store."

"Don't even try that, you've been in remission for over five years," Bea barked. A tight and fragile flicker of pain passed over Christy's face. Her mother slowly got up, opened the fridge door, and stood there, not picking anything out, just staring into the cold light.

Bea put her head on the table. She'd left New York twelve hours ago and she was already down a well, falling. Buying the plane ticket was the first productive feeling she'd had since she'd made the derecho pitch, but now that she was here, the feeling was replaced by something caged and mean. The two of them hadn't lived under the same roof since Bea was thirteen and she'd forgotten how much she hated the person she was around her mother. Growing up, Christy tried to argue with Bea about how there were a million different ways they could live, how they didn't have to drink the Kool-Aid. Did Bea really need a training bra? What was she training for? How could she be sure Girl Scouts wasn't a fascist cookie scam? Had she ever met anyone who bought the shortbread ones? Even as a child, Bea knew Christy's questions weren't as groundbreaking as her mother made them out to be. After all, if you name a child Beautiful, you shouldn't be surprised when they develop an eccentricity intolerance. But Bea was no longer a child, no longer Beautiful, and there was no longer the myth of some romantic bohemian dream keeping Christy's promises interesting. Bea did the math. All this time, she'd been doing the math—for both of them. They were running out of options, out of possible lives. The money was nearly gone.

"If I was going to steal a tablet, I would've stolen a much nicer one, believe me." Christy closed the fridge. "We're out of beer."

Bea didn't believe her, but she didn't push the issue, either. She'd gone too far and it'd been so long. She was already here. "What's with the rubber cement?" she tried. Her mother perked up.

"You really want to know?"

"Don't make me regret asking."

Christy disappeared into her bedroom. After a minute, she returned with what looked like a tattered roll of butcher paper. Carefully, she unrolled it on the table. Bea gaped.

A sprawling patchwork of papers, quilted together with mismatched tape and staples. Printouts of Wikipedia entries, hand-drawn outlines of family trees, grayscale topographic maps, sticky notes and torn notebook paper and takeout napkins. There were lines intersecting and pointing, phrases highlighted in thick, bleeding slashes of pink and yellow and blue. Diagrams from a poorly photocopied library book, a printed screenshot of a flood description, a Polaroid of a mining shaft. It took up the entire table, and everywhere Bea looked, there were more notes, more arrows, more information. It was warlike and endless and Bea had to stand up to see it all at once.

Bea watched her mother smooth out various bits of paper, carefully unfolding corners and wiping away nonexistent crumbs. Bea pointed at a section where a photo of a quail was crossed out in highlighter. "What is this?" she asked, though she wasn't sure if she wanted to know.

"LunaGirl and MiniTaco's boyfriends told them—"

"The people from your Scrabble chat room?"

"Scrabble? I haven't played that in forever, not since chemo," Christy scoffed. "No, they're lifting friends, said these guys on their boyfriends' gaming stream talked about a rich guy who buried a million bucks out in the middle of nowhere ten years ago for someone to find. There are clues in a poem he wrote and everything. This guy's family doesn't even know where it is, but you're a millionaire if you find it." Christy tapped a coffee-stained Subway napkin in the lower left-hand corner with her handwriting on it. "This is a line from the poem: *Where weather and water meet.* Thought it was pretty. As I read up on it, people kept referring to geographic coordinates and town names. I started printing out maps and taping them together so I could see everything better, you know? I'm such a visual person, I had to get it all in one place, and then . . ." Christy quieted, fingertips hovering just above the papers, until she caught herself and cleared her throat. "Tape isn't sturdy enough now with all this weight, but I think rubber cement should do the trick."

"Hold on, you're on a shoplifting forum?"

Her mother ignored her and kept talking. It'd been almost a year since the girls online had told Christy about the hunt, all of them saying it'd be the biggest haul any of them could hope for, more than even a walk-out with a Chanel bag or a MacBook, which were the ultimate gets (most notably achieved by the infamous user FangChix, who nabbed three first-gen rose-gold iPhones on the night of the product's release, praised by everyone when she posted a photo of the stacked white boxes and said she'd sell them for half price, only to be banned when a user wired her the money and she disappeared).

Shoplifting wasn't about the thrill of getting caught, though that was obviously a part of it, Christy explained. No, it was about the pile of stuff after a good day at the mall, proof of beating the system. It was like getting a hickey: the action itself was half the fun, sure, but the pleasure lay in the aftermath, when you looked in the mirror and there was physical evidence you had gotten something you wanted. And like hickeys, some preferred to hide their hauls and some loved to flaunt them. Most of the women on the forum—and they were almost all women, Christy insisted, though there were a few complicit boyfriends and flamboyant teens—routinely racked up hauls worth thousands of dollars. Some accounts revealed evidence of wealth: a marbled countertop in the background, a reference to a guest bedroom, talk of sorority sisters. For most, though, it wasn't just for sport. There were photos of diaper boxes, bulk-sized ovulation tests, puffy winter coats, prom dresses, wedding makeup, printer ink. Detailed accounts of how to walk out with razor heads and tampons, outlining the exact movements, glances, and timing it took to acquire each item. They never watch the greeting card aisle, or itching armpits is the quickest way to bra-stash. Critiques were expected, though never of the items themselves. Whenever someone would sass a user's haul (ur posting US Weekly from a fuckin gas station? r u serious lol???), the replies were always ten times more savage (stfu u hag those mags r fuckin amazing i'm reading one right now how are u spending ur weekend u pathetic bitch). The guiding maxim was: If it was stolen, it was needed.

"What about people's identities? Do they steal those, too?"

"Don't be ridiculous, they're good people." Christy said. Once she found out about the treasure, she spent less and less time with the shoplifters. Not that she stopped lifting, but this was something that required more than quick hands and the invisibility of being a woman over forty. Plus, it was from someone who *wanted* you to take what they had. "I thought the whole thing must be a scam," Christy said. "I mean, a poem with clues to a buried treasure? Really? But then I did some more research, and it's real. There's an entire website dedicated to it. And it's worth more than a million dollars now. Inflation, you know."

Bea strangled the neck of her empty beer bottle. "Inflation doesn't work like that."

Christy held out the tablet, its lime-green leather cover swinging open. "If you don't believe me, you can look at the site yourself."

The forum hadn't been redesigned since the early aughts. It was the vintage internet of grayscale grids and clashing fonts, the poster's username—1ShOtMcGeE, xxxallgoldnofoolxxx, GREG3871—and pixelated cartoon picture above each boxed comment. There were signatures below most of the responses, relics of customizable online anonymity, all blinking star clusters and Comic Sans song lyrics. Some had clichéd outdoorsy quotes from the likes of Muir ("the mountains are calling . . .") or Thoreau ("I went to the woods . . ."). The occasional Abbey, though those were rarer. Most often, they had a list of coordinates, each annotated with "failed, Aug 2013" or "attempted, Jan 2011."

"ChristineM52? Do you know how obvious that is?"

"I didn't say you could look at my profile." Christy snatched the tablet back. "Most people think it's in Idaho or Montana, which is smart, right? So much space out there to hide something. But I think they're wrong." Though she had only been involved in the hunt for about a year, Christy was convinced Utah was the answer. After reading through dozens of pages of old forum threads, scouring the poem, and reading old academic periodicals on Southwestern hydrology ("One of the lifting girls gave me her college library login"), she had had a breakthrough. "Canyons. Utah canyons. These canyons." Christy tapped the map with a long, blue fingernail. A circle, a town called Mercy.

The sun blazed in from the front window and the house swelled with heat. Bea wilted, head between her elbows. This was exhausting, her mother was exhausting, this was always how it was. Bea went to the fridge. Her mother was right, there was no more beer. Somewhere, a thousand miles east, there was an excellent curry restaurant that would deliver in less than twenty minutes, a guy who'd show up with a variety of sativas in less than thirty. "Do you have any other booze?" Bea asked.

"Under the sink."

The cabinet under the sink was filled with small bottles of essential oils and one large bottle of rum. Bea drank straight from the bottle. It was spiced, thick. "How long have you been doing this," she asked, motioning at the map.

"A year? Maybe a little more."

Bea did the math. "Before Grandma Gertie died?"

Christy joined her at the counter. She crossed her arms. "And?"

"Did you move out here for *this*? Because of this forum?"

A shrug.

"You moved to Salt Lake City because of a fucking treasure hunt?"

"It's cheap here."

"You hate snow."

"I grew up in New England, kid, I can deal with some snow."

"You're insane."

"Is that really the worst thing?"

"You could've gone anywhere. Anywhere."

Christy took two mugs out of a cabinet and poured them each a shot. She held hers up to Bea. "You could've, too."

◄▬

Medical bankruptcy should've been much more interesting. It should've been a revolt of the body, a total refusal of care. Anarchy, after all, is the guiding maxim of cancer, your body working in unpredictable and unfeeling ways to destroy itself, treatment just varying attempts at mitigation. What could be more bankrupt?

Christy, apparently. She had hidden the neon envelopes under a wad of supermarket circulars earlier that week, too bored to deal with them. The notices and voicemails weren't her first. She'd been hounded by persistent phone calls and brightly colored letters ever since her daughter was in diapers. Christy always struggled to take them seriously, mainly because they were caused by decisions she'd never made, results of the impulsive choices of her ex-husband or the mitochondria in her left breast. She'd listen to the stern messages about collections and past due and this is the last time we'll call before serving, and the melodrama of it all would always make her laugh. Like the $48.22 in Florida back taxes from when she worked at a mall piercing booth: she'd only worked there for a couple of months, back when they needed some extra cash to pay for a new car seat. For years, salmon-orange envelopes emblazoned with bold text would appear, each a screaming flag among the coupons and magazines. After all these years, surely the postage outweighed the debt, she thought, and then she wouldn't think of it again until the next one showed up.

Her ex-husband would claim Christy didn't take money seriously. Money, he'd yell, is *everything*, and we don't have *any*. You're a spoiled little rich girl from Connecticut. She'd laugh at that. Weren't you the one who said I should drop out of high school? Weren't you the one who said I'd never need a job? Weren't you the one who didn't like condoms? You're from *Westchester*, she'd hiss. He'd tell her to grow the fuck up and then Christy would land her closing argument—*just wait until my mother dies and I have enough money to leave you*—and then he'd throw something past her, usually a half-full beer, and storm out the door.

Pregnancy changed everything, though only for nine months. Her husband became an actual partner, doting on her with McDonald's apple pies and late-night foot rubs and pharmacy runs for antacids. The sex was tender, prolonged, and he would help her shower afterward. They lived in Delaware at the time, their tiny duplex close to the Dover Amtrak station. Gertie despised the husband, hated him ever since Christy announced she wasn't finishing her junior year of high school because she fell in love with a salesman. He was twelve years older than her. They were moving in together. "He gives me flowers," Christy had explained. Gertie was astonished, furious, and they didn't speak for years. But the pregnancy changed that, too. Gertie showed up at the Delaware duplex with a monogrammed baby blanket, a rocking chair on order, and the promise to stay until the due date. When they got home from the hospital, they stood around the bassinet, the baby sleeping under the new blanket. Gertie and the husband exchanged trembling, toothy smiles. Watching from the rocking chair, exhausted and torn apart, Christy was overcome with a warm, heavy peace. It was only later she would recognize this as happiness.

Eventually Gertie left and, in time, the husband did, too. The baby was colicky, up at all hours. Christy took to sleeping in the rocking chair, a habit that didn't change until Bea was nearly in kindergarten. Her husband, meanwhile, took to sleeping anywhere but their home. Monday was numbers day, when her husband had to call his boss with the tally of the prior week's sales, and on Sundays he'd sometimes show up with a customer and regale them with lies about Christy's cooking, hoping to seal a final deal. Every Sunday at sundown, Christy would put on a bra and makeup, dump a Stouffer's meal into a baking dish, preheat the oven, and wait. Sometimes, he'd show up. Most of the time, the hours would slip by like grease: TV muted, lasagna a puddle on the counter, lipstick smeared, baby fussing in her crib. Around ten o'clock, Christy would pour a gin and tonic and drink until she could no longer read the closed captioning.

The catch was, he was a catch, or at least seemed to be. His charm was addictive, expansive, winks and jokes that vacuumed all the attention in the room. There were boasts of the latest deal, the three-piece suits, the unsolicited business advice. Christy wanted to point out the gray streaking his shoulder-length hair, his rosacea and jowls. It's fake, she'd mutter, whenever someone complimented his watch, but no one seemed to listen or care. Christy didn't think she could afford to leave him, not for years, not until he disappeared. At first, his absence was unsurprising and convenient. She and Bea tucked away in a condo in Rhode Island, a town small enough for Christy to consider making friends, but after nearly two months of not hearing from her husband, and not getting any of his paychecks in the mail, she figured she should investigate. She called his supervisor and got an address in Burlington. She and Bea drove up after school the next day. The drive was nearly six hours, traffic horrible, and Christy was in a terrible mood when she walked into a slummy apartment and was greeted by lit candles and Van Morrison, her husband bare-assed and tangled around a co-ed. Christy laughed, said they were lucky his daughter was asleep in the car and wasn't here to see this. Her husband sneered, pants around his ankles, and said don't be a fucking prude, Christine, our daughter's nearly in high school. Christy pointed at the girl. Not much younger than her, then? At that, he lunged at Christy, and the co-ed screamed, and then Christy finally left.

Christy and Bea moved in with Gertie, who was kind enough not only to welcome them to the Stamford house but also to never mention the ex-husband. A lot had changed since Christy last lived at the house. The once meticulous yard was overgrown and weed-wild, the toilet in the downstairs bathroom no longer flushed, and the dining room wallpaper was curled and stained. But it still smelled like Windex and cinnamon, the oven light was still permanently left on, and the topmost stair still squealed. It was home. They were able to enroll Bea at the local middle school just in time to start eighth grade, and Bea seemed thrilled about it, especially when Gertie insisted Christy buy her daughter new clothes for the school year.

"She's practically in rags, Christine," Gertie said. They went to the mall, Bea only wanting the preppiest polos possible, and Christy would've been disappointed had she not also treated herself that day. Tiny purses, oversized coats, platform sandals, wide-brimmed hats, all in bright colors and dizzying patterns, everything her ex-husband hated. That day, she decided she would wear his ring as long as his credit card worked. It did, so she did, through the fall and into the new year.

It'd been months since they'd heard from the ex-husband when Christy's name started to appear on the brightly colored envelopes. Christy had never gotten so much mail, so many phone calls, and she ignored them all. Until that spring, when a stout, whiskered man showed up at the front door. He asked if Christine Macon Caldwell was home. She didn't know Christine *Caldwell*, Christy told him, but she'd be happy to pass along a message. The man shuffled in place, a large manila envelope in his hand, and didn't meet her eye. Christy stared him down, smiled wide with teeth bared, until he left. After that, every time the clerks at the stores ran Christy's credit card: declined.

Turns out, her ex had been fired for not hitting his numbers. That was a few weeks ago, the supervisor explained over the phone. The ex had stayed in Burlington, but rumor was he recently followed a girl to Montreal. Christy demanded an address, a phone number, a name. Did he know people wanted to take her to court, she yelled. She—they—had a daughter, did he know that? But the supervisor didn't know anything, only remembered the tavern near the lake her husband liked, how he took customers there. Sorry for your troubles. All men are trouble, she said, and slammed down the receiver.

Gertie couldn't be much help. There was a reason for the house being the way it was, why Gertie left the country club, why she hadn't bought new clothes in a decade. There was a translucent pink Mac in the Stamford kitchen, and Gertie loved to talk about the new technology, usually sitting in front of it when she called Christy, the computer's clicking and beeping punctuating Gertie's questions about her granddaughter. Christy had always been proud of Gertie's quick acclimation to the internet. Proof of her mother's intellect, she told herself. Even after moving back into the Stamford house, Christy wouldn't question why Gertie would spend hours in front of the hulking desktop, and it wasn't until Christy asked Gertie for a loan that she found out why her mother loved the internet. Poker, hours of it, and with real money, specifically, the money her long-dead father left behind, the money that Gertie was supposed to leave behind, the money that was nearly gone. Gertie was sheepish but unapologetic. Christy stole the Mac's Ethernet cord and gave Gertie a pack of cards. She told her mother it was all right. And it was, because Christy finally opened her own credit card.

The money didn't feel real because it wasn't. It worked for a while, making minimum payments, hitting limits, and then opening another. By summer, Christy knew she was living off financial fumes, knew that there was maybe a couple hundred dollars left on the Connecticut Credit Union Silver Saver Express. She went to the store to stock up on canned soup and butter noodles, peanut butter and beans. "Y2K isn't real," Bea muttered as they heaved bags of rice onto the checkout belt. The card declined. Christy handed over another card, but it, too, declined. Eventually, Bea pulled out some wrinkled bills from a back pocket. Christy refused to cry, or at least she held off until they were in the car, and Bea asked if she should pick up extra babysitting jobs to help pay for groceries.

Gertie knew someone who knew someone who was married to a lawyer. The lawyer told Christy that divorce was good, but bankruptcy was better. She could do the latter without the former, but it'd be harder, what with the joint accounts. "Bankruptcy no matter what, though," he said, rubbing his gigantic eyebrows. He smelled like cigars and burnt steak, like nothing that really mattered. His body was almost a perfect circle, and he was probably too old to get hard. When he told Christy he was doing this session pro bono but the next meeting would be two hundred dollars an hour, Christy still considered it. He shook his head. "I can't believe these banks keep approving you."

Christy could. That August, right before Bea started high school, she found a card through a local theme park and bought the plane ticket to Burlington. Tracking down her ex-husband took a few days of asking around, eventually getting a name and neighborhood in Montreal, where she found not only him and the co-ed, but also a four-month-old baby boy. Christy was overjoyed. A baby, she assumed, meant he wouldn't fight her on the divorce. A new family, a new marriage, a new life. But the ex-husband refused. The girl had a faint Boston accent and feathers braided into her blond hair and spoke a lot about energies. She referred to herself as a hopeless Catholic, thus the resistance to divorce and birth control. Christy pointed out babies out of wedlock were condemned by the Church, but that didn't seem to matter to him or the girl, who was a girl, technically a teenager and hardly older than Christy was when she first met her ex. But the girl believed in family, loved family, and Christy was family. Christy should stay, the girl insisted. The ex-husband, when the girl left the room, demanded Christy leave. Would he sign? He wouldn't. Christy stared him down, holding the divorce papers, the baby cooing next to them. The bankruptcy, the money, the credit cards. Christy didn't see any other option. The girl returned. Christy smiled. Christy stayed. Weeks went by, Christy sleeping on their couch in exchange for helping with the baby, hoping to slowly wear down their stubbornness by being both relentlessly helpful and completely in the way. She'd sit down with the girl and help get the baby latched, give her tips about when to apply Vaseline to diaper rash. From the other room, the sound of her ex-husband kicking a wall, and Christy would grin, which would make the baby giggle. She loved his giggle. Christy would call home to check in with Gertie. "I'll be home soon," Christy promised. "I just need to finish up a few things here."

When Christy was pregnant her friends told her they hoped, for her sake, it was a boy. Boys were easier. In Quebec, Christy could also see how the boy was simpler: she didn't compare herself to his fits or confusions, didn't overexamine why he didn't sleep much, didn't judge how slow he was to start crawling. Christy thought of her daughter and all the moments she was missing—the first day of high school, the first time she forgot her locker number, the first panicked pop quiz—and a deep ache glowed in her ribs. Her daughter was a teenager, nearly grown and fully sullen, refusing to come to the phone whenever Christy called, but the boy was full of potential and cuddles. Whether it was because he was a boy or because he wasn't hers, Christy never asked. It's easier not to look in a mirror.

Word got around that Christy, this mysterious American friend of the ex-husband's, was helping with the baby, and soon a white British family approached Christy about part-time work for their pimpled ten-year-old twins. Anxious for the extra pay, for any money at all, Christy lied and said she was fluent in French, but the parents didn't seem to care. Their children were spoiled and petulant in ways that Christy found ridiculous. "They despise croissants," she told Gertie. "It's buttered toast or nothing." Gertie had to remind Christy how she hated cheese as a child. Still, the twins were terrors. When they weren't glued to their video games, they tortured the baby, shoving candy wrappers and dead leaves down his diaper, pinching his ears, and stealing his rattle. They screamed for biscuits and screamed harder when, the dough warm from the oven, Christy realized they meant cookies. They never slept, peed in the potted plants, and purposely pulled out Christy's hair. The parents laughed when Christy told them about the twins' misbehavior, said they were happy they were raising such spirited children. They were monsters, the entire family, but they paid on time and in American dollars. After a few months, Christy earned enough to cover the cost of Bea's first cell phone, though her daughter refused to answer her calls.

Time disappears with children, evaporating like mist. She'd been in Canada for nearly a year when the ex-husband finally caved. The girl's cousin had seen him kissing another woman at a local bar the night before and he hadn't yet come home. When he eventually walked through the door, the girl screamed about his lying, stupid, ugly, old face and how dare he, how dare he, throwing bowls and mugs at his feet, toddler wailing. Christy stayed quiet, the boy wrapped around her legs. The girl told the ex-husband she was leaving, and then did, taking the boy with her. She didn't come back, not later that day or later that week, and the ex-husband became desperate. The girl wouldn't talk to him, the grocer wouldn't look at him, the bartender ignored him. He wept on the couch, choking back platitudes about his son, his beautiful boy. Disgusted, Christy pulled out the divorce papers and said he could make it right, and he finally did.

Christy didn't. She should've left the next day, should've got on a plane just in time to help with Bea's PSAT prep, help pick out a homecoming dress. Instead, Christy stayed in Canada for another three years. In America, she'd be divorced and bankrupt, a bad daughter and a worse mother. Bea still refused to come to the phone or answer Christy's weekly letters. Every so often there'd be a kick in her upper throat or deep in her gut, her body remembering how far she was from her daughter. But Christy pushed these feelings aside, knowing they'd eventually lessen. The nannying job was her first paycheck since high school. The money was hers and hers alone, no longer contingent upon anyone else's whims or charity. She sent money back every week, enough for Gertie to thank her for it, which is how Christy knew it was needed. One day she'd explain to Bea how important this was, how the money made her feel like a good person, even if she wasn't. One day, her daughter would understand. Christy told herself this until the last day she was in Montreal, the day she was laid off because the twins were headed to boarding school in England. She told it to herself when she landed in New York and when the taxi pulled up to the house in Stamford. She told it to herself for years, throughout all the unanswered calls, until she got sick and her daughter finally spoke to her again.

———

When Bea said she was coming to Utah, Christy had been overjoyed and then immediately overwhelmed. How to welcome her daughter, make her comfortable, make her happy? The tree was a limited edition, part of a four-part seasonal release. The artist was a Salt Lake local and Christy had been on the waitlist for a tree long before moving to Utah. She got the notice minutes after Bea's plane had taken off from JFK, which Christy took as a sign. The Autumn Aspen. It was gorgeous, more intricate, and made with better materials than most of the other plants in her collection, and the artist had only made a dozen or so. The price tag reflected its exclusivity and craftsmanship, but Christy was thrilled to hand over the wad of cash. The leaves, the branches, the color, the timing: finally, the perfect gift.

There had been tie-dye sweaters and blinking dolls and light-up trucks and books—so many books!—and then, later, the delicately colored beads and the woven scarves and the poutine mixes she'd ship to Connecticut from Montreal. Once Christy had moved back to the Stamford house and Bea was in college, she found all the gifts piled in the back of Bea's closet, most still in their original packaging and tissue. Christy tried to donate them, but Gertie insisted Bea may want them one day. Give her time, Gertie said. You never know. Which was true, Christy had never known. Her daughter's desires and interests seemed fairly straightforward—neutral colors, sensible footwear, analytical nonfiction—and yet she couldn't seem to crack the perfect gift. They were still in the back of the closet when Christy prepared the house for sale. It was one of the last boxes she handed over to the volunteers at Goodwill.

The aspen was going to be different. All this time, Christy had been trying to find things that would appeal to her daughter, things Bea would use and enjoy. But the point of gifts isn't utility. The point is the surprise. The aspen was going to be Bea's surprise, something useless but nonetheless beautiful. Something that would make her think of Christy, and smile.

After picking up the aspen and sending a photo to Bob, Christy went shopping for breakfast burrito ingredients. They had been Bea's favorite, she explained to Bob in the grocery store parking lot when he called to ask what the aspen had to do with the treasure hunt. "I thought you were realigning our strategy toward the mountains," he muttered, obviously relieved. Christy's stomach had fluttered at his use of a possessive. *Our!* she mouthed to herself as he proceeded to lecture her about how they needed to reexamine a recent post on floodwaters. He was always like this, even before these daily phone calls, back when they were only swapping messages on the forum. A lot of theory, not a lot of feeling. By the time Bob hung up, Bea had texted saying her flight had landed. Christy hurried home. She wanted to have enough time to unwrap the aspen and unpack the food, to make sure each surprise was perfect.

It wasn't. Her daughter was unimpressed by the aspen, barely looking at it, and the meal was twenty minutes of silence, Bea delicately using a fork and knife to cut her burrito into smaller and smaller pieces, eating none of it. Christy knew the burritos weren't any good, but she ate all of hers, just to make a point. She got the map out thinking it'd be a good way to connect with her daughter, show how she'd found purpose and friendship since Gertie's death. A conversation starter, at the very least. But it'd been a small disaster, her daughter speechless and awkward, making an empty excuse about needing to get some fresh air after the flight. While Bea was on her walk, Christy did the dishes and a glass broke on the counter. It was a pretty glass, delicate and ornate, the best of the mishmash of glassware that had come with the house. Christy had always loved having a tonic water in it each night, had always looked forward to the routine, and had served it to Bea hoping she'd notice it. As Christy held its shattered pieces, she choked back hot, embarrassed tears. Dinner, Christy decided, would be different. She texted Bob for advice. He suggested quiche. Scrambled eggs poured into a premade crust and heated in the oven until no longer runny. Christy watched a lot of cooking shows, mostly for the ambiance, so even though Bob didn't have an exact recipe for her, she didn't think it would be that hard. Her daughter wouldn't look her in the eye, but she could deal with that, just like how she could deal with her daughter showing up in Utah with only a day's notice, wild-eyed and skittish, like a feral kitten.

Aside from the drinking glass, the table was the only thing about the house Christy liked. During the move-in tour, the landlord had offhandedly mentioned how the table had been his grandmother's. The landlord was dumb and arrogant, always chewing something whenever he called and never saying goodbye before he hung up, but including a family heirloom among all the dingy particleboard was, to Christy, the worst offense. She ate greasy soups on the couch and slammed the flimsy cabinet doors, but she was respectful toward the table. A solid, heavy pine with spindle legs and an oiled top, it was the only furniture in the house that had been obviously cared for. The meals and conversations that must've been centered around it, the feelings and memories it must've anchored. Christy was careful to respect it.

The quiche wasn't quite done, but her daughter was already seated at the table, so she carefully pulled it out of the oven. She sprinkled chopped spinach on top—*a dinner should always include some lovely greens*, she remembered cooking show hosts saying—and brought the pan over. Her daughter didn't look up, didn't offer to help, but that was fine. It wasn't until Christy went to place the quiche on top of the pile of mail that Bea made any movement at all, snatching the pile of brightly colored envelopes, leaving nothing to protect the table from the hot pie tin. The quiche was already collapsing into its steaming, runny center, and Christy didn't dare move for fear it might splatter to the floor. Panicked, she asked Bea to put the mail back, please, this thing is hot and will ruin the table's varnish. Bea scoffed, said to put it down, the table's not theirs, who cares. *I CARE*, Christy bellowed, and her daughter slowly slid the mail back to where it was, eyes wide.

Both women prodded the quiche with their forks, the middle too liquid to consume. After a long silence, Bea mentioned a neighbor she'd seen on her walk and how the neighbor had four kids whose names all started with Z. "Zander, Zayn, Zara, and Zola, all under ten, too." Bea shook her head, amused.

Christy knew the Zs, as she called them. They lived across the street and their parents, Abigail and Andrew, were excessively friendly in the hard-eyed, high-pitched way that indicated they were terribly unhappy. The kids, though, were chubby-cheeked clowns. They once pranked Christy by throwing a rubber snake in front of her on the sidewalk. Christy had fallen for it, screaming HOLY SHIT loud enough for Andrew to run outside, the kids shrieking with laughter. The Zs shouted it to her whenever they saw her, a chorus of singsong *shit*s, which Christy found deeply endearing. She often offered to babysit, and wanted to, but Abigail and Andrew had always demurred.

"You know you need to pay your bills." Bea pointed her fork at the mail under the pie pan. "Or, I'm supposed to pay them. You're at least supposed to open them."

The middle of the quiche had become a gelatinous yellow soup. Christy stirred it with her pinkie finger. "You're right. I should. I also should've left this quiche in the oven for another ten minutes. You live and you learn."

Bea put down her fork and began to rip open envelopes. "Some of these are from months ago," she said, examining the contents. She held up a pink letter. "You know you can't drive without paying your car insurance, right?"

"I hardly drive."

Her daughter opened another. "*Past due for your annual install-ment of the Martha Stewart Home Magazine Collectors Bundle*? Are you serious?"

"She has some great cleaning tips. A national treasure. You know your grandmother would see her at the market sometimes? Said she was always wearing lipstick. Always."

"How are you even getting these things? You don't have a credit card, you barely even have a credit score."

Christy had not just one, but two credit cards, a fact she didn't plan to tell her daughter. Bea reached for the remaining pile. Christy let her, the quiche cooled, its crust slimy and limp. She smashed sections of it under her fork while her daughter read the mail aloud. Mostly bills and well-disguised coupons, though one envelope, to Bea's chagrin and Christy's glee, held an offer for a credit card. Her daughter launched into a lecture about Christy's bankruptcy and lack of GED and how she had to be more careful, how people target people like Christy and doesn't she understand how serious this can get? Bea was her father's daughter, and though Christy made sure to never mention their specific similarities, Bea's tendency toward haughty sanctimony was always a chilling reminder. She was used to Bea's lecturing about budgeting and QVC and email fraud. These lectures had anchored their conversations for years. Christy would usually politely nod through them, because it seemed like the only way to get her daughter comfortable enough to eventually talk about more interesting things, like why she came all the way to Utah to cry in the shower. Christy pushed the eggy mess around the tin and chewed a canker sore on her tongue. Her daughter meant well. Her daughter cared. Her daughter paid the rent. When Bea finally ran out of steam and asked what they were going to eat now that Christy had pulverized their dinner, Christy smiled. She went to the kitchen and came back with a roll of tin foil. "Put this on," she said. Bea didn't understand. "Wrap it around your waist, like a skirt or something. I can show you how." Bea hesitated. "Didn't you say you're hungry? Just trust me." Her daughter took the tin foil and Christy went to get the car keys.

⋯▶

When Bea was in high school, celebrities talked about a secret. The secret was simple: All you had to do was think about something hard enough, want it deep enough, and it came true. Thought and truth, direct correlatives. Think you were happy and you were. Think you were successful and you were. Think you were home, and well, look where you were.

Bea believed it. She'd already done it. Christy had always said her name was the only word she thought the entire time she was in labor, which made it Christy's favorite word, and what better way to name your only child? It was Beautiful, but to Bea, it was torture. The looks, the clarifications, the laughter. It only took until second grade for Bea to understand the need to avoid her full name. On the first day of class, she would go up to the teacher and quietly ask to please call her Bea Macon, thank you very much. When she walked across the stage during her high school graduation, speakers blaring, Christy wasn't there to witness how the crowd murmured and shifted when they called her up to the stage. Taking her diploma, jaw set, Bea vowed it'd be the last time her name would embarrass her. That fall, during her first semester of college, she spent her eighteenth birthday applying to legally become Bea Macon. Over a dozen years later, no one was any wiser. Think it, say it, and so it was.

Bea had decided getting fired didn't matter. She had two months of severance. Plenty of time, she figured, to find another job. Sure, she'd reach out to recruiters and network with colleagues at other banks, but otherwise Bea decided she deserved to take a breather. After nearly a decade of round-the-clock analysis, she could spend her time attempting to relax. Self-care, she told herself. She deserved something nice, like a diamond laser facial that made her cheeks peel for days; three loud, tropical print linen dresses from Neiman Marcus, all on sale, none in her size; breakfast sandwich delivery every morning, extra bacon; a standing desk that she never assembled, the boxes stacked next to her bed, blocking the light from the room's only window; a vibrator controlled by Bluetooth that Bea could never figure out how to set up. Just this once, she told herself as she typed her now-memorized credit card number, she had earned it.

But despite all the self-care, Bea couldn't sleep. She tried a meditation app. The reviews insisted on the efficacy of a specific episode that detailed every bird on a fictional tropical island, squawks identified by a syrupy male voice. It didn't help. The last of the bird calls would trail off into a haze of surf and wind and Bea would sigh, turn over, and restart the track. This went on for almost three weeks. Tired of avian insomnia, she signed up for a BodyCore yoga class. Bea typically avoided yoga, mostly because her mother had been an enthusiastic adherent throughout her childhood, pulling the car over during long road trips to perform acrobatic displays of stretching in park-n-rides. But Heat Up BodyCore Level 2 was not Christy's yoga. Fierce and focused, it required a heart rate monitor and raised voices. For thirty-five dollars and sixty minutes, success was possible and determined by ranked cardiatric data. It wasn't clear if sneakers were necessary, but Bea brought them just in case. She was going to become someone who exercised, who planned their days around when they would sweat with other people. BodyCore, Bea decided, would make her sleep, which would finally let her think, and then, maybe, she could figure out what she should do next.

Class, mat rental, and BodyCore-branded electrolyte water totaled fifty-one dollars and sixty-two cents. She handed her last functioning credit card to the Lycra-bound woman behind the front desk when Martha walked in, ponytail swinging and arms outstretched, saying she didn't know Bea was a BodyCorer, wow wasn't this a coincidence, it was so great to see her, it'd been too long, and had she heard about Grant and Carolyn? Wasn't it just perfect?

Bea had nothing against Carolyn, though, of her freshman year roommates, it'd been Martha with whom she'd connected the most. Despite her trust fund and private schooling, Martha didn't take field hockey or cotillion too seriously. She never asked where Bea bought her clothes or if she went to summer camp. She drank beer. Carolyn, meanwhile, was shier, more reserved. She drank a very specific brand of Nordic vodka, wore silk tops in pale colors, and kept one hand in her lap while she ate. Freshman year, Carolyn quickly entered into a near-royal relationship with Charlie St. Stephens, the two of them shiny brunette members of dynastic Virginia families. They moved to New York together after graduation, but it only took a few months before Carolyn discovered Charlie preferred a different flavor of partner, specifically an off-Broadway tenor named Lukas. Meanwhile, Bea had signed a lease on a two-bedroom in Brooklyn. She'd long lost touch with Carolyn and Martha, and the few friends she had from college were far-flung, doing admirable but low-paying work in small cities or remote countries. Bea had posted to the alumni Facebook group looking for a roommate. When Carolyn reached out to ask if the room was still available, Bea could hardly believe it. People moved to New York hoping everything would change, and with Carolyn Alderman as her roommate, it might actually happen. Carolyn meant galleries and galas, lunch reservations and private dining clubs. Bea immediately and enthusiastically responded to Carolyn. She didn't even bother with a lease. "The least I can do," Bea said.

Decorators arrived with beautiful, neutral-colored furniture.

Workers fumigated the apartment, repainted the walls. Overnight there were cast-iron pans, delicately painted plates, an overly complicated juicer. After it was all set up, Carolyn arrived, said hello, and then never left her bedroom. Bea would sit on the couch and hear various sobs from the other side of the wall. Bea would knock and offer tea, but Carolyn wouldn't open the door. For the month she lived with Bea, Carolyn would order the same dinner: chicken pad thai, mild. Every night, Bea would tip the delivery guy and leave the takeout bag outside Carolyn's door. Every morning, the bag and to-go containers would be neatly tucked into the trash. Martha would text Bea asking for updates and Bea would send increasingly desperate messages—What's Carolyn's favorite tea? Should they try a movie night? Does she even like tea?—hoping to help. It wasn't until Bea mentioned the nonstop pad thai that Martha left her internship in London and showed up at the apartment straight from JFK, bags over each shoulder and under both eyes, and told Bea she'd take it from here, thanks, could they please be left alone for a bit? It was a rainy summer Sunday, and even though she knew it'd be flooded with tourists, Bea spent the day wandering the Brooklyn Museum, brushing up against the whining teenagers and whispering Europeans, savoring the people more than the paintings, wondering if they should order ramen that night as an homage to the microwavable cups they shared freshman year. But when Bea returned that evening, a bottle of Nordic vodka in hand, the apartment was empty. For the first time, Carolyn's bedroom door was open. Her bed was made, the floor clean, the closet vacant. There was a note and a check for a month's rent left on the dresser. This should cover any costs. They were taking a trip and they'd let her know when they were back in the city. Thanks for everything. The room was white and soft and spotless, as if Carolyn had never been there at all.

Carolyn never came back, never called, not even after Bea saw a post about her moving into a SoHo loft with Martha a couple of weeks later, on which Bea dutifully commented a heart emoji. Bea figured she should remind Carolyn about the furniture she had left behind. It was the polite thing to do. She hadn't been in the room since Carolyn left, and when she opened the door, she was met with an acrid, eye-watering stench. It didn't take long for Bea to discover the mason jars under the bed, dozens of them lined up in rigid rows, all filled with fermenting yellow vomit and capped with tight silver lids. A hand towel pressed against her face, Bea carefully threw each jar into a trash bag. She texted Carolyn asking her to call her when she got the chance, but Carolyn never did. Leaving the jars was confession enough, Bea figured, and there was no need to make it more than it was. Better to wait until she could gently bring it up in person, maybe even mention her own compulsive avoidance of creamy sauces, Gertie's two-chews-and-done rule. Bea drank fresh-pressed oranges from the juicer and cooked Gruyère frittatas in the cast iron, but her texts inviting Martha and Carolyn over for brunch went unanswered. Bea once ordered the pad thai, just to see what the fuss was about, and found it chewy and bland—which, she supposed, was the point. Eventually, Bea listed the bedroom as furnished, this time on Craigslist. A rotating cast of roommates moved in, each memorable in their own way (the midnight opera singer, the incessant farter, the two-hour showerer). No one ever mentioned a smell.

She finally saw them again years later, when they were all on the other side of thirty, a chance encounter on Orchard Street—Carolyn manning the door of a gallery opening while Martha swayed wine-drunk on the sidewalk. Bea wandered past and made eye contact long enough for Carolyn to notice her. There was a suggestion to catch up soon, which none of them thought would ever happen, but then, a few months later, they ran into each other at a restaurant, which led to an invitation to a party last spring on Martha and Carolyn's SoHo rooftop. This was the party where Bea had met Grant, an old high school friend of Carolyn's, the night filled with loud music and lukewarm vodka. Martha and Carolyn were nowhere to be seen, Bea knew no one else, and so when Grant had asked if she wanted to get out of there, his hand on her lower back, she said yes. From there followed so many hurried, blurry nights with him, the texts and the fumbling, the hours spent waiting, the months of hoping, all of which led to that moment in the yoga studio, Martha squealing about how Carolyn and Grant made such a cute couple, didn't they, and they had known each other for so long, I mean it almost makes you believe in fate, it almost makes you dizzy. Bea smiled and nodded too many times before claiming to need the bathroom and rushing out the door, feeling like she was living a life that surely couldn't be hers.

The feeling then had not been unlike the feeling Bea had now standing on a Salt Lake sidewalk wrapped in tinfoil. How glaringly, stomach-wrenchingly apparent her idiocy was, how deserving she was of humiliation. Her mother, of course, did not understand the problem. "C'mon, it's just a promotional thing, they don't care, I do this all the time." But knowing it was a regular occurrence for Christy only made it worse, and Bea refused to go inside, so her mother pushed through the door alone, the foil flashing as she waddled up to the counter. A cluster of college-aged girls at a table openly stared, hands over their mouths. The two workers behind the counter, a young boy and an older girl, greeted her mother by name. Bea didn't believe it. She didn't want to believe it. And yet her mother ordered food, expertly motioning to the fajita veggies and salsa verde, tinfoil arms crinkling. When Christy finished, she pointed at Bea. The boy shrugged. Christy waved her arms to summon Bea inside. The girls at the table took out their phones. Bea smoothed the foil around her waist. She reminded herself she did not live in this city, she did not know these people. She thought: They'll never see you again. She thought: This doesn't matter. She took a deep breath and went inside.

The girls snickered. One of their phones had the flash on. "Make sure you tell them it's for the promotion, it won't work unless you say it," Christy said as she made her way to a table on the far side of the dining room.

"The promotion," Bea said quietly, face grim. The table of girls openly laughed and the boy looked over at them. He had a faint pencil mustache and sweaty temples and was no older than sixteen. He bit back a smile and asked which tortilla she wanted. "Flour. With chicken. Please." After she finished going down the line, she asked if she could get a fountain soda, too.

"Drinks aren't free with the, uh, thing," he said, gesturing at Bea. "And you should tell your mom or whatever it's only during Halloween you get a free burrito with a burrito costume, but even then it's only for, like, the first fifty people or something."

"Don't forget the tip," Christy yelled, mouth full. There was a flash as the girls took another picture. They were ten years younger than Bea, but that made it worse, knowing she would've done the same at their age, or even now. They laughed again. Bea's skull burned. She struggled to get her wallet from her back pocket, the foil twice-wrapped around her shorts, and started to rip the stuff off in handfuls. "You know what, I'll just pay. I'll pay for hers, too." Bea said. She handed the boy the first card she could pull out. Tinfoil littered the counter between them in sharp, silver blooms.

Declined. The boy tried again, and when the card declined again, he looked over at his coworker. The girl was busy emptying frozen beef onto the grill, the meat steaming up in clouds of plastic and cumin. Bea shoved a couple of bucks into the tip jar and said to forget it, abandoning the burrito and the credit card on the counter. She was halfway across the dining room when the girl called her over. "Our manager is out," the girl said, pushing the burrito and two cups across the counter. "Plus, your mom's the only person who ever tips."

The group of girls walked past while Bea was at the drink station. She moved the cups between the Diet Coke and Sprite spigots, careful that each cup got an equal amount of both. "We love your outfit," they sneered. Bea froze, the machine gargling with ice, until the doors jingled closed. Her throat was tight; the cups were cold and sweating in her hands. She took a long gulp of one and then refilled it, and then repeated the same thing with the other cup.

Bea sat down and Christy immediately began to explain how

the best deal was to ask for half chicken, half pork, but not as a dou-ble meat order because—but then her mother sipped her drink and broke into a huge grin. "You made it our way!" Christy squealed. The soda combination was their secret recipe. Whenever they drove to meet Bea's father in whichever city was their new home, they'd string fast-food stops along their way, ordering a Half-Half at every drive-through—half Coke, half Sprite—and they'd drink them while sing-ing along to Fleetwood Mac and never mentioning her father's name. Bea smiled, throat loosening, and lifted her cup in cheers. Another group of teenagers walked into the restaurant and Bea didn't look their way.

The burrito was better than Bea expected, full and well por-tioned. She poured on extra hot sauce before each bite. Her mother was absorbed in her tablet, frantically tapping at something. The two workers behind the counter had disappeared into a back room. A handwritten sign hung above the drink station: *Refills $2*. "I'm going to get some more soda, do you want any?" Bea asked, but her mother didn't look up. The girl was back behind the register by the time Bea's cup was full, but Bea didn't try to go over to pay and the girl didn't seem to care.

Christy held up the screen when she got back to the table. "What does this look like to you?" Her mother had zoomed in so close the photo had become a cluster of fuzzy, overblown pixels, red and beige with a black mass in one corner.

"Artsy," Bea said.

Christy huffed and pinched the screen until the photo sharpened into focus. An empty blue sky and a red rock cliff, taken from the ground below.

"It's a cliff," Bea said slowly.

"Obviously."

"In the desert."

"Obviously."

"You asked what I saw," Bea said. "I don't know what you want me to see."

"What do you see right here, right at that spot?" Christy zoomed in on the black mass. Squinting, Bea could make out branches.

"A dead bush."

"Do you have a pen?" Christy asked. Bea didn't. Christy went up to the register and came back to the booth. She scribbled BUSH? DEAD? on a spare napkin.

"You know you can download apps that can let you take notes directly on the photo, right?" Her mother didn't look up. "And you know there are a lot of dead bushes in the desert, right?"

Bea watched, sipping her soda, as her mother took more notes— AQUIFER LEVEL? POWELL?—manically shifting between the tablet and the napkin, her mother's tinfoil shirt loosening. Christy was hunched over the tablet, zooming in and out on the canyon wall, over and over, enough to make Bea worry. She put her hand on top of the tablet screen. "Are you going to tell me what this photo is?" Christy pushed Bea's hand away. Bea put it back. "I'm serious, what is this?"

"He says he's found it and posted this as proof." Christy pointed at the screen as she spoke. "He agrees with me about the desert. Everyone else thinks it's got to be around water, probably rivers, because the poem mentions headwaters. But we think desert, we always have. We were supposed to figure it out together, in fact, he thinks we're very close to figuring it out. We are, together. I know he had nothing a week ago, but then I posted about my washout theory last night, and boom." Christy dropped the tablet and threw up her hands. "Suddenly he has a photo. Says it's over. He's got it. He didn't even text me before making a thread about it. He didn't even warn me." Her mother shook her head. "I can't believe it," she said softly.

"If this guy's got it, why's he posting a photo of a cliff and not gold doubloons or whatever?"

"Because he's too old and dumb to actually climb up there and get it, but he wants to hire someone to do it for him. It's one of the reasons he's posting a photo of the actual location, to convince someone to help him. Says he'll give them ten percent of the haul."

"Well, he's an idiot, because that's a terrible fucking deal," Bea said, picking up the tablet. She messed around with the photo, but it was still just a cliff. There was the sky, the rock, and the dead bush.

"He didn't even tell me." Christy put her head in her hands. Her mother sighed so deeply she made herself cough, which made her eyes water, tears dribbling around her nose. "I feel like I've been staring at this damn photo for hours and sometimes I see something and sometimes I don't. I feel like I'm looking at clouds, like sometimes it's a dog eating a turkey leg and sometimes it's just a damn cloud. Is it real? Or does he want me to think it's real?" Christy took the tablet back and brought the screen close to her face. Bea was no longer sure her mother's tears were from coughing. "Everyone else thinks he's insane. I feel like I'm going insane."

"You said it, not me."

That made Christy smile. She sniffed, zoomed in and then out. "You sure you don't see a million dollars?" she asked.

"Does this guy—"

"OnlyBob."

Bea snorted, but her mother was serious. "Sure, okay. Any chance he knows you're in Utah?"

"Yes."

"Aside from the fact you shouldn't tell an internet stranger where you live . . ." Bea paused for effect. Christy grabbed a handful of fresh napkins and rubbed the entire stack on each cheek. Bea continued. "Anyway, he's the only other person who agrees with you about the desert as a possible location, right? He's obviously trying to jump you on whatever information you have. At the very least, he thinks your theory is credible enough that he went so far as to scope out viable options in the area. You made him nervous."

Her mother's mouth twitched. "You think?"

"Why else would he go out there now and not a week ago? Look, when I sense an analyst on an earnings call has an inclination about something, that they might know something no one else does and is hinting at it in one of their questions, what do I do? Follow their lead, brainstorm possibilities, research and calculate, and hopefully beat them to it. Try to get there first. That's obviously what this guy is doing. He must think you're on to something with desert stuff. The real question would be why he would post a photo that everyone could see. It's a fake-out. He's buying himself time because he didn't find anything."

Christy squeezed Bea's hand. "Who taught you to be so smart?"

Bea felt a surge in her throat. She told herself it was only acid reflux. She sipped some soda and the knot lessened. "I should tell you something," she said, but her mother was busying herself with the tablet. Bea considered what it would mean to tell Christy about her job, her finances. Their finances. Her mother might wave her off, tell her they'd be burritos in the meantime, it was no big deal. But it was. It was her career. It was her life. Their life. And her mother seemed happy. A bit delusional, sure, but aren't all happy people deluded?

Bea pantomimed a phone call and slid out of the booth. A fake nod, a grimace, a *sure, of course, let's get our broker on it*. Her mother watching, Bea wandered across the dining room and wrapped her declined credit card in some spare tinfoil. She threw it into a trash can. After a fake laugh, she tapped at her phone to mimic a hang-up.

"I thought you were on vacation," Christy said as Bea sat back down.

"You know how work is." Bea picked up her phone and refreshed her inbox, letting the circle spin, spin, spin.

They had another round of refills. Christy poked at the cliff photo, Bea checked her credit card balances. The girl behind the counter came up to them, mentioned closing, and asked if they wanted some of the leftover chips. "We throw them out otherwise," she said. "Saves us a trip to the dumpster." And before Bea could open her mouth, Christy smiled and said, sure, happy to help.

It's not rocket science, though it might be harder than rocket science, considering the amount of automation in modern rocket science. But to use a phrase that people use: it's not rocket science. Less math, more gut. Not often do people dedicate themselves so thoroughly to a poem, mining its word choices down to the syllable, investigating eighteenth-century derivatives, cross-referencing phrases to historical flood graphs. Typically, such work is reserved for the underfunded and overstressed populations of later-year doctoral programs. Rarely does the general public take a fine-tooth comb to any sort of literature with such scrutiny and dedication.

The poem itself wasn't particularly artful or inventive—many wouldn't consider it a poem at all. It didn't rhyme, was filled with clichés, and had simple lines like *where man walked yards before* followed by the even simpler *and walked yards again*. No one on the forum ever argued if it was a good or beautiful poem, but their dedication to decoding its meaning and intent, memorizing lines and debating style, counted for something. Any high school English teacher would tell you how impossible it is to get anyone excited about poetry, let alone verse dedicated to the pastoral mundane. Then again, most teachers aren't deciphering metaphors with buried treasure as a possible reward.

The hunt forum was just as rife with humble bragging as any other part of the internet, but instead of personal news or political polemics, posters would brag about having discovered the latest water levels of an Idaho lake, the elk migration patterns across the Colorado Plateau, and the hygiene habits of Wyoming Pony Express riders. Research prompted by overwrought interpretations of stanzas, line breaks, and diphthongs. Literary devices sifted and raged over by people who not only knew the specifics of advanced canyoneering but also had enough free time to argue about it.

A favorite word was *amateur*. It didn't show up in the poem, but it appeared constantly in posts. Mostly, accusations of being one, or a question revealing someone as such. last frost is typically way after Mother's Day in MT, a user would helpfully reply to another post, before signing off with u fuckin amateur. Or a thread would begin with an innocuous question—what's your favorite satellite phone?—only to devolve into replies of: lol amateur; amateur hour over here; sooooo fuckin amateur. An embarrassment which, according to the forum's parlance, was worse than your post not getting any responses at all. Expertise was respected but rarely recognized. The only user who seemed to have any unimpeachable sway over the place was the founder of the forum itself, MadMax, or MM, as he was commonly referred to in the forum threads. MM was not the author of the poem—or so he said—but he also seemingly had no interest in finding the treasure. Instead, he merely claimed to appreciate "the conversation." When things went haywire—threats of doxxing, references to nudity, gun braggarts—MM would show up and lock down the offending thread, announcing in genteel all-caps: ENDING THIS OUT OF RESPECT FOR THE CONVERSATION. Thus everyone, even journalists, referred to the forum as the Conversation.

Though he claimed not to have an account and never posted, the Poet was aware of the Conversation. He posted on a blog hosted on his personal website, which was also the only place his self-published memoir was available for purchase ($19.99 plus shipping). The book was a relentlessly clichéd and self-mythologizing account of his travels and adventures as a white guy in the American Southwest during the 1960s. He saved his best writing for the very last chapter, where he revealed he had buried his life savings in the wilderness, discoverable only by interpreting the poem that concludes the book. When he first published it in the mid-2000s, the memoir was the only place one could read the poem. Now, a decade later, encrypted PDFs and fuzzy scans were readily available on the Conversation. Aside from a buy link for the memoir, the Poet's blog was mostly his meandering, indulgent musings, ranging from a lengthy description of a theoretical wasp-moth cross-species ("like the modest mule, rumpy and infertile") to an ominously brief pan of ketchup ("worthless, watery jam"). With an email address, readers could comment at the bottom of each post. Discussion was usually quiet except whenever the blog referenced the treasure, and then the comments were endless, filled with breathless conjecture and pleas for more information. The Poet would never respond, continuing to blog about insects and condiments as if the comments were never there.

At one point, the Poet gained a modest level of notoriety due to charges of illegal antiquities dealing in Durango. An article about his arrest referenced his memoir and the associated treasure. The Poet was found guilty, but not until after a regional news frenzy, which spilled over into the blog's comment section. Overnight, hundreds of responses appeared at the end of each post, even the ketchup one. The website crashed.

The Conversation cropped up while the Poet's site was offline. Some die-hard and longtime blog commentators knew each other's email addresses and wanted, nay, *needed* to discuss the treasure in the blog's absence. Forum lore was that MadMax was the only one who knew anything about coding, though no one was exactly sure how he became the moderator. MM didn't advertise the Conversation, but the Poet wrote about it once his blog came back online. He commended MadMax by username, saying he supported any gesture toward community, something the Poet was thinking a lot about during his court-mandated three hundred hours of community service. After the blog was posted, a few dozen accounts on the forum snowballed into a few hundred and then a few thousand, each anonymous username clamoring to take part in one big Conversation: Where was the treasure?

The next day, Bea went out on a walk, because she didn't have anything else to do, other than what she'd been doing since midnight, which was compulsively refresh her email. The morning ahead was a wide, empty mouth. Christy had been asleep when Bea left, and if her mother still slept like she did when Bea was young, Christy wouldn't emerge from her room until noon. Noon was two hours away. Bea queued up an aggressive electronica playlist and headed toward a trail close to the house. She tried to make her thoughts blur to the music's heavy bass line, for all the math and emails and credit cards to become small and distant, but it didn't work. A small creek ran alongside the trail, and when Bea found a shaded spot, she sat down and opened her email. Nothing but coupons. She went to her text thread with Phil. She last reached out the day before, right before she boarded her flight, to tell him she was headed to Utah to help take care of her mother but she'd be available for a call. That's wonderful. Have a great time. No need to worry about me, he replied. She was not worried about him. She was worried about how he hadn't taken her up on any of her offers to meet for a coffee or find a time to talk. She had worked for him for nine years. She knew his wardrobe well enough to recognize a sweater was new, knew the exact brand of hand lotion he preferred, knew he hated tomatoes. Bea's thumbs hovered over the text box, but there was nothing to say.

"Whales," someone said.

Bea startled. An old man stood next to her, a little off to the side, just far enough that it was difficult for her to turn and face him. She pulled her headphones off. "Excuse me?" she asked.

He was slim and white and ancient, with a baseball cap and high-belted pants. "I used to swim here when I was young. Water came up to my nipples." He patted his shirt pockets where, apparently, his nipples were. "Wow," Bea said, looking back at the water, moving to put her headphones back on.

"But now there're no more whales."

"Here?" The creek looked barely knee-high. "Are you sure?"

The man scoffed. "Of course. Don't you see all the gulls? It's a sea."

"I thought it was a lake."

"They're called *sea*gulls."

"We're pretty far from the ocean."

"My goodness, dear girl, why do you think they're the state bird?"

A jogger came upon them. He was a young guy, college-aged, and gave them a quick nod. Bea waved and stood up. The old man said something about miracles and Bea started to jog behind the guy. She ran with him for about a minute, long enough for him to glance at her a few times, and then stopped when she started wheezing. Convinced the old man wasn't following her, she stepped off the path and doubled over. The guy carried on without looking back.

By the time she caught her breath, Bea poured with sweat. The day was already hot and only getting hotter. She was tempted to wade into the creek, especially as the sun grew stronger and higher, but didn't want to give anyone else the opportunity to approach her. Everyone here was so eager to engage with each other, uninhibited in their good mornings and how you doings and what a nice days, Bea giving a curt smile each time. It was bizarre, this overt and insistent friendliness, and she didn't trust it. Better to stay on the move, keep walking, not give them pause enough to say more. The Uber driver was wrong. It wasn't like New Yorkers weren't hospitable—they were, generously so—but they also understood when people wanted to be left alone. The only people in Utah who ignored her were pushing strollers, but even then, the babies would stare out at her, eyes wide with astonishment. They certainly didn't know about the whales.

The beautiful delusion of New York was its intimate anonymity. Nail clipping on the subway, crying in high-rise elevators, heavy petting on street corners: everyone acted out their private in public because the boundary between those two worlds is so gloriously, dizzily indistinct when you share an island with a dozen million other aching, horny, farting souls. It gives you the sense you might do anything, anywhere, at any time.

After a few years in the overstimulated morass, this freedom feeling could warp itself into the why-the-fuck-not of Bea wearing yesterday's sweats and no bra to her local bodega, because not once had she ever seen anyone else she knew there aside from the jittery dude from 2A. A few months ago, when Bea shouldered the door to the familiar handful of bells, intent on a very specific Gatorade flavor (blue, the one she intuited had the most healing properties), she saw him, and, of course, this was after she had sworn off him for good because he had ghosted her—again. And yet there he was, bent over the freezer even though it was early spring, overcast and slushy, no one buys ice cream in this weather, a fact Bea said aloud and which made him stand up with the last mango ice pop in his hand like it was some sort of accomplishment. The look on his face, the genuine pleasure to see her, made her forget all about her Gatorade and bralessness and everything else. "Hey, Bea," he said. The shock of it. The inevitability. That's what the city did: create a mirage. Anything was possible, anything could happen, which never felt more true than when Bea invited Grant back to her apartment and he actually came over, for the first time ever, and then he kept coming back, right up until the week she got fired.

Christy had forgotten about the lipstick. She'd been biting her nails while Bob spoke, phone pressed against her ear, and now each fingertip was smeared in bright red. He asked what coordinates they were going to hike to and she said he'd have to be patient and find out when they got there. He didn't like that, grumbling for a while, until she asked him what shoes to bring. As he explained all the necessary equipment, she licked her fingers, but the lipstick remained. "Does the hotel have room service?" she asked, interrupting.

"The hotel? Christine, are you serious? It's a motel, not a Hilton."

"We should tell the front desk we're there to celebrate. Maybe they'll leave us something fun in our room. They do that sometimes."

"We're not celebrating anything. Not yet, at least."

"Just because we haven't found it doesn't mean we can't have a little fun." Christy missed the old days when she could curl a cord around her fingers. Instead, she pulled at her hair. "Right? I mean, didn't you say there was some sort of party happening?"

"It's a town hall meeting, not a party. There are going to be very important people there, the kind of people who've lived in Mercy for generations. The kind of people who know things, things we need to know."

Christy sighed, long and dramatic. "It's our second night to-gether, can't we do something fun? I'm sure these people go out to the local watering hole afterward, wouldn't it be easier to interview them then? Everyone likes to talk about family secrets after a couple of drinks. I can't imagine people talking during a town hall, sounds like that's more of a listening kind of thing."

"Don't be an idiot, all right? They only have these a few times a year. This is a huge opportunity. It's the whole reason we're going next weekend."

"I thought we're going next weekend because you have Friday off of work."

"Right." He cleared his throat. "You can skip the meeting, but I'm not, and that's that."

"All right, all right. But you're buying me a drink afterward. Something fun, like a cosmo. I've never had a cosmo."

"Cosmo?"

"You know, like from *Sex and the City.*"

There was a long pause. Then, "I don't think there's a bar that serves those kinds of drinks."

"But there is a restaurant," Christy said, her voice a wink. "You're taking me there."

"You're *meeting* me there," he said. "Remember the plan: Pat's Grill. It's across the street from the hotel, you can't miss it. Call me when you get to town and I'll meet you there."

"Didn't you say they have great steaks? How's the wine list?"

"Look, I'll be around, but I'm meeting someone beforehand to get details about who will be at the town hall."

"Should I come early? To go with you?"

"No," he said sharply. "No, not necessary. You know what we figured out, I'm people and you're place. Bring your map and we should be fine. On Friday you can stay at the hotel until I'm done or you can go to the restaurant early, I don't care. Get a booth."

"I just can't believe it's happening," Christy said wistfully. "Can you believe it?"

"I'll believe it when I'm out there and I open the chest myself. Until then, I've—we've—got to stay focused. No distractions. If you bring any of those crystals or oils or whatever down here, Christine, I swear—"

"Oh, don't worry. My daughter got rid of them all."

"Your what?"

"My daughter's in town. She flew in yesterday. It was unexpected, I think there's something going on. There's been a lot of crying, but it's nice to have company. You've never visited me."

"Does she know?"

"Know what?"

"About the map."

"Of course she does. It takes up my entire dining table."

He didn't respond. Christy bit her lip, hard. "She thinks it's silly."

"Silly?"

"She makes fun of it. But she'll have to go back to New York soon, she has a very demanding job. The hotel doesn't have internet, does it?"

He caught the hint. "It's not great. I mean, it's the middle of the desert."

"Exactly." Christy nodded to herself. "Nothing to worry about."

"If you say so."

"We've planned this for so long."

"It's time," he said firmly.

"It's time," she said, smiling.

The trail veered away from the creek and, after a few hundred yards, intersected with a golf course. The grass was bright green and littered with crushed bottles and goose shit. Sweat pooled in Bea's bra. She didn't have a hat or sunglasses. Panting, she made her way toward a pergola next to one of the tees. She sat down on a bench under its shade, her thighs slipping against the composite wood. In the distance, the metal spikes of a refinery and the clear, wobbling blur of a lit flare. There was still an hour and a half until noon.

Pulling out her phone and clicking through to Grant's profile was more habit than decision. The most recent picture was posted over a year ago. He wore a checked tangerine button-down that only works on a particular kind of man with a particular kind of jawline.

The photo was taken in the sprawling kitchen of some unknown home, Grant leaning against the marble countertop. It was his laugh in the picture that always got Bea, the way his head was tilted just enough for a few strands of hair to dangle in his eyes, hand outstretched toward the camera as if to say, I can't believe you said that, stop it, c'mon. There was no caption and seventy-two likes. She had followed his account ever since they met, and she compulsively checked to make sure she hadn't missed any new posts, even now. He told her he didn't really use social media, which Bea assumed is why he never followed her back and still didn't after she mentioned it. Bea had decided it was for the best. After all, distance was a form of privacy, and Gertie always told her that to give someone their privacy was to give them your respect. Bea was nothing if not respectful. Which is why she never liked the laughing photo, though she had looked at it hundreds of times. Did she sometimes imagine she took it? Yes, of course. But did she ever give it a small red heart? Never. Associating Grant with anything close to a heart, even if it was a like, was a bridge too far.

She tapped over to Carolyn's profile. It was a grid of bleached-out beaches and bouquets. Never any captions, always a location tag. The kind of profile that didn't have to strain for cohesion because it documented a life that was already immaculately curated, Carolyn literally being an art curator. Bea had liked every photo Carolyn had ever posted, except one from earlier that day, one Bea hadn't yet seen. They were outdoors at a wrought-iron table, green grass and blue sky, a beer and a wineglass suspended midclink. Their faces were out of frame, though the hand holding the wineglass was obviously Carolyn's, the dainty rings and fashionable manicure. The hand holding the beer was tanned and large-knuckled, sleeves of his checked tangerine shirt rolled up below the elbow.

It had always been dreamlike: only on weekdays, close to or just after midnight. His roommate's solemn nod at the door, Grant's crooked grin, his hand guiding her into his room. The beer and the whiskey and the weed and, occasionally, the drugs. Anything he consumed, she did, too. Their nights were blurred and scattershot, hardly whole. Afterward, they would sit on his couch eating microwaved quesadillas, watching a show about the bends in the space-time continuum, and he'd look at her and wait until she looked at him, and then he'd dive into her shoulder and make strange, honking noises, which never failed to make her laugh. Eventually, she'd leave, and for weeks she'd replay the night, over and over, while her texts went unread and posts went unliked, and when it seemed like the memory was almost too precious, almost too unreal, his name would appear on her phone, as if he knew, because he probably did.

There was no charade, no pretense. The nights in his apartment—and, later, the string of nights in hers—were the two of them at their most honest, Bea thought. They did what they did without any of the anxious messiness of other people or obligations. Bea had never had a boyfriend, and despite numerous suitors from dating apps, never got past the coffee or cocktail phase. But she and Grant were a tight, tidy world of intimacy. Sure, he wasn't much for foreplay, and sure, he frequently struggled to perform because he was usually drunk or stoned or both, but they were still young. Wasn't that what Gertie told her when they watched *90210* together and Bea would cover her face during the make-out scenes? *Ah, you're still young.* The real pleasure was afterward, in bed or on the couch, when Grant would become loose and relaxed, almost tender. They'd spend hours together hanging out, drinking, laughing, legs intertwined. He'd ask about her favorite band. She'd ask about a bruise on his thigh. They'd order food, and he'd do the shoulder-snorts. For Bea, it was enough.

"Seagulls. Right over there." It was the old man, the same one as before, standing in the shade of the pergola only a few feet away. "Sea. Gulls," the man said slowly. He was right, there were seagulls, three of them standing erect in the sandy bowl of a nearby trap. He held out a hand toward the birds, fingers bent into a gun. "Bam." The hand shifted to Bea. "And you didn't believe me," he jokingly scolded, waving his finger-guns at her. "Best place to see the whales is off near the North Shore. They only come out at night, though, and only if you don't wear any bright colors. It's worth the wait."

Bea wasn't scared, but wondered if she should be. "Are you following me?"

The man raised his hand. "Blessed be the observer," he said. He paused expectantly. Bea pinched her thighs, thumbs pressing into her skin, making sure she could feel it. She could. The man turned and slowly shuffled away. Bea watched until he disappeared around the bend of the trail. No one else was near, no one else had seen. Bea opened her phone, wanting to tell someone what had just happened. The screen was still Carolyn's photo, the checked shirt and the drinks. Grant had liked the photo. His red heart, for everyone to see, right at Bea's fingertips. Before she could like the photo, her mother called.

"Christ on a fucking cracker, leave a note before you disappear next time. Where are you?" There was noise in the background, a man yelling and some clanking.

"I had a business call," Bea said, remembering the lie. "I went on a walk to take it, I didn't want to wake you up. What's up?"

"Flint is here, and he would like to talk to you." Her mother's voice was unnervingly sweet and high-pitched.

"Who's Flint?"

"Our wonderful landlord. Oh, look, he just took a bite of his doughnut. Do you want to swallow first? No, okay, here he is."

There was shuffling of the phone being passed and then the smacking of lips. "Yeah, so, uh, your mom broke the AC unit." A shout in the background and Flint turned away from the phone, though Bea could still hear him chewing. "Okay, ma'am, if you didn't break anything, then how'd all this smelly oil get all over this?" He turned back, voice louder. "We're going to have to replace the whole system."

"Okay," Bea said. "That's what the security deposit is for, right? If I remember right, it was about twelve hundred dollars, that should be more than enough."

A loud, wet smack. "Nope, this is different."

"How is this different?"

"Oils. Voids the warranty."

"I believe the warranty is your problem, though, as the landlord."

"No, ma'am, don't think so."

"Let's reread the lease, then."

"AC wasn't on the lease. Your mother asked for it."

"So you're saying it was a gift? You're going to charge us for a gift?"

"Look." Flint's tone became hard. Bea could hear exactly how his tongue moved around his mouth. "You're going to have to sort this out with your mother, but this isn't a window unit. She poured stuff directly down the vent and now someone has to pay for it."

"That's what a security deposit is for, though."

"I got a guy coming by to give a quote. You can negotiate with him."

"A quote? For what?"

"For the system," Flint said with noticeable exasperation. Bea heard a knock. There were rustling noises, her mother saying hello. "Hey, buddy," Flint said, and then to Bea, "We're going to need you here as soon as possible. I'm gonna need a deposit up front."

"You just showed up, how do you even know how much it's going to be?" But the landlord didn't answer, already talking to some other person in the room. Bea kept asking if he was listening, but he clearly wasn't, and after some fumbling, hung up. She called back, but there was no answer. A group of golfers, all white-haired women in broad visors, walked toward the pergola. Bea checked her email. There was a new message from a recruiter she'd reached out to the other week. *Sadly because of my relationship with your former employer, I cannot . . .*

<hr>

Christy didn't question the need for a repair, or the need for AC, though she insisted she could go without. She didn't question when the repairman showed up and clearly pretended the situation was worse than it was—Christy married an HVAC salesman, after all, and knew there was no condenser down that vent, knew there was a labyrinth of metal ductwork that eventually led to a machine, but a few drops of oil would hardly travel far. In any case she knew the machine was old, from about the time her ex-husband first started selling them, and was corroded and undermaintained, but she didn't question them. She questioned why her daughter let the landlord hug her when he said hello. She questioned why her daughter believed the landlord when he said the lease didn't cover the HVAC system. She questioned why her daughter nodded as the repairman said the issue was irreparable and the cost nonnegotiable. She questioned why her daughter flinched as he mentioned the price, why she asked to pay with credit, why she paid at all.

"Are we sure, honey? I mean, why don't we get a second opinion?"

But they ignored her. Christy was used to this. In fact, she preferred it this way. She knew her daughter wouldn't listen to her about anything money related and she knew the men wouldn't listen to her about anything home improvement related, but if she questioned them, and they heard her question them, then it was enough. It wasn't passivity, no—Christy saw it more as quiet confidence. She was always here, right here, should they want to ask what she thought. No repair should cost that much, the system was already on the outs, and the men were playing into her daughter's obvious anxiety. A scam, plain and simple, but her daughter didn't bother—or want—to know her opinion. That'd been true since Bea was in diapers, and Christy had made her peace with it long ago.

If there was anything she would apologize for, it was her bad timing. She met Lindsey a couple of months ago at the local library. Christy was there to use the printers, methodically opening every Conversation link she'd emailed herself the night before, when Lindsey sat down at the desktop next to hers. There were plenty of other computers available, but Lindsey had chosen the one directly to Christy's left. This would usually annoy Christy, put her on alert, but Lindsey was young, noticeably so, and had the energy of a not-yet-potty-trained yellow Lab. The girl kept humming to herself as she clicked through her social media pages, conspicuously looking over at Christy. Christy eventually said hello, just to see what the girl would do, and the girl was unsurprisingly thrilled. "Hi!" she nearly screamed. "I'm Lindsey!"

Lindsey loved essential oils, loved how they smelled, loved how they were made, loved how they were packaged. She had some in her bag, did Christy want to see? Christy was printing nearly sixty pages of research. Christy would be at the library for a while. Christy said why not. Eventually, they moved to a table. Lindsey asked about Christy's life, what she was doing, where she'd been, and what her future was. Christy hadn't been asked these kinds of questions in a long time—she and Bob had not yet started their nightly phone calls—and was touched by the girl's curiosity. Once Christy mentioned her bout with cancer, though, Lindsey blossomed. "Thank goodness I found you!" the girl yelled again, enough for a librarian to turn and glare. Turns out, these oils could do anything, help anything, heal anything. Would Christy like some? Christy thought it was an offer, a gift. It wasn't, Lindsey apologized. There was an edge of desperation in the girl's voice when she mentioned three young kids at home. Christy was feeling flush from the sale of the Stamford house. She bought a dozen little dropper bottles and was blindsided when it cost her a couple hundred dollars. The girl followed her to the ATM and thanked her about a dozen times. Lindsey told her to follow her on her social media and waited for Christy to pull out her phone and do so, after which she left and Christy never heard from her again.

The oils were fine, if a bit overperfumed. Christy enjoyed putting a few drops of lavender in her bath and would sniff a bit of peppermint on sluggish mornings, but she never noticed any of the more medical benefits Lindsey insisted on. She still struggled to fall asleep and her back still ached. The rental house, though, always smelled faintly of cigarettes and strongly of mildew, and no amount of scented candles or room freshener covered it up. One morning, she'd been adjusting the air-conditioning and thought: two birds, one stone. Planning to spend the few hours with background HGTV while browsing the Conversation, Christy chose the vent closest to the couch. The bottle of patchouli was fairly full—it was her favorite and she'd been saving it—and the cap with the stopper was refusing to open. She twisted fairly hard until finally it popped and the bottle slipped out of her hands and shattered onto the vent. After Christy got most of the glass swept up, she thought the only issue would be how intense the scent concentration would be (but it was, she thought, a very lovely musky smell, much better than smoke-and-mildew), but then the AC wouldn't turn on. Christy poked around the outdoor compressor, suspecting the corroded coils were the issue, and told the landlord as such. With Bea in town, Christy had followed up with the landlord on the lack of AC. She never thought he'd show up so quickly, and now here he was, insisting the oils were to blame. "Disgusting," the landlord kept saying, nose wrinkling.

The repairman came suspiciously quick and had an obvious ease with the landlord. If her daughter was at all street savvy, she'd recognize this and demand the service call fee waived, but Bea didn't.

Christy opened a bag of chips and sat at the kitchen table while the others crouched around the vent in question, her daughter flustered about which credit card to use, always focused on the money and not the people. The chips were stale, but Christy ate them loudly, each bite making a satisfying crunch, and still they wouldn't look at her.

Christy didn't know when her daughter planned on leaving. Back in Connecticut, Bea would walk through the door and immediately announce the exact train she was taking back to the city. That she had come to visit Utah, and so suddenly, was surprising enough, but there'd been no mention of going back to New York. Her daughter was obviously hiding something, probably heartbreak, and that was fine. Christy could wait. The bag of chips was empty. Christy tossed it aside, bored. The men were leaving and Bea was apologizing again. Christy wiped her hands on her blouse. There was no way her daughter would stay more than a week, she knew. There was no reason to tell her about the trip to Mercy, not yet.

A person does not become a high school valedictorian, go to an Ivy League school on scholarship, and take the first job they're offered without a profound fear of the unknown. Bea knew this about herself. In college, it seemed the easiest way to make money—stable money, long-term money—was to work with money. She never considered any career other than Wall Street. She never again wanted to be the person who tallied up each lemon and onion in her cart, never wanted to debate between new shoes or a new coat. She never wanted to do the math, which is why she studied math. She was good at it, too. The way the numbers would cohere around a proof into a static, unquestionable outcome: it was intoxicating. The control of it, the predictability, the power. Once you learned the rules and functions, you could bend and combine them into a quantifiable reality. As she moved into meteorology, the math became bigger, realer. Her datasets and calculations, if they were good, could be reflected in actual events, backed by material consequence. There was a rush that came with an accurate prediction. A holiness, a godliness. Her mother would never believe her, but Bea considered it an art form. The formulas and tables and graphs were a world she created and adjusted as need be, a world wrought by study and imagination—a world that, if she did it right, reflected her lived reality. What was that, other than art?

Of course, she wasn't infallible. The derecho wasn't the first mistake she'd made, just the biggest. The first few years on the desk were littered with numerical accidents: the misplaced decimal, the inverted pivot, the missing dataset. She'd realize her mistakes and then lie awake at night cursing her stupidity, convinced she'd be fired the next morning. Phil, though, would always gently correct her before any of it got out, protecting her from the desk's frantic wrath. Their work was predictive analysis of weather systems; the margin of error was generous. When it became clear Bea wouldn't lose her job over a few botched Excel cells, she became complacent. Mistakes became routine, normal, and no one, least of all Phil, seemed to care. Years went by. Her colleagues who'd been summer analysts at the same time as her had long since been promoted into senior positions or left the bank, and she eventually became the longest-standing junior analyst on the desk. Bea would ask Phil for advice about promotions or responsibilities, but he always dodged her. He'd promise a holiday bonus or a modest pay raise, and would make good on those promises, but a title change was a dead end. By the time Phil had his seizure, Bea felt like she not only deserved more but needed more.

Bea sat on the front steps and did the math. The subletter's first payment would come tomorrow, but she'd have to save it for rent. There was Christy's rent, too, and then there were her loans and utility bills. It'd been a week since the AC repair, seven days of pretending to take important work calls while really avoiding the landlord's calls. Eight hundred and fifty dollars. She double-checked the lease. *Intentional harm.* The only exception to repairs. She did the math until there was no math left to do. If she paid the repair bill, there would be the credit cards, but not much else. The money, her money, would be gone. She planned to go out on another walk that morning, and had gotten as far as the gas station a few blocks away, when the wind picked up, air metallic and humid. A storm was congealing over the plains, dark clouds thickening with moisture. The morning was bright and warm, but Bea knew it wouldn't be for long.

She peeled open the pack of cigarettes. Bea had smoked occasionally through college, mostly as a way to fit in, and Grant had a pack-a-day habit. It wasn't something she sought out, but buying a pack felt better than asking the gas station clerk where the nearest state liquor store was. She told herself she'd quit once she went back to New York and, as she lit a cigarette, refused to think about when that might be.

Truck brakes groaned from the nearby highway. Somewhere, a leaf blower. A few crows hopped into the yard, scratching at the ground. They watched Bea and Bea watched them until the door across the street banged open and the Zs tumbled out, jostling each other, and the birds flew off to the roof, beady-eyed and suspicious. Each kid was turtled with an oversized backpack, sleeping bags cradled in their arms, and they wore matching lavender T-shirts that said WASATCH WARD WARRIORS 2016. One of the girls shoved one of the boys and after a minute of fake crying, they sat on the curb and began a complex game of throwing pebbles. One bounced a few feet from Bea. She tossed the pebble back and the Zs screamed, hands over their heads. *Holy shit what are you doing holy shit you're ruining the game holy shit holy shit is she going to throw her cigarette next holy shit.* They were still screaming when a white school bus rolled up. The Zs disappeared into it and reappeared at the windows, their noses up against the glass. Bea waved and one of them stuck out their tongue, spit smearing across the window. The bus left. Above, one of the crows shat, the white paste flecking the steps next to her. The wind picked up. She shivered and texted the subletter to ask if all was okay. The response was immediate. Could she empty out one of the dresser drawers? Her boyfriend was staying over a lot and wanted room for his clothes. Bea didn't respond. She went to her inbox and read market reports out of habit, thoughtlessly noting the temperature shifts over the South Pacific, already mentally drafting a summary email to Phil, only to remember Phil, and everything she'd always done for him, was no longer her problem.

The door opened behind her. "You need the car?" her mother asked. Bea shook her head. Typhoons likely, Bea typed into an email draft to no one. Christy began talking about a store, something about a midsummer sale. Bea continued to type. Late August winds building across the southern seas. Disruption to main corridor shipping routes. Autos and tech. Bullish.

Christy sat down next to her and looked at her expectantly. "Want to come?"

"What?" Bea exhaled. Christy waved the smoke out of her face.

"I just told you, the store. Tomorrow. It's the best of the year."

"Best what?"

"Sale. You wouldn't believe the deals. Want to come? I'm going to leave first thing in the morning and try to get there as it opens. I'd love some red beryl. It's rare, but apparently this place specializes in it. Can get it for hundreds less than normal."

"Hundreds? Of *dollars*?"

"They're extremely rare crystals, honey."

Bea had been the primary executor of Gertie's estate. After Gertie died, she went over the numbers. There wasn't a lot left, not enough to sustain her mother indefinitely, especially since, to Bea's total shock, Gertie had a startling amount of gambling debt. Bea had expected her mother to be bereft, but Christy had been infuriatingly casual. How did sweet Gertie even know about online poker? Who told her? Christy shrugged. Every mother is a mystery, she'd said to Bea, which only made Bea suspect it was Christy's fault. They'd been forced to sell the Stamford house, and for much less than either Macon woman had hoped. Christy soon announced she was moving to Utah. Bea encouraged it—cheaper than Connecticut, she figured—and agreed to pay for Christy's rent and health insurance out west. How her mother could pay for anything else was unclear. Christy had always been able to get by without any sort of recognizable job or career, somehow managing to make do, and Bea had never let herself think about it too deeply. Better to not know, better to not ask. But that was Bea's stance when she still had a career, when her future was still knowable and plannable. Just last night, she got another email from a recruiter declining a phone call. Bea dragged on her cigarette, willing herself patience. "If you can afford a rock that costs hundreds of dollars, then you can afford rent."

"If you don't want to go with me, that's fine," Christy said, unbothered. "But I really think this crystal is going to do wonders. Red beryl is known to draw good energy toward you while promoting calm and confidence. It's also an aphrodisiac. Can't put a price tag on that combination, if you ask me."

It happened only with her mother, this immediate fury, how it snapped out of her in a quick, hot instant. "If you want some good, calm energy around here, how about you start paying the fucking bills."

Christy stiffened. "Look," she said. "I know the AC unit wasn't a fun situation, but I also think the repairman—"

"I think," Bea snarled, "it's time for you to start paying rent. Next month, actually."

Christy stared at her evenly. After a long, quiet moment, her mother went inside. Bea's breathing became hitched and shallow. She told herself it was from the cigarette. She put her phone down and waited for her anger to subside. The rage was reflexive, a muscle she'd been using since Montreal, and though she didn't regret her words, she regretted her delivery. Too harsh, too impetuous. She needed to be better than that. More controlled. Her mother would never listen otherwise. Bea breathed. A hand on her back, her mother's, the other holding out a narrow piece of paper. A check.

"For the AC," her mother explained. It was half the cost of the repair. "I can stretch a dollar when I need to, but I don't think I can cover rent yet. Maybe in a couple of months. There's a farmers' market at the park by the golf course. I was thinking I'd start making my herbal soaps again. Remember those? With how much people love all-natural stuff out here, I could charge ten dollars a bar. More if I add oats and call it baby-friendly." Christy dropped her voice and pointed over her shoulder into the house. "And I think I'm on to something. I could find it. I really think I could."

It took Bea a moment to remember. "The treasure?" Bea said, nearly laughing. "You're serious?"

"Dead serious."

She was, Bea could tell by the way her mother said it. Bea considered the check. She did the math. A plane ticket, maybe. A sliver of her Brooklyn rent. About half of the Utah rent. None of the options were fixes, but they were options nonetheless. She took the check from her mother and the relief was so instant, so heavy, that Bea fought the urge to close her eyes.

"We could stop by the bank on the way to the store," Christy said. "If you need to," she added.

There was edge of concern in Christy's tone and Bea realized her mistake. She had never taken money from Christy, not once. It was never an option and therefore never a question. Bea had always been the provider. All of the weekend plans canceled, all of the friends who lost touch, all of the hours at the desk: Bea would insist it was all to help Christy and Gertie. She did it for them, because who else would? If she had a job, she would never accept the check. She would've told Christy to keep it, to spend it on groceries. She would've told her mother to stop being so dramatic. And Christy knew that.

They didn't have to pay the repair just yet, she decided. She could hold off a bit longer. In the meantime, she'd figure out something else. She always did. "Not necessary," Bea said breezily. She tore the check in half. "I already paid the repair."

Christy sat down and motioned to Bea's cigarette. "Next time do that closer to the road, you're getting the smell inside and then we'll never get the security deposit back. Flint is an absolute idiot about smoking. The other month he thought my incense was some sort of drug and went ballistic. He accused me of being stoned and when I told him it was nag champa, he said I was speaking in tongues. These people have no idea what they're talking about. Remember how upset the neighbors in Stamford got when I started composting? The *looks* they gave me! Told me I was out of my mind. Now everyone has those little bins under their sinks. But this landlord, he'll definitely recognize cigarettes." Bea snuffed out the butt on the steps. "Well, no need to waste one, the damage's already been done," Christy said, taking the pack. "Want to split one?"

"I thought you hated smoking. You told me it was antifeminist."

"That doesn't sound right."

"Remember when you found me out by the driveway last year around Christmas? You tried to hit the cigarette out of my hand. Look, I even have a scar." Bea pointed at a knuckle where there was a faint, glossy spot of skin. It could've been a scar or a wart, Bea wasn't sure, but she remembered how wild-eyed Christy had been, screaming outside in the snow in a short-sleeved dressing gown about how irresponsible Bea was being. Bea had demanded to know who was actually the irresponsible one here, who was actually paying all the bills. The feminism comment happened. More yelling, their words becoming clouds in the cold, and then the scuffle for the cigarette. It went on long enough that a neighbor came outside and asked if he should call someone. Christy had fled inside, gown open. Bea was supposed to stay the weekend and help trim the tree; instead, she called an Uber and lit another cigarette. While she waited for the car, she caught sight of something glinting in the sidewalk's dirty slush. Her mother's earring, a dangly beaded one that Bea knew was a favorite. Bea had kicked it deeper into the snowbank.

"My mother was dying. I was upset and I knew it was her last Christmas and I couldn't handle it."

"I was upset, too," Bea said. "I was stressed and sad, too."

Christy pulled back her hair with both hands and then, after a moment, let it fall, curls bouncing. "I know," she said, as if it were an apology. They sat in silence for a minute, each ignoring the urge to reach for the other.

Christy lit a cigarette, inhaled, and then handed it to Bea. "I can't smoke the whole thing myself unless I want cancer again."

The wind picked up. They passed the cigarette back and forth until ash blew into their faces, the sky darkening, the crows disappearing. The leaf blower picked back up again, and there was the faint roar of the highway. There was thunder. There were so many things to listen to, to notice. *Blessed be the observer.*

lol i wish i could do this to my wife's crystal bullshit
@MadMax is this kosher?
DUUUUDE LMAO
i don't see what this has to do with the Convo
Not cool, Bob. This is not what I want to see first this morning. @MadMax
probably not great to do that on quartz, buddy, like literal bad vibes
woooooooooow lol
This is really inappropriate. Flagging @MadMax
hey bob you trying to tell us your stupid desert theory is a dud? fuckin knew it.

The photo was of piss. Of Bob pissing. Or, at least, of someone pissing. It was a selfie, taken from about chest-high, a strong yellow stream in full view as it splashed onto a pile of quartz. Christy zoomed in. Though the body was out of frame, and it was posted from his account, Christy could tell it wasn't Bob. The shoes were wrong—new, trendy sneakers—and he'd know better than to do something like that to quartz. It must be some sort of joke, one that no one would understand except for her, but she didn't get it. She wondered if this was Bob telling her to call him. She zoomed in and out, analyzing the photo for some sort of clue, anything she might've missed, and before she knew it, her daughter was over her shoulder and peering at the screen. Christy tried to pull the tablet into her chest, but Bea was too quick, snatching it out of her hands. "Holy shit, is this a picture of someone *urinating*?"

Bob hated crystals, told her she looked ridiculous holding rose quartz as she consulted the map. He thought it was immature, or as he called it, *unserious*. He said it made a mockery of the scientific research they did together. She said the crystals were harmless, something she enjoyed, and it didn't have anything to do with him, so what was the big deal? But Bob wouldn't hear of it, said as much the last time they spoke. "Stop sending me these stupid rocks," he said. And she did, hadn't sent anything to him in days. She'd missed his past few calls. He texted asking if she was ignoring him, but she wasn't, she was just busy with Bea and the AC, she told him. The last text she sent mentioned the crystals sale, how she was excited about the chance to buy more. She meant for it to be flirtatious, a teasing reference to their disagreement. But to respond like this! Everyone on the Conversation knew Christy was the crystals person. He'd never been so public, so blatant, about their connection.

Bea put down her coffee and scrolled the Conversation. "Wait, this is OnlyBob? The same guy from the cliff photo? Why did someone write, 'Christy knows what this means'?"

Christy took back the tablet. She hadn't seen that comment. NC-Guy. Never heard of him, but that didn't matter. A lot of people knew her. She was, she was proud to admit, a bit of personality on the site. "It's an inside joke, they're being funny."

"Funny? It's fucking *gross*." Bea pantomimed a gag.

Christy pulled up her texts. Funny, but the crystals aren't going anywhere. I'll call you tomorrow when I'm on the road. The text was immediately marked read, but he didn't respond, and she didn't expect him to. Christy saw the time. "We have to go," she shouted to Bea. "We're going to be late for the sale!" The store was across the city and the drive took longer than expected. By the time they pulled up, the store had been open for over twenty minutes and there was a line wrapping around the parking lot. Christy's heart sank.

"This many people want some overpriced rocks?"

Christy didn't dignify her daughter with a response. There weren't any open spaces in the lot and she had to loop around the block before pulling over. She gripped the steering wheel, the car sputtering.

"Are you going to park?"

"Pointless," Christy said. The tiger's-eye would be one of the first crystals to sell, she was sure of it. She drove away.

"Where are we going?" Bea asked.

"Home," Christy said.

"What about the crystals?"

"Don't need them."

"Are you sure?"

"Positive."

She was leaving tomorrow, she told herself. The weekend—their weekend—began in mere hours. Her and Bob, in the desert, on the hunt, together. Despite it being all she had thought about for weeks, Christy couldn't shake her dark mood. Bob was already there, like they always planned, but who was in the photo with the crystals? Maybe he met someone at the hotel, some dirtbag he befriended in order to learn more about the area. That's what they needed, after all.

A local to give them the literal lay of the land, to show them how to navigate the canyons. Maybe he got drunk with some kid and they decided to have a laugh together. It was a joke, she told herself. The photo wasn't funny, but it didn't mean anything. Besides, she'd see him tomorrow and could ask him about it in person. They'd laugh about it together. Maybe she should turn around and go back to the crystal shop, buy him some new quartz. Christy almost put on her blinker, but then it started to hail. No matter, she thought. Better not to, keep her luggage light. That's what he always told her. She could nearly hear him say it. No need for crazy, Christine, just keep it light and simple.

They pulled up to the house. Christy didn't notice it at first. Bea did. Her daughter asked what was on the front door, she got out of the car and pulled it off the door. Bea slapped a hand over her mouth. Christy scrambled out of the Chrysler. "What?" she yelled. Her daughter yelled something back, but Christy misheard, or thought she did.

"What do you mean, eviction?"

Christy was not a quiet person, but most of what she knew about parenting revolved around knowing when to be quiet. There was a lot Christy wanted to talk to her daughter about, like why Bea thought she was entitled to the bathroom at all times or why she had barely mentioned her boyfriend, Grant. But what she most wanted to talk to Bea about was money.

Ever since they got the notice the day before, Bea kept saying how the eviction was ridiculous, asking if Christy could believe it. Christy could and did. Never trust any man who chews that much gum. Still, it was her daughter's reaction that gave her pause. Bea was anxious and angry, clearly, but not at Christy. In fact, not once in the twenty-four hours since the notice had her daughter tried to blame her, and Bea blamed Christy for most things. Her daughter had left the notice on the kitchen table. Christy read it. Failure to pay for damages. They had one week.

Christy had always trusted Bea with money matters. She wasn't proud her daughter supported her, but her daughter seemed proud to do so. Bea was a math whiz and the financial guru, everything Christy wasn't. This had always been the family narrative, one that all of them, even Gertie, had repeated. Thank god for Bea. What would we do without Bea. Ever since Montreal, Christy had always been able to make do, scraping together spending money with various side hustles, mostly crafts sold at farmers' markets—at one point her soaps had a cult following in Fairfield County, everyone from Darien housewives to Wilton Quakers clamoring for her squares of flower-embedded lye—but her daughter was, without a doubt, her lifeline.

This was doubly true after her cancer wiped out her Montreal savings, triply ever since Christy moved to Salt Lake and, for the first time, had a lease. Christy had never paid rent because she had never had to. Her ex-husband's company paid for their short-term rentals and the Stamford house was in Gertie's name. Now that she did, she wasn't even sure how to, and was grateful, deeply so, that she didn't need to. Her daughter always took care of it. Or at least, her daughter always took great pains to make it seem like she had taken care of it. Now, as they sat next to each other on the couch, both partially obscured by their screens, she wasn't so sure. She spent the afternoon debating if she should say anything and decided she should. She was leaving for Mercy the next morning and didn't want the eviction to cloud her trip. Christy chose her words like she pulled off price tags in a store: carefully, but without remorse. "The eviction said it was due to a failure of payment for damages. You said you already paid him. Do you need to tell me something?"

Christy could see Bea's jaw clench. "No."

"You sure?"

"Yes."

"I'm happy to help. I can write another check, maybe call Flint and talk to him about a payment plan. I'm a good tenant, even the Zs' parents say so—I guess the people before me were wild, playing loud music all the time. He's an idiot, but he's not stupid. I'm sure we can figure something out."

"Mom," Bea said. "I paid him. What he's doing is extortion, but I'm handling it."

Her daughter sounded so confident, Christy thought. It would impress her if her ex-husband hadn't been the same way. "Sorry," she said. "The notice seemed so official. I got worried."

"I told you, I'm handling it."

Christy pretended to poke around on her tablet. She asked one big question, why not another? "Also, when are you planning on going back to New York? I don't think you ever told me."

Bea didn't miss a beat. "You can just tell me if you don't want me here."

Patience, Christy reminded herself. She inhaled through her diaphragm. Exhaled. "You're welcome to stay as long as you'd like, but you should know I'm spending the weekend in the desert. I'm leaving tomorrow morning and I'm taking the car with me. I'll be back Monday night."

Bea's head jolted up. "Hold on, you're *leaving*?"

"I would've rescheduled if I had known you were going to be here for this long, but it's too late to cancel the hotel reservation. It's only for a couple of days." Christy had prepared. She had bought sturdy sneakers from Goodwill, lifted a pair of workout leggings and a hot pink sports bra from Target. Everything packed in a bag at the foot of her bed. All that was left was an oil change for the old Chrysler, which was supposed to happen today, but she'd forgotten about it after the crystals and then eviction crisis, so it would have to wait until tomorrow. That was fine, she could deal with some hiccups, because everything else was planned: the hikes, the routes, the gear, the meals. Their meals. A whole weekend of just the two of them. They were meeting in real life. Christy didn't expect Bea to still be in Utah, but the time alone in Salt Lake might be good for her daughter, as Bea, it seemed increasingly clear, needed to get her head on straight. A restorative weekend for them both. Christy got up and went to the sink. She ran the tap at full blast, numbing her hands under the cold water. "You're welcome to stay here," she repeated.

"Did you somehow forget we're getting *evicted*?"

"That's not until the end of the month."

"Which is in a week."

"We've been planning for this for weeks. It's all sorted. It's not a question."

"*We?*" Bea laughed meanly. "I should've known. And who's paying for this romantic getaway, huh?"

Christy viciously scrubbed a plate, careful to keep her voice even. "I don't need your permission."

"No, you need my money."

Christy tossed the sponge across the counter. "How many Thanksgivings did you spend on your laptop while Gertie and I cooked? How many times did you leave Stamford a day early to prepare some report? When you showed up here with hardly any notice, I was *thrilled*. I thought you were actually here to surprise me, to *visit me*. But it's been, what, almost two weeks? This is the first time I've seen your precious work laptop. And now there's an issue with paying the landlord. Be honest, do you even have a return ticket?"

Her daughter froze. "I took PTO," she said finally.

All those years ago, whenever they moved to a new town, chasing her ex-husband, Christy would drop Bea off at the local ice cream shop with ten dollars and encourage her to buy a cone for herself and a friend, saying how any kid would appreciate having a free cone, why doesn't she go say hi. Christy would pretend to run an errand, only to park around the corner and watch her daughter from across the street. Bea stood patiently in line, the other middle schoolers jostling and yelling around her, until eventually ordering a cone, always with sprinkles. She'd pay, pocketing the change, and then Bea would sit on a stool and lick it, slowly and methodically, so still and nondescript none of the other kids would bother her. After a few agonizing minutes, Christy would pull the car around. Bea would already be standing on the sidewalk, a stray sprinkle stuck on her perfect cheek. Her daughter was withdrawn as she climbed into the back seat, answering Christy's questions in a clipped, serious voice. Yes, she had fun, yes, her friend had ordered the same thing. Christy remembered how, when she asked what Bea's friend's name was, how her daughter would pause, wipe the sprinkle off her face, and ask, could we please go home now? Christy would curse herself for following her ex-husband all those years, pulling Bea out of all those schools and camps. The constant change had hardened her daughter into a stoic, she'd cry to Gertie after Bea had gone to bed. There was no way to protect your child against disappointment, Gertie had told her. You do your best and then you have to let them find their way.

Christy rolled her shoulders and turned back to the sink. "I'm taking the car for the weekend. You can call me if there are any issues." Bea didn't respond.

When she was done with the dishes, Christy prepared a bowl of baby carrots and a block of cream cheese, one of their old snacks, and brought it to the couch as a peace offering. Bea put away her laptop and broke a carrot in two, dipping both pieces into the cheese. Christy pulled Bea's legs into her lap and Bea let her. Christy flicked on the TV. A movie was on, an older one about high schoolers played by actors with cocaine problems and greasy hair. Christy watched for a moment, remembering when it first came out in theaters. She'd gone alone since her husband deemed the movie immature. The boy at the concessions stand gave her free popcorn. The actors were running through hallways. Christy didn't remember this part. The concessions boy had been cute and her age. Christy went back three more times, telling her husband she loved the soundtrack. Each time, the boy gave her free popcorn and then, eventually, his number. She called him once but hung up when he answered. Christy snapped a carrot between her teeth.

Bea changed the channel to the nightly news. A fire had started in one of the canyons. The anchorman discussed how people had lost their horses, aerial footage of burnt stables. The rain should help, the weatherman said with a perfect smile. It always does. "Sad," Bea said, flipping to the next channel. It was Christy's favorite celebrity gossip show, a show so ridiculous she wouldn't normally want her daughter to know she watched, but she no longer had the energy to care. "Keep this on," she said. Bea, mercifully, said nothing. They watched quietly, side by side, carrots crunching, as a segment about a pop star began. The star had been struggling ever since her biggest hit, a beloved earworm from when Bea was in high school, and who was now more famous for her tabloid appearances than anything else. They kept playing clips of her performing the song and then cutting away to humiliating, late-night paparazzi shots.

"That was such a great song."

"And she always seemed like such a sweetheart. I would hang out with her."

"Remember the underwater thing? When she was a villainous mermaid?" They both laughed. "Like, why did she need a gun underwater?"

"And that hair!" The pop star had famously red hair. "You can't argue with that hair. But she should've stuck to her roots and stayed with the ballads. I always thought she had a beautiful voice, but then she covered it up with all that electronica nonsense. It sounded like shoes in a dryer. Remember her football show?"

"You mean the Super Bowl? When she tripped?"

"And she did that magazine cover with the matching bathing suits."

"Right! With her sister!"

"They did everything together, huh?"

"It was creepy. They were touching each other too much. Remember the boyfriend, that dancer guy? He got her to wear all those hats, the ones with the feathers." They laughed again. They were ridiculous hats, even the pop star eventually admitted it. "I don't think she even makes music anymore." Bea wiped at cream cheese that fell onto her sleeve, a white smear across her gray sweatshirt. Christy took Bea's arm, licked a thumb, and rubbed. The white smeared deeper into the fabric.

"I feel like she fell apart when she fired her mother as her manager. Maybe that's for the best. Maybe she's happier now."

"Are you happier?" Bea asked, suddenly serious.

Christy hesitated. "With her not making music?" she asked, letting go of her daughter's arm.

"Being in Utah. Do you like it?"

"Sure," Christy said carefully. "I don't miss Connecticut, if that's what you're asking. It's gorgeous and cheap and easy. But you're too far away."

Bea sucked on her lower lip. "You're definitely leaving tomorrow?"

"Yes."

"Is it for the treasure thing?"

Christy nodded.

"And this person you're going with, are they a treasure person?"

"He is."

"Were you ever going to tell me about him?"

"Maybe," Christy said. "Eventually," she added.

"That's so dumb."

"Don't call it dumb. It's not dumb."

"Meeting a stranger in the middle of nowhere? Staying with him for an entire weekend? Not telling me about it? How is any of that a smart idea?"

"I would like to see him, to make sure it's real. To know it's real," Christy said softly.

Bea scoffed. "Don't tell me you're in love."

"Are you in love with Grant?"

"It isn't like that."

"Exactly," Christy said. "Exactly."

A long moment, the TV announcer discussing a forthcoming romantic comedy about populating Mars. Finally, "I'm coming with you," Bea said. "I didn't fly all the way out here to be alone, and I don't want to be around if the landlord shows up."

"Why?"

"He's evicting us, Mom, I don't think he'd show up with cookies. I'm coming with."

Christy was surprised at how relieved this made her, so much so she nearly forgot about Bob. He was a parent. Or was he? She couldn't remember. He must be. Something about the way he gave advice about Bea. He'd understand, she thought. He had to. "Fine. You'll have to get your own hotel room, though."

"Obviously," Bea snorted and, despite herself, Christy did, too.

An HVAC salesman, Bea's father traveled the country evangelizing the miracle of high-efficiency, low-cost heating and cooling. Never sweat or shiver! Comfort starts with temperature! Control your climate, don't let it control you! Family dinners were spent debating how best to sell baseboard heat to Phoenix suburbanites or Arctic-simulating window units to Fargo homesteaders. Whether her father was any good at his pitch, however, was unclear. The Macon family's tenure in any given locale seemed less beholden to sales numbers and more to her father's inability to commit. There was more than one afternoon where Bea came home from school to find a note on the kitchen counter explaining San Jose's burgeoning condominium boom and Christy should call the central office, they'll explain everything, he'll see them when they made it out. Christy would spend the rest of the evening yelling profanity-laced demands into the central office's answering machine. Mostly: how dare they, don't they know this is a family, and if they didn't tell her which hotel they put her husband in she'd be sure to tell them exactly how small their genitals were. Bea didn't remember Christy ever leaving these messages for Bea's father.

Leaving, in Bea's childhood, was just as abrupt and unsurprising as acne. Unwelcome, usually accompanied by some deep ache, but an expected part of growing up. Once she found a soccer team that served orange slices at halftime or had a successful slumber party with other Jonathan Taylor Thomas enthusiasts, it'd be time to go. Her father would look at her and Christy over his morning coffee, eyes bright, and announce, *Tampa*, as if the city were the second coming. Or there'd be the note on the counter. Or there'd be nothing at all, not until someone from the central office finally called Christy back, and then they'd head off to State College or Fort Wayne or Vallejo. He was a goddamn traveling salesman, he'd yell whenever Bea asked if she could sign up for summer camp, who knows where they'd be by summer! But isn't that exciting? Besides, honeybee, camp is expensive; the road is free.

When the time came to leave, Christy and Bea would pull the suitcases out of the closets and begin their routine. Never-hung pictures were tossed into the car trunk. Kitchen utensils dumped into a shoebox, sheets stuffed into trash bags. Only Christy's plants were packed up gently. Despite how many times her father would try to throw them out, or how many times Bea would complain about them, Christy insisted the plants come with. Bea and Christy would spend an entire day carefully tying back the various plastic branches and cloth blooms, and then the fig and ivy and clover and cacti would sprout out from the back seat of the old Chrysler, blocking the rearview and rustling on the turns, quiet compatriots to the Macon women's every move.

This time, as Bea and Christy left Salt Lake City for Mercy, only the aspen bounced on the floor of the back seat. Her mother didn't think it necessary, but Bea had insisted. "It'll keep me company while I'm off doing Conversation things," she said happily, but her mother remained sullen and unimpressed. Bea knew she was interrupting, knew her mother had been excited about her weekend and now was sullen and careful, delaying their departure with unnecessary chores and bathroom breaks. Bea called about another room at the hotel, but when she heard the nightly price, she hung up. A quick internet search brought up an RV park across the street that had rustic cabins for rent. They'd have to stay through Monday to meet the nightly minimum, but Bea could use her credit card points. Her mother said Bea should save them for something fun. Bea told her this could be fun if Christy ditched the creepy dude and stayed in the cabin with her. Christy didn't respond, only closed her eyes, fingertips on her temples.

But Bea didn't care, because Bea was in a fantastic mood. That morning, a recruiter had reached out over email. *Would you be interested in a call today or tomorrow . . . the hiring process is already underway. . .* It was a no-name freight research firm based out of Los Angeles that peddled low-level data reports, the kind of reports Phil would purchase if a broker pushed him for an impact analysis, which almost always went unread, since the report's existence was usually enough justification for them to make the trade. The firm hoped to expand into meteorological predictions and was staffing up a newly opened Manhattan office. The recruiter didn't clarify the exact position that was available, but did mention Bea's "highly sought-after expertise" and "years of experience" as reasons they wanted to interview her ASAP. The research firm would be a demotion, a job that would be awkward to admit to should she ever run into any of her old coworkers, but that didn't matter, not now. Bea responded immediately, saying she was available at any time. Feeling generous, and suspecting she'd have to go back to New York promptly, if not immediately, Bea promised her mother elaborate car games and a deep dive into their astrological birth charts. But when Bea climbed behind the wheel of the Chrysler, Christy took the back seat. Her mother said her knees were bothering her and she needed to stretch out. After a few miles Christy was asleep, tablet on her chest, snoring faintly.

Bea didn't mind, not until she pulled the car onto the highway. She switched radio stations until she found something recognizable and forced herself to hum along. It was like riding a bike, she told herself, if the bike was two tons of steel and had to maintain a minimum speed of sixty-five miles per hour in the right lane. Bea got her license at sixteen and, like most teenagers, zoned out during driver's ed and confused the gas for the brakes at least once. In Stamford she had access to the Chrysler, but Gertie kept the car on retainer for her unreliable schedule of bridge, grocery runs, and hair appointments, so throughout high school, Bea took the bus or hitched rides with friends. Bringing the Chrysler to college was never an option and driving was unnecessary in New York. The six-lane highway snaking along the Wasatch Front was her first time driving on a major highway in nearly a decade.

It was a hazy morning, the inversion thin and gray in the rearview mirror. Bea let go of the steering wheel just long enough to turn on the hazards. She calculated how much room she needed to give the monstrous semitrucks surrounding her. Driving wasn't that bad. People do it every day, frequently multiple times a day, sometimes all day. Totally normal, she thought. Totally fine. A few panels of plastic and metal between her and the person driving in the next lane, everyone hoping everyone else would abide by a barely-agreed-upon set of rules dictated by painted lines on the ground. As if people were naturally cautious and courteous. As if humanity were gracious and rational. Not to mention weather, wildlife, and random fucking chance. The sun goes behind the clouds, the sun comes out from behind the clouds: both have been reason enough for someone to panic, jerk the wheel to the left, and obliterate themselves in a tangle of metal and glass. Idiots, everyone, idiotically maneuvering around mountains in near-guaranteed death machines, like it was normal and boring and not one of the statistically stupidest things to do. Why did we build our entire society to be dependent on mobile combustion engines of probable suicide, nothing holding you back but your own dumb sense of self-preservation? Bea's armpits were damp and cold and she pushed the brakes to remind herself she could.

Bea was never old enough to drive during their cross-country travels. Christy never left any of the major highways, always choosing efficiency over scenery. Who knew what her father was up to, her mother would mutter as she blazed over the speed limit, stopping only to pee, stretch, or refuel. But there was no father to chase now. After a close call with an oversized tractor trailer, Bea pulled over and programmed her phone to avoid highways and tolls. The backroads added an additional two hours. When Christy groggily asked Bea why they were on a single-lane road in the middle of farm pastures, Bea said it could be part of Christy's research. A way to get the true lay of the land, to know what you're dealing with down here. In truth, Bea figured backroads would be less trafficked and thus more amenable to her consistent, low-grade panic attack. Her mother didn't seem to care, quickly falling back to sleep. Bea flexed her fingers over the steering wheel, the joints sore and cramping from constant gripping. Her shoulders relaxed when the speed limit halved and she became the only car on the road.

The Utah backroads were more back than anything Bea had ever seen. No house or building for miles, rolling grasslands and endless wire-and-wood fencing. An occasional hare streaked across the road, ears straight up and twice its size. Occasionally, the flat sprawl of alfalfa bisected by thin spokes of irrigation arms. And then a town, no more than a few double-wides and derelict farmhouses, maybe a gas station or post office, empty except for a wandering dog or gaunt horse. But tractors moved in the fields, splays of dust clouded out from behind them. In one town, Bea looked over quick enough to see a hand flip a sign in a roadside store to OPEN. People, somewhere, out here.

It was disorienting for Bea to realize, or remember, how the country was so vast. How most of it was not apartments and late-night delivery, public transportation and overcrowded bars. Most of America was broad, wide expanses of land scattered with towns that were no bigger than a few seconds in a car. In New York or Chicago or Seattle there was no question that in ten, fifteen, fifty years it would still be a place where people lived and loved and worked. Six hours may get you from Los Angeles to New York in a plane, but that wouldn't get you through the full length of Utah in a car. These were broad western spaces, spaces so overlooked that an area the size of Connecticut could be designated national wilderness the same year the personal cell phone debuted and most wouldn't even know where it was on a map.

Slowly, the land shifted from snowmelt-fed mountains, thick with spruce and aspen, into vast, flat prairie, until, finally, they drove through arid canyonland. The road curved between red cliffs as high as skyscrapers. It was hard not to feel alone in this kind of place, the endless sky and land, huge and open. But instead of a kind of loneliness, Bea recognized an excitement, an awe. For the first time since she left New York, the future felt near and coming.

PART TWO

Glory Be to the Money Diggers

Some sources close to Joseph Smith claim that in his youth, during his spiritual immaturity prior to his being entrusted with the Book of Mormon plates, he sometimes used a stone in seeking for treasure. Whether this is so or not, we need to remember that no prophet is free from human frailties.

—ELDER DALLIN H. OAKS, FROM A TALK GIVEN AT BRIGHAM YOUNG UNIVERSITY, AUGUST 1987

S pend enough time in the desert and you'll get to know its rain. It doesn't come often, but when it does, it feels like it won't leave. Monsoon season. The wild, furious time when dust becomes mud becomes flood. A horrible river that engulfs anything in its path, tires and toddlers and lawn chairs and cows, a giant gargling mass thundering along the ground while a thousand white fingers rip open the sky. The flood churns, thick brown blood coursing through canyon veins, until it exhausts itself into Lake Powell or a flat-brimmed wash, heavy with debris and death. But when it ends: life.

This is how it's supposed to rain in the desert, the way it has for millennia, far before the first humans trawled across its lands, hunting, worshipping, and moving on. Before another set of humans came with different animals and different worship. They didn't leave. They didn't know the land or the rivers, but they stayed. They claimed sovereignty, purity, paradise. They murdered, stole, farmed. Eventually, different rains came.

They told no one it was happening. Not the ranch towns to the east or the reservations to the south. Ignored, too, were the tortoises and hares and coyotes and vultures. The testing sites were deemed worthless, nothing and nowhere. The blast a colossal bellow. The sky went silent for a moment and then everything rippled, a rug shook out. Children stopped and laughed while they headed to school, touching the ground, wondering if it would happen again. Women ran outside and then back in, babes at their breasts, milk spilled on the table. Men paused on horseback or tractors and looked west, saucer-eyed, as the cloud bloomed upward and outward. Their cows bolted, their dogs cowered, and all the birds vanished.

It was an eerie, long, silent moment. Then the rain started. A fine, fluttering gray. Not quite snow, not quite ash. Something more glinting and dark.

The children were outside, shoving and screaming. When it began to fall, they all looked up, opened their palms. As it settled on the ground, they scraped it up and balled it in their fists, taking bites. It crunched on their tongues, warm. They threw it at each other, they rubbed it into their hair, they shoved it down their pants. Later, much later, those who remained would think back and remember how before they knew what it was, it was the most magic their town had seen in a long time. How they laughed and played, ash on their lashes and between their toes, their teachers looking on, hushed and wary.

The lambs died first. It began with bloody vomit and angry sores before shifting in a bloated, drawn-out agony, the herd looking on as their young screamed, bubble-eyed. The ewes died next, in the same way, though not as quickly. Those that survived gave blue-tinted milk that tasted a day away from rancid. Horses refused to eat, losing hair and becoming gaunt. Dogs formed giant lumps behind their ears and under their haunches. The birds were still gone. For weeks, whenever it rained, the raindrops were gray and heavy and smelled of metal.

They knew something happened, and was happening, but they didn't realize how much had changed until years later. Breast, lung, ovary, anus, skin, lymph. Point to a part of the body and a tumor would appear there, cells dividing and colliding into chaos. Movie star or rancher, teenager or grandmother: no one was spared. It took years, generations, before Washington admitted to the fallout. It was because of the wind, they were told. Unpredictable, unknowable. Whenever storms roared in from another state, loud and merciless, no one in the area could be completely sure if they were from god or government.

Desert rain comes from desert earth, a cycle, round and round. The ash that fell that day seeped into creeks and washes and rivers. It dissolved into the air, formed clouds, and then fell again. It swept out into floods, into crops, into cups. It settled deep into the earth, far underground, until through pressure and stone and mining, it gurgled up, pooling and warm. When you kick and float and dream in the water, it's there, all around you, lessened but still inflamed, still glittering.

"Well, isn't this the most charming little place you've ever seen. I can't believe it's a log cabin made with actual logs. I didn't think they made them like this anymore. What if I cancel the hotel room and get the cabin next to yours, what do you think? Look at that sunset!" Christy held her tablet out and took a picture, shutter noise at full volume.

The Petrified Forest RV Park and Cabins sat at the edge of town and overlooked endless shadowed mesas, miles of brush and sky. Bea sat in the rocking chair on the cabin's small front porch. Inspired by her mother, she took a photo of the sunset. It'd be a good one to post with some caption about finding herself or taking it all in, beautiful and brag-worthy, but she couldn't bring herself to pull up the app. Who would care? Who would respond? Carolyn had posted twice in the past hour, near-identical photos of her in a tiny straw hat at a beach, posing in bright green dress. Location tag: *Long weekend.* Bea liked the post. She took another photo of the desert, but it was still just the desert. The yucca, the cabins, the pinking clouds: Bea imagined the dozen likes, a pathetic amount, and some lame comment from a co-worker or old classmate. She texted the photo to her mother. The tablet chimed. "I already took this photo," Christy said, confused.

"You should post it to the forum."

"Conversation," Christy corrected, and though her mother admitted it was a nice view, she wouldn't post it. They had to keep a low profile; they didn't want other hunters to know they were there. "Undercover," Christy said, grinning, before heading off to the restaurant next door to find some caffeine. Bea pulled out her cigarettes and then saw the NO SMOKING sign. She flipped the lighter instead. A hulking gray RV was to the left of the cabin, pumping shit and piss into tanks, while two men watched baseball on an outdoor TV affixed to its side. Women in ankle-length dresses and long braids walked through the campgrounds, their arms full of laundry. The breeze was hot, the sun was high. The lighter clicked, clicked, clicked. Bea refreshed her inbox, waiting for the recruiter to email her back. She daydreamed about what meal she'd order when she got back to the city. A classic, she decided: bacon, egg, and cheese on a roll with ketchup and extra hot sauce. Christy rounded the corner from the main road. Her mother was in a teal linen shirt and matching wide-legged pants, and held up a plastic to-go cup.

"You'll never guess what I found." Christy shook the cup. "Iced coffee!"

"Everyone drinks iced coffee."

Her mother lowered her voice and nodded toward the long-skirted women as they walked toward a different cabin, arms now empty. "Isn't caffeine off-limits?"

"Did this place have a bar?"

"Decent wine list, even better whiskey."

"So why wouldn't they serve coffee?"

Christy reached over the railing and offered Bea the chewed nub of her straw. "Would a sip make you less grumpy?"

Bea rubbed her eyes with the heel of her palm. "You know, a six-and-a-half-hour drive isn't really a walk in the park."

"Speaking of walks, I'm going to that national park information center down the road and ask about some maps. I can't check into the hotel until tomorrow afternoon, so I thought I would go on a little hike in the morning. No use sitting around and twiddling my thumbs. I'm going to go out looking. Hunting!" Her mother pointed off the porch with her coffee, ice sloshing. "There's gold in them hills!" At Christy's shout, the men from the RV looked over. Christy turned back to Bea. "You want to come?"

"Why not." Bea shrugged. "Could be fun."

"Fun? This isn't about fun, honey. This is serious business. I'll handle all the details, how about you go get some sleep. No need for you to worry."

"I'm worried," Bea said.

"You're always worried, but you won't be worried soon." Christy winked. "Because millionaires don't worry about a damn thing."

The canyon was, as the guidebooks described, the "most stunning geologic formation outside the Grand Canyon" and the "most untouched beauty of the United States." A number of years back, when the area was declared a federally protected national monument, the president himself had posed under the shelf of sandstone, his shirt tucked into his jeans, a slight scruff shadowing his jaw, the rock behind him glowing an impossible orange-red. Somewhere, out there, was America being beautiful, and the Macon women intended to find it, if only they could figure out where it started.

The ranger at the information center had advised Christy against the hike. "He said it might be strenuous for someone my age," her mother scoffed. The ranger was younger than Christy, but not by much. "No spring chicken," Christy told Bea. "And this book says most trails are manageable with the right equipment. Good thing we have these books, huh?" She held up the stack of guidebooks. Bea turned off the highway, asked if the books mentioned anything about the upcoming access road. She didn't ask about the PROPERTY OF THE

BUREAU OF LAND MANAGEMENT labels on each of the books' spines. Christy flipped through a few pages. "Bumpy but manageable," she announced. Bea imagined a rock-strewn gravel drive. Instead, the road tossed Bea and Christy against their seat belts, the Chrysler barely clearing hulking boulders and hidden holes. Christy hollered and whooped in the driver seat, while Bea sat pale and silent. They pulled into what appeared to be the parking area, a flat sprawl of dirt where there was a dust-covered Subaru and nothing else. Bea squinted against the early sun, a tightness behind her eyes growing. They had slept late and there had been no time for coffee. Christy handed Bea her homemade sunscreen. "The skin is the largest organ of the body, we shouldn't clog it up with chemicals." Egg whites are no match for UV rays, Bea argued, but Christy wouldn't hear of it and Bea forgot to bring her own. The cream had the consistency of flu snot, and after they smeared some over their arms and necks, they grabbed their bags and laced up their shoes.

The plan was to hike two and a half miles northwest, where they'd then crisscross down a wash and into the canyons before heading toward a natural amphitheater called the Cathedral. Christy would take notes for her map while Bea would make sure they followed an actual map. After Christy was satisfied with whatever details she was looking for ("The treasure, honey. I'm looking for the treasure"), they'd turn around and head back to town in time for Christy to check in at the hotel. According to the ranger, it would take them about five hours including the hour drive to and from town. No more than five miles round trip, tops. Very popular, the ranger said. Tourists did it all the time. "Good thing we're not tourists," Christy said, winking.

"Did you ask where the trail started?"

"To the northwest," Christy said, clipping the breast strap of her backpack.

"Do you have a compass?"

"We don't need a compass, we can go by the sun. Look, that's north, that's west, so that's northwest." Christy pointed in front of them. "The ranger said some trail-finding was involved, but just to keep an eye out for the cairns and we'll be fine."

"A cairn?" Bea itched the back of her neck. A thick wad of egg lodged itself under her fingernail. She regretted not bringing a hat.

"Man-made rock piles, stacked up in a row. They mark back-country trails. What a goofy little word, huh? I should post something about cairns on the Conversation, people will love it."

Bea couldn't see any evidence of trail-guiding rock piles. It was the desert. The whole place was rock piles. But her mother was already picking her way down the slickrock below the parking area, so Bea followed. Bea had insisted on carrying all the water for the hike, feeling like an honorable daughter as she slid the bottles into her backpack earlier that morning. The backpack now sloshed back and forth with every step, forcing Bea to slowly shuffle down the hill.

Christy wasn't faring much better. Arms straight out, her mother put one foot carefully in front of the other as if performing a roadside sobriety test. She would occasionally yell about how fun this was, only to trip a few seconds later.

It went on like this, sweat and slosh and stumble, until they made their way off the slickrock and onto dusty solid ground. Ahead, the gnarled expanse of desert, buttes, and mountains hazy and far-off. In front, a small stack of fist-sized rocks next to a dimpled trail of sand.

"Cairn," Bea guessed. Christy cheered. They headed down the path. A lizard skittered around Bea's shoes. Another cairn. A long lick of sweat down her spine. Cairn. The scream of some low-flying bird. Cairn. Shriek. Stumble. Sand. Cairn.

Bea had gone on hikes before, wandering through the thick forests of the Upper Hudson on an office retreat, climbing the forgiving swells of the White Mountains during freshman orientation. But those trails were ribbons cut through the landscape with handrails and carved steps and trash cans. Here, instead of a large double-paneled sign describing the flora and fauna, there was nothing but the stretching horizon, punctuated by jags of piñon and rabbitbrush. Bea was so focused on spotting the next pile of rocks—there, a dozen steps ahead and then there to the right, fifty steps—that when Christy grabbed her backpack to stop her, Bea yelped in surprise. "Water break," her mother croaked. They knelt in the shade of a scrawny piñon, the sun high and hot and not a cloud in sight. As her mother tipped a water bottle over her face, Bea checked her cell phone. They'd been hiking for almost an hour. Both guidebooks described the distance from the parking lot to the beginning of the canyons as "no more" and "a little less than" a half mile. Her pedometer app said they'd walked nearly a mile. But these apps were notoriously inaccurate, Bea told herself, and, in any case, the phone had been in her backpack the entire time. Hardly an accurate measurement, especially with all of those water bottles tossing around. "How far do you think we've hiked?" Bea asked.

"I'm just trying not to step on a rattlesnake. You're the Lewis to my Clark here," Christy said, slathering more egg whites on her shoulders. Bea drank from her water bottle and studied the trail descriptions. Her mother snapped photos in every direction and when she told Bea to smile, Bea flipped her a middle finger. After Bea decided they should go westward, they got up and headed off to find another rock pile. Her mother hummed as she walked. Bea followed, checking the pedometer app every few yards.

Christy's humming became panting. The heat was heavy. Around them, endless expanses of the same trees, the same rocks, the same bushes, the same dirt. Blisters forced Bea into a limp. No cairns, no piles. No one else, not even the haggard screech of a bird. Christy guided them around a giant boulder and Bea slumped into its shade. After catching her breath, Bea consulted the guidebook maps. They were cartoonish, hand-drawn, and not to scale. Utterly useless, made by and for idiots. She looked for more water, but there was none, the bottles all empty, Christy pouring the last it over her head. Bea pulled out her phone to check the time and saw a blinking notification. A missed call. A New York City area code. The recruiter.

She frantically redialed, but there was no service. The call failed. Bea cursed and it came out choked, her tongue too bloated, huge, and dense and sticking to the roof of her mouth. Coughing, she slumped onto her side. She couldn't catch her breath. She couldn't focus. Her heart started to pound, chest tightening. She couldn't stop coughing. The world went fuzzy and then dark. Bea began to shake. Hands became fists and her chest became so strained, to touch it would be to burst. There was no one here and no one knew where they were and there was no service and they didn't even think to bring real sunscreen or a hat or even sunglasses and all she had on were stupid fucking running shoes and who does that other than a total fucking idiot, if only they had a map that wasn't totally fucking useless, but no, they were total fucking idiots who were totally fucked, the hike, Utah, derecho, all of it totally fucked, and now here she was, totally fucked in the middle of fucking nowhere with no idea what the fuck she was doing and no fucking service and no fucking job and what the fuck was she doing here.

What the *fuck* was she doing here?

"Did you say something?" Her mother's voice cut through the pounding feeling. Bea's chest clenched and then softened, enough that she was able to sit up, head swimming and hands jittery. The guidebooks were next to her, and she picked them up and threw them as far as she could, one after the other, their pages fluttering against the dry desert air.

"What are you doing?" Christy squawked.

Bea bent over and croaked out what should've been sobs, but no tears came. "We're," she said, gasping, "lost."

"Oh, honey, of course we are. But I thought we were having some fun, you know, exploring? Seeing what's out here? It's beautiful, isn't it? But if you're not feeling well, we should turn around, okay? We're going to have to find our way back to the car, so I'm not sure why you threw those books, okay, because we both know I have no sense of direction."

"We could die out here."

Christy cocked her head. "That's a little dramatic. There was another car in the parking lot and the ranger said this is one of the more popular hikes around. I'm sure we'll see someone soon."

Bea tried to say something about how they didn't have any water, but she was hyperventilating, her heart drumming, her entire torso shaking. Her mother put an arm around her back, told her in soft tones to lie down, c'mon, let's take some deep breaths. Six in, eight out. Nose then mouth. Six then eight. Her mother repeated it while she pulled off Bea's sneakers and rubbed her shoulders for a bit and when Bea was breathing to the beat, said she was going to go look for those books, all right, but you stay here, rest. Six in, eight out. Can you do that for me? Six then eight. Bea kept her eyes closed, the blisters on her heels screaming against the air. She repeated the numbers, numbers always comforting, as her body curled into a jittery ball. Six eight six eight six eight. She rolled back and forth on the ground, her heart a jackrabbit, lungs sore and shallow, everything a frantic buzz.

After what could've been an hour or a minute, her brain quieted into a soft, lazy thrum that slowly morphed into words, like how it's gorgeous out today and what's your name and my daughter's just over here. A hand on her back, but this one was bigger than her mother's, wider, its fingertips barely touching the fabric of her tank top, gentle but hesitating.

"Hey, I think you might be dehydrated and heatstroke is no joke, all right, you should try to drink some of this and then I can try to help you and your mom get back to your car, okay? Here, take it. It'll help." A man squatted next to her, thighs bright pale, shoes cloth and tight, and held out a Gatorade.

Christy appeared behind him. "Look who I found. His name is Chase."

"Tag, actually. Short for Taggart." He didn't seem offended. Sunglasses hung around his neck, tapping against his bare chest as he squinted at her. He twisted open the Gatorade and held it out again.

"He was climbing in the canyon. Did you know there's a canyon right there? You wouldn't believe it; he and his friend were only a few yards away. I told you we'd be all right! You guys probably heard us talking, didn't you? Anyway, I told him we were lost and you weren't feeling too great." Christy dropped her voice even though she stood right next to Bea and Tag. "She's been talking to herself," she told him.

Tag nodded, still in a squat. Bea took the Gatorade. It was a relief. Not necessarily in terms of thirst, but in that the person handing it to her was someone who seemed competent and confident. Solid, Bea thought, in a way where it'd be hard to push him over. She tried to thank him, but he was distracted, because her mother wouldn't stop flirting with him.

"You know, I've always loved men with long hair."

"Where's your shirt?"

"Do you need any sunscreen?"

Bea let her. Her breath evened between sips and soon her fingers stopped trembling. The guy stayed close, deep in a squat, and responded to each of Christy's questions with polite, concise answers. Thank you. In the canyon. No, thank you. When Tag failed to laugh at a joke Christy made about it being hotter than a whore in church, her mother got bored and wandered off. Tag turned to Bea. "How many fingers am I holding up?"

"Four," Bea said quietly.

"Good," he said. "That's good."

"I'm Bea." She held out a hand.

"I heard." Instead of shaking it, he pulled her up. "Tag."

"I heard," Bea said, but then her mother shouted about finding another one, come here, quick. Bea and Tag joined Christy at the canyon edge, and sure enough, at the bottom of a shallow canyon was another shirtless man. He was scrawnier than Tag, a concave chest covered in wiry black curls, arms too long. He had a giant black square of vinyl strapped to his back, the same shape and size of a large dog bed, and wore a wide-brimmed hat. Both men were about Bea's age. Compared to Tag, though, this one didn't seem all that concerned about two lost women in the middle of the desert. He was more preoccupied with the discarded literature. He held up the guidebook. "You know, you can't throw this away out here, all right? 'Leave no trace' exists for a reason."

"Meet Hank," Christy said brightly.

Bea limply waved. "Sorry," she said. "My fault."

"Why do you even have the ranger copies of this," Hank grunted, sliding the pad off his back and fumbling with a drawstring backpack that was underneath. He pushed the guidebook into it, scowling.

"You guys know how to get back to the Red Wash Trailhead?" Christy asked. "That's where our car is."

"Damn, no wonder you're out of water, that's what? Eight miles away?" Tag whistled. "Were you trying to go to the Cathedral or something?"

"Damn," Hank echoed. He looked genuinely impressed. "You really are lost."

"We'd love to see the Cathedral, if you two boys don't mind showing us the way," Christy said. "I have some important research to do in the area."

"You're definitely not making it there before dusk," Hank said, looking at his phone. "It's already past two and it'll take at least an hour and a half to get to the wash, plus another half hour to get to the slot." He motioned at Bea. "More if you're going barefoot. Do you even have a hat?"

"No," Bea admitted.

"It's a miracle we found you boys, then," Christy said. Bea watched in horror as her mother put her arm around Tag's waist. "I mean, we could've died out here, huh?"

"We should be heading out," Hank called up. "We have to get to work soon."

"Where do you work?" Christy's arm was still around Tag.

"A restaurant in Mercy," he said, stepping away.

"Pat's Grill?" Bea asked.

"Yeah," Tag said, surprised.

"We're staying next door, at the Petrified Forest cabins."

"We could give you a ride back, if you'd like."

"You're sweet," Christy cooed. "Do you have another Gatorade?"

"The quickest way back to the truck is through here." Hank pointed up the canyon. "You two ever climb before?"

The large black vinyl square on Hank's back was a crash pad. The men told Christy and Bea that they should try their best to land on it. The drop wasn't too bad and it'd take too long to set up a belay. Bea pretended to know what they were talking about, nodding as she put her shoes back on. Her mother, meanwhile, didn't hesitate. Christy lay down on the ground and pushed off. "Catch me, Hank!" she squealed as she disappeared over the edge. She nailed the landing, though her forearm hit an outcropping on the way down, blood dripping down into her palm. She was fine, Christy assured Hank, smiling as he fumbled in his pack for a bandage. A war wound to brag about later.

Bea was not as enthusiastic. Tag promised he would be there to make sure everything was fine. Offered his hand as she lowered herself onto her stomach, told her how to position her hips and where to look. "Remember to push off," he said. "It's easier than you think," he said. Bea ignored him, terrified. The sand and rock dug into her sweat-thin tank top as she wiggled out over the ledge, the drop a terrible downward yawn.

Her fall was not elegant or smooth. It was not a movie-magic collapse into the arms of waiting men. It was a series of humiliating moments, the knees hanging over, then her stomach, then her chest and then all of it went slipping, Bea trying to grab the edge but the edge was nothing but dust and stone, not an edge at all, and when it was clear gravity was taking over, Bea fell backward into a sun-blinded blink of air and prayed for the best.

The landing hit her awkwardly, painfully, but not horribly. Her shoulder and knee throbbed, but no worse than her feet and their weeping blisters. She could walk. She could stand. Tag cheered, Christy asked when was the last time she had this much fun, and Hank scowled. After Tag dropped down—easily, seamlessly, as if hopping out of a car—the four of them made their way through the winding slots. The canyon walls were blanketed in spiders and striations, heat pulsing off of them. After a while, Bea couldn't feel any specific part of her body, everything numb and salted and aching. The guys chatted about their climbing routes, which they'd do again, which they'd avoid. Christy would occasionally lag behind to rub Bea's back and say they were almost there, though they weren't and both of them knew it. Bea, exhausted and empty, would grunt until her mother left her alone.

The ground sloped uphill and soon they emerged from the canyon and onto a wash. The late afternoon sun glinted off glass on the horizon. Windshields, Bea realized, and she whimpered with relief. She and Christy followed the guys to a green, beaten pickup and threw their bags into the bed. Bea lay across the back seat, head on Christy's shoulder, as the guys packed up. She listened as they argued over the right way to tie down the crash pad, both of them vehemently disagreeing with the other's knot choices. A fist of a headache clenched behind Bea's eyes. Her mother gulped a fresh Gatorade and declared herself human again. She offered it to Bea. Bea took it but couldn't be bothered to bring it to her lips. Her eyelids were fifty pounds each, her head even heavier. The guys piled into the front seats. The engine groaned to life and then revved over the bumps of the access road. The group fell into a silence, the only noise the faint bluegrass from the radio and the low moan of the engine. When the ground shifted from the crunch of gravel to the hum of pavement, Bea fell instantly, blissfully asleep, her head in her mother's lap. She began to snore. Tag glanced in the rearview mirror and watched as Christy gently stroked her daughter's hair.

Pat's Grill was L-shaped, booths lining windows and a bar hooked off the back. The sun had only just begun to set, but the place was crowded, tables loud with families and hikers and elderly couples, while unshaven men stared into pints at the bar. Bea sat in the corner booth, as her mother instructed, and considered her phone. The recruiter hadn't called her back. Bea wanted to call after they had gotten back to the cabin, but her phone was dead. By the time she was showered and her phone had a full battery, it was past seven in New York. Bea reminded herself how a phone call that late would've been annoying, but not unusual. Returning a phone call at seven, she figured, would reveal her as the kind of person who worked that late, which she was until a couple of months ago. Seven was nothing. Seven was late to appetizers, midway through happy hour. There were three long, dull rings and then a voicemail. *CLT Recruitment, please leave a message with your name and number and we'll* . . . She spoke for too long, apologizing for a family emergency, her mother, a hike, sunstroke, and then gave her number and spelled her last name. She hung up and immediately felt like an idiot. She refreshed her email. Nothing.

Bea's wet hair hung limply, fat soapy drops dripping onto the laminated menu. The shower earlier had been excruciating. The sunburn across her shoulders and legs, the blisters on her feet and between her thighs: all of it screaming against the lukewarm water. She had to bite a knuckle while scrubbing the dirt and dust off her ankles. She rolled her neck and examined the food options. She was going to order it all, she thought, nibbling at her peeling lips. Extra fries. Double pours of beer. The cheesecake. Her stomach groaned. She reloaded her email. Still nothing.

"Nice shirt," the waiter teased. Bea didn't recognize him at first. His hair was pulled back into a small kiss of a bun, and he wore a floral short-sleeved button-down, like something from Hawaii. After an awkward moment, he pointed to his chest. "Tag? From earlier?"

"Oh, shit, hi," Bea said, horrified to remember she was wearing her favorite sleep shirt, a gray frayed rag with LIVE LAUGH ARGUE across the chest, a relic from her high school debate team. She crossed her arms. "Thanks."

"Sure," he said politely. "You feeling better? You look better."

Bea flushed, sending chills through her sunburn. "Yeah, thanks. You guys really saved us out there. My mom was convinced she knew where she was going." Bea gave a weak laugh.

"Don't worry about it. Happens more often than you'd think. Sometimes I've needed to get saved, though Hank's usually the one saving me." He smiled. "You thirsty?"

Bea picked up the menu and pretended to focus. "What's your best beer on tap?"

"Honestly, the Coors."

"Sounds great. And two waters, please," Bea said, staring at the menu. "With extra ice."

"You got it." Tag left and she exhaled a ragged breath. She cursed herself. Christy had insisted on the restaurant, saying it was where she was meeting her friend, and Bea insisted on joining in order to assess the friend. She hadn't considered the guys from the hike, hadn't considered her outfit or her hair or makeup. She wondered if she had time to go to the bathroom and see how awful she looked, but then her mother ran past the window, hair flying. Christy had on a purple dress, long and tied at the waist. She was out of breath by the time she sat down at the booth, fresh blue eyeliner rimming her lashes. Silver rings, silver bracelets. Perfume, mascara. "God, I'm sweating like a pig. How do I look? Do I look sweaty?"

"You look great," Bea said, and she meant it. "Pretty."

Her mother pulled on her earlobes. "I forgot my earrings. I

should go back to the cabin, I feel naked without them. Can you order me a chardonnay?"

"You look great," Bea repeated. Tag appeared with two waters. "She'd love a glass of chardonnay," Bea said to him.

"Could you bring another set of silverware, too, please?" Christy asked. "And another water, but with no ice?"

Bea had so far refused to ask any details about Christy's weekend, mostly because she wasn't entirely convinced it was going to happen. The snafu at the hotel only made it seem more unlikely, the woman behind the desk not having any reservation under Christy's name and Christy refusing to mention her friend's name, despite both Bea and the woman at the hotel asking for it. Instead, her mother had rushed back to the cabin with her luggage to get ready for dinner, while Bea had gone to the restaurant. She watched as her mother fiddled with the salt and pepper shakers. "Is your friend actually coming? Or do I need to add you to the cabin reservation?"

"He should be here any minute." Her mother used her tablet camera to reapply lipstick. She asked Bea if there was any on her teeth, but when Bea just glared, Christy sighed. "Bob said he's very excited to meet you, but if you'd rather have dinner elsewhere, you're more than welcome. I think there's a pizza place down the road, inside that outdoor shop."

"Hold on, it's *Bob*? The guy who posted piss pics? Are you fucking *joking*?"

"I don't need one of your lectures right now," Christy snapped. "You're only here because you insisted on being here."

"One chardonnay and one Coors." Tag placed the glasses on the table, glancing between Bea and Christy. "And the extra silverware and water. Are we ready to order, or are we waiting on someone else?"

"Oh!" Christy yelped. Her lips trembled and then, haltingly, formed a smile. "He's here."

He wore a flannel shirt, ironed blue jeans, and a plain white baseball cap, taken off when he saw Christy. A thick gray mustache, slightly curled at the ends, and a paunch. *Squat* was the first word that came to mind. Christy scrambled out of the booth, smoothing her hair. The two smiled at each other, nervous and awkward, and then after a long moment of shuffling, hugged. He was shorter than her, not by much, but enough to notice. He made eye contact with Bea from over Christy's shoulder. Broad and bloated, his face had a placid, unrushed expression, as if he was watching television. His face, Bea thought, was extremely punchable.

He was the first to pull out of the embrace, though he kept his hands on Christy's shoulders. "You're good-looking," he said with noticeable surprise. Christy smacked his arm and giggled.

Tag waved at Bob. "How're you doing, sir?" But Bob was too busy listening to something Christy was murmuring to him, both of their faces serious.

Bea touched Tag's wrist, lightly, but enough that he looked up. "Do you have liquor here?" Bea whispered.

"Like whiskey?"

"Like a double whiskey."

"Best I can do is a single," Tag said.

Bob snapped his fingers above Christy's head. "Get me a Coors, kid."

Bea pushed her beer to the other side of the table. "Have mine."

"Why, thank you." Bob slid into the booth next to Christy. The vinyl squeaked under their weight. Bob reached out a hand fuzzed with gray hairs. "You must be—"

"Bea," she said, arms crossed.

He rapped the table with his knuckles. "Pleasure to meet you. I'm Bob."

"Not Robert, only Bob?" Bea asked, not unkindly.

"The one and only," Christy said. She picked a piece of lint off of his shoulder.

Bob ducked away from Christy's touch. "Your mother's told me so much about you," he said. Tag put a glass of whiskey in front of Bea and handed Bob a menu, but Bob waved him off. "You know I don't need one of those. Do you still have that steak special?"

"Yessir," Tag said.

"Great," Bob said. He pointed at his water glass. "I'll have some ice, too."

"Yessir," Tag said again, leaving.

Christy blinked, eyebrows stitched together. "I thought you hated ice."

Bob ignored her and turned toward Bea. "Christine tells me you live in New York City," he said. No one called her mother Christine except for Gertie. Bea picked up her menu and flipped it over, making a show of not responding. Christy drank a long gulp of wine. After a beat, Bob added, "She says you work in finance, something about a bank?"

"She works in commodities," Christy said.

"Really?" Bob asked, voice lilting. He was impressed. So was Bea. Her mother never took any interest in Bea's career. Gertie would ask how the office was and Christy would silently leave the room. If Bea canceled plans to visit Stamford because of work, her mother wouldn't respond to texts for days. She didn't think Christy even knew she was in commodities. She glanced at Christy from behind her menu. Her mother gave her a sharp, indecipherable look. Bob cleared his throat. "You know, I grew up on a cattle ranch outside of Reno. My dad always had a lot of talk about corn and feed pricing, loved to follow the markets. Never had a head for numbers, but my older brother did, so he took over the place. He died a few years ago. My niece wants to make it into some sort of dude ranch, though I'm not sure people come to Reno for that sort of thing." Bob paused. He looked out the window, eyes blank, as if he forgot he was talking.

"I've always wanted to go to a ranch," Christy said, urging him on. "I love animals."

"You're terrified of horses," Bea said, sipping the whiskey.

"That's not true. I had those fancy figurines growing up, the horses with the giant, fluffy hooves. You know the ones, from the Budweiser commercials? I loved brushing their hair. Did you have horses like that, Bob?"

Bob explained the difference between draft horses and riding horses, giving an in-depth description of hands and musculature, while Bea counted the ice cubes in her drink. When Tag appeared asking about food, Bob announced he was paying and that they should order whatever they'd like. He ordered the steak special, medium rare, extra fries. Even though she usually tried to avoid red meat, Bea asked for the same. Christy overenunciated *Caesar* and asked for the dressing on the side. Tag hummed thoughtfully at each order, his Adam's apple wobbling. Bob fell into a long story about his childhood dream to become a farrier. Hooves, he kept saying, are beautiful mysteries. Christy kept trying to catch Bea's eye, but Bea swirled her whiskey and stared at the TVs above the bar, focused on keeping her brain as empty as possible. Dusk had started to roll in, the sky a smear of pink, clouds skinny and glowing. The motel across the street had NO VACANCY lit even though the parking lot was empty. The whiskey was sharp and cheap. Christy made a joke and Bob laughed for real. He sounded like a mattress squeaking, which wasn't the worst sound, but after a while, it could be.

Bea knew her mother didn't like to be alone and had always gone to great, dramatic lengths to avoid it. Montreal was the ultimate proof of that, and when that failed, it wasn't long until her mother found another back to rub or collar to fuss over. There was Mattias, the soft-spoken, goateed handyman who fell through the ceiling of the Stamford house while checking for a squirrel infestation. Then it was Xander, a bulky and vaguely European man who never sat down and claimed vegetables were only healthy when eaten raw. During Thanksgiving her junior year of college, he taught Bea how to smoke a gravity bong and then promptly disappeared after the pies were served. There were one-offs: the ones from the macramé class, the park, the delivery guy. By the time Fran was in the picture, Bea was long out of college. Gertie insisted Bea visit and meet her. Fran had built a rocking chair for Bea and it was critical that Bea come to collect it off the front lawn; the ladies from Gertie's bridge circle were starting to talk. Bea didn't think a rocking chair could be a big deal until she saw it. Fran was a conceptual artist, Christy explained, whose specialty was outsize perspective. The chair was a tractor seat suspended between two enormous metal hoops. It was bigger than the Chrysler parked next to it in the driveway and painted a sickly pea green. Christy told Bea that Fran had been waiting all day for Bea to sit in it, excitedly motioning at a step stool next to the closest hoop. Fran squatted at Christy's feet, silent, fingers picking at the grass. Bea climbed onto it, and at first the chair held Bea's weight. She then tried to rock it, since it looked, after all, like a rocking chair. It immediately collapsed. Grandma Gertie helped Bea out of the mangled metal while Fran ran inside, screeching about her art, Christy rushing after her. Fran didn't leave the bathroom until Bea offered to pay her for it. With a curt sniff, Fran looked at Bea's check for three hundred dollars and asked Bea what working on Wall Street was like. Seven hundred and fifty dollars later, Fran happily took the check and said she always knew Bea would appreciate art, knew it the moment Christy told her about her accomplished daughter. Bea was shocked, almost impressed, and avoided Fran for the rest of the night. Eventually, there'd be Marcello, Angie, Lawrence, Sam, Sebastian. Bea would say hello over the phone and like the selfies Christy would send, but after Fran, Bea refused to meet any of her mother's paramours.

Bob was different. It wasn't because he met her mother on the internet and sent strange, questionably sexual photos—Bea wasn't a hypocrite—no, it was how Bob used his thumb to flick something out of his left nostril, how he belched into his fist and didn't apologize, how he leaned across the table toward Bea, pointing his knife at his steak, and said, "You know what, this might be even better than the last time I had it." For someone who just met their not-girlfriend's daughter, Bob was noticeably relaxed, maybe even enjoying himself. Bea finished her whiskey. "How long did it take you to drive out here, Bob?"

"Oh, a couple of hours. I drive up from Arizona all the time."

"You live in Arizona?" Bea asked.

"I thought you lived in Reno," Christy said.

"Used to," Bob said quickly.

"Tell me, Bob, do you usually send women pictures of you peeing? Or was that something special for my mother?"

Bob turned to her mother. "You showed her that?" he asked softly. Christy became very focused on her croutons, pushing them around her plate.

"She didn't have to show me anything—you posted it on a public forum," Bea said coolly. She shoved a fry into her mouth. The restaurant was both loud and empty now, only one other booth occupied, a younger guy in a green hat who kept looking over at them. "You think you found the treasure, right? My mom showed me pictures of the cliffside in Arizona. Seems pretty convincing to me." The guy caught Bea's eye and grinned. Bea looked away.

Bob shoved a forkful of steak into his mouth. "It might be."

"It might be? Are you telling me you left a million dollars behind to drive to Utah and see my mom?" Bea had three fries in her mouth, maybe four, and when she smiled at Christy, a half-eaten one fell out. "How romantic."

Christy did not smile back. "We're having a nice time," she said. It was an order.

Bea wasn't angry. It was a deeper feeling, like when you sense yourself slipping on ice and your mind goes sharp and shifts your weight, saving yourself from the fall. "Have you found someone to help you get it yet?" she asked. She shoved another fry into her mouth.

"You know, you see—" Bob started, but Bea interrupted him. "I know someone who can help," Bea said. Tag stopped wiping down tables when he saw Bea waving. His hair had fallen loose from its bun. "Did I forget to bring over the ketchup? Sorry, I always forget the ketchup. I can grab some right now."

"I have a question for you." Bea made her voice syrupy, which was easy after the whiskey. "Tag, have you ever rock climbed in Arizona?" Her mother started to speak, but Bea talked over her. "Because Bob is looking for someone to help him out. He's offering, what was it? Ten percent? You'd get a hundred thousand dollars if you could climb up a cliff for him. Show Tag the photo, Bob." Bea hiccuped. One drink wasn't usually enough to get her drunk, but she didn't usually drink after being lost and dehydrated in the desert for most of the day. She sipped water as Tag waited awkwardly. "C'mon, Bob. Show him."

Christy glared at Bea and lifted up her plate. "We'll take the check, Tag, please." Tag took her dish away, visibly relieved.

"You need someone to climb a cliff in the desert and Tag found us after climbing a cliff in the desert. You leave treasure behind to come here and now you won't even take advantage of a real desert rock climber, right here in front of you?" Bea shrugged. "I'm a little confused, Bob."

"You're a little drunk," Christy snapped. The younger guy from the other booth was on his way out the door, but not before making eye contact with Bea. He smirked. A jolt shot through her gut, sour and hot, but Bea dismissed it as indigestion. When was the last time she ate steak? She never ate steak. Bob stared out the window, face blank again, while Christy muttered an apology. Bea's phone binged. The subletter wanted to know if she could paint one of the bedroom walls black.

Bob paid in cash, pulling from a thick wad of bills. Bea's steak had gone sticky and cold. Christy said she and Bob were leaving. Bea said nothing and poked at her food with her fork. They left. Bea chewed ice and checked the bill. Bob had left a thirty percent tip, which just made Bea angrier. The TVs had switched to cartoon reruns and the kitchen clanked with dishes. The sun had set, the sky watercolored in purple and crimson.

Bea sat at the booth long enough to watch Christy and Bob walk past the restaurant windows. Christy pulled her suitcase behind her. They headed to the motel across the street. Bob went in first and didn't hold open the door. Her mother might not be a paragon of romantic success, Bea thought, but she was in a hotel with a man who liked her enough to drive across state lines and spend significant cash on her unfriendly daughter. Back in New York, Bea could hardly get someone to buy her a drink. She stabbed the steak with her knife and fork, leaving both utensils sticking out of the calcifying flesh. Tag came by and asked if she wanted her food wrapped up. Bea asked for another whiskey. He apologized. They were closing up for the night, but, hey, any chance she liked karaoke?

Hi Bea,

Just got your voicemail. No problem at all, I'm sorry to hear about your mother, hope she recovers soon. I'm headed out of the office, so no need for a call, but if you could do the attached project as soon as possible, preferably before Sunday, that'd be ideal. We'll need an updated resume, too. Apologies for the rush, the hiring committee is already screening candidates and I'd like to get you in the mix. I'll be online all weekend and can pass it along as soon as I hear from you. Unfortunately, I won't be able to answer specific questions about the project, but judging by your (amazing!) work history, I'm sure you'll find it fairly straightforward.

Thanks,
CLT Recruitment

The crowd inside the pizza-parlor-cum-outdoor-gear-shop down the street from Pat's Grill mostly ignored the singers so the guy's overly enthusiastic Eminem went largely unnoticed. Hank, though, could hardly hide his exasperation. "What is it, 2005? Who is this guy?" he said loudly. Tag shushed him. "You can't be the only one who sings," Tag whispered. The guy tried to get people to put their hands in the air. "Shut the fuck up," Hank barked, impatient. The guy glanced over. He wore a green trucker hat with BEST CLUCKIN' BREASTS written in bright yellow letters. He was young and short and vaguely familiar. Bea wasn't sure if he heard what Hank said, but the guy wouldn't break eye contact with her as he rapped. At first, Bea was amused, giving a thin smile, but the guy's intensity soon made her uncomfortable. She shifted on her bar seat, sipped her beer, turned to Tag. Tag, in a seeming effort to be apologetic, motioned at the hat and gave the guy a thumbs-up, but the guy didn't stop staring, not until the bartender cut the music and asked if anyone owned the black F250 parked outside, because there's a dog losing it in the kennel. The guy dropped the mic and hurried out the door.

Despite it being a Friday night, there were only a dozen or so people scattered on barstools between racks of fleece and spandex, all of them drinking beer. Bea pulled at the hem of her dress. She'd run back to the cabin before they went over to the karaoke bar, mistakenly thinking her T-shirt and shorts would be out of place, but now she was the only person not wearing performance fabrics. Hank was up next, singing "Thunder Road." "The only song worth singing," he said, grabbing the mic stand. He alternated between eating a slice of pepperoni and fumbling through the dusty beach roads and rusted Chevrolets. "He never gets the lyrics right," Tag said, clearly amused. Bea asked Tag if he was going to sing. No, he said. "I'm just here to support. Are you?"

"Nope. My mom would, though. She loves karaoke. Joan Jett is her signature, 'Bad Reputation.'"

Tag clapped as Hank went into an air guitar, fingers strumming what was left of the pepperoni slice. "You should call her, we could use someone up there other than this idiot."

"She's with her new boyfriend," Bea said. "And I don't think he's the karaoke type."

"Bob?"

"You know him?"

"Yeah, and he's definitely into karaoke. He was here the other week. Was pretty incredible, actually. Did a whole Elvis set, hips and everything. Really brought down the house, but yeah, he's here all the time."

Bea froze, beer at her lips. "He's here all the time?"

Tag frowned at Bea's sudden seriousness. "Started showing up, what, a month or two ago? Apparently he's got business out here or something. He really loves the steak special at the grill, always orders it whenever he's in town. Thinks we keep it on rotation for him, but really it's the special for the entire summer. You had the steak to-night, right? What did you think? Chef switched up the seasoning on it, which I thought was risky, but I guess Bob didn't notice—" Hank rejoined them at the bar. Tag elbowed him. "Hank, that guy Bob, the one who loves the steak, how long has he been coming around town?"

Hank was grinning from finishing his song, pointing at a couple of people across the room, but he grimaced at the mention of Bob. "Too long. Remember how that pervert wanted me to go out into the canyons with him?" Hank shuddered. "Total creep. Why?"

Bea realized she'd crushed the plastic cup in her hand. She opened her fist, fingers sticky with lukewarm beer. "He's my mom's boyfriend."

Hank laughed. "Are you serious?" When it was clear Bea was, Hank whistled. "Your mom seems cool, but she has fucked-up taste in men."

"Oh, I know, trust me." Bea drafted a text to Christy, to call her

ASAP, but then thought of their moment on the couch in Salt Lake, how excited Christy was, how quiet. Bea deleted it.

A middle-aged woman approached the microphone stand and the early strands of "Hotel California" began. Hank winced. "Looks like Linda's back," Tag laughed.

"Who?" Bea asked, putting her phone down. She'd deal with her mother later.

"Linda's crazy," Tag explained to Bea. "She struck it rich with coal shares like a million years ago and now she collects parrots and goes to Europe every spring. She comes back when the desert flowers peak, which should be around now. Joke's on her, there's been absolutely no rain, but she never misses karaoke night." Linda sung the backup singers' echoes. She was, Bea thought, pretty good.

"It's not like she has a job," Hank said dismissively.

"I don't have a job," Bea said. "I don't," she said again. When neither of the guys responded, she added, "I got fired." It felt strange to admit, dizzying.

Hank shrugged. "Cool." Bea wanted to say more, almost did, but his tone made her feel young, as if she'd been scolded.

"You know, I'm here because I lost a job," Tag said.

Hank rolled his eyes. "Dealers don't get fired, they get killed."

"Do I look dead to you?"

"You look like someone who won't give me your recipe." Hank motioned at Tag, but didn't look away from Linda, who was now singing Fleetwood Mac. "Did you know this kid used to make the best edibles in Santa Barbara? But now he won't make them, says he's retired. Doesn't even eat mac and cheese anymore!"

"You're from Santa Barbara?" Bea could see it. The long hair, the slow response times.

Tag was about to say something, but before he could, the bartender announced they were doing an intermission, singing to resume after they fixed the bathroom. Please don't put paper towels down the toilet, the bartender sighed into the microphone, speakers buzzing.

Linda came up to them and asked Hank how he was doing. Hank started to talk about the town hall the next night, whether or not they should go, but Linda seemed more interested in playing with Hank's hair. Bea watched, stunned, as the woman methodically wrapped chunks of black strands around her thumb, pulled, and then released. Hank never stopped talking. Bea turned to Tag, but Tag stared straight ahead while studiously eating a slice of cheese pizza. Awkward, and unwilling to make it seem like she thought anything was strange, Bea pulled out her phone. Martha had posted a new photo, a group posed around a poolside table. Sunglasses, fresh flowers, cloth napkins. Bea vaguely recognized some of the people in the photo from college. There was also Grant's roommate, the one who would open the door for her and give her a solemn nod, the one who sat on the other end of the couch when Grant had mentioned a weekend vacation in front of Bea, before the ghosting and the Popsicle.

Grant sat in the background, holding a glass of white wine. Carolyn was next to him, one hand on his thigh, the other holding a cocktail. They were all smiling with perfectly straight teeth. Bea liked the photo and typed a comment. The cocktail emoji and a blue heart. Carolyn would see it and think nothing of it, if she noticed it at all. Grant, though. Would he even look at the photo? He was tagged. There was enough of a chance. Bea sent the comment and then finished her beer in one swift gulp. Tag ordered another slice and asked if Bea wanted one, too. She'd be right back, she said, but Tag didn't seem to hear her. By the time Bea slipped off her stool, Linda had climbed into Hank's lap, her hand scalp-deep in his hair.

The motel sign glowed yellow and red down the street. At some point since dinner, the NO in NO VACANCY had gone out. The night was long and quiet aside from the occasional reverb of music. Bea stepped out into the middle of the street. It was a nice town, she thought, lighting a cigarette. She tried to take a photo, thinking a post would be a good follow-up to the comment, but her phone showed nothing but purple darkness and indeterminate shapes. Better to not post, she figured, and maintain the illusion she could be on some re-treat. Claim she was staying present and aware, which is why she hadn't responded to the subletter about the drawer or the paint. Down the road, a light blinked off in one room of the motel. In another, the strobe of a TV. Would they watch TV? Would they talk? What would they talk about? She thought of the postcard on Christy's fridge, the B. Her mother probably sent postcards to him. Christy loved the mail. When she lived in Montreal, she'd send letters to Bea every week. Bea couldn't remember what they said, only that they were always multiple pages. Bea kept the fat wad of envelopes hidden in a box in her closet, tucked under some old gifts. She wondered what happened to them. Long gone, probably. Bea inhaled and let the smoke burn the back of her throat.

The creak of the bar door. Tag walked up. "Sorry about Hank." he motioned behind them. "They can get weird like that."

"She really likes his hair."

Tag chuckled. "They're quite the pair, that's for sure." He kicked a rock. "So how does Mercy compare to Reno?"

"I've never been to Reno."

"I thought Bob was from Reno?"

"He is. Or might be. I have no idea. I'm from New York, I'm visiting my mom. She lives in Salt Lake."

Tag raised his eyebrows. "New York, huh?"

"You ever been?"

"Nope."

"Don't believe the rumors, the people are great. I don't know about Reno, though. My mom and Bob met online." Bea chewed on the butt of the cigarette and stared at the motel. Another light had gone on and figures moved behind a curtain. "He always orders the steak when he's here?"

"And always sits at the same booth by the door."

"For how long?" She imagined grease dribbling down his mustache, the squeak-laugh.

"Until he finishes his steak usually."

"No, how long has he been coming here?"

"Maybe since Memorial Day?"

Months, Bea noted. "Does he tell you why he's here?"

Tag paused. "It was funny you mentioned the climbing stuff earlier. Bob asked Hank to help him out with something a week or two ago. He offered to pay for his time and everything, but refused to say what it was for. Hank was creeped out and said no."

Bea sighed and flung her cigarette into the street. "My mom is such an idiot about these things. You know how often she gets conned? I've explained Nigerian princes to her maybe a hundred times, but this treasure hunt with Bob is next level. That's why they're here, by the way. To look for buried treasure. It's this whole thing, there's a website and everything."

Tag searched the ground for her littered butt. "I haven't heard anything about a treasure," he said as he crouched and picked it up, the end smoldering. Bea pulled out her phone.

"It's apparently all here in this poem," she said, holding up the screen. "The guy who buried it is a poet. There's a million dollars hidden in these words."

"A poem?" Tag took her phone.

"I wish I was lying."

Tag read the poem aloud. It was as bad as Bea remembered. Tag said it was nice. "You know, sounds like it could be somewhere around here," he said. "But I don't know how you're going to find an exact location from a poem."

"That's because it's not real! It's a scam or a joke or some random guy having a good time. It's a waste of time. My mother's wasting her time." She took her phone back and lit another cigarette. "What do you think my mom and Bob are doing right now?"

"I don't know if you want to know."

A light went off in the motel. "That's what I'm worried about."

Tag followed where she was looking. "Bob's a weird guy, but he's harmless."

"I don't know if I believe you." Bea dragged the cigarette. Tag watched as she exhaled. "Want one?" she asked, holding out the pack.

"I'm good, thanks."

"A dealer who doesn't smoke?"

"It was a long time ago. And I wasn't a dealer. It was more like I was a chef."

"Of mac and cheese?"

"Dank and Cheese," Tag corrected, grinning.

⬤▶

Taggart Rae Peterson was from Seattle, more specifically Tacoma, though it was easier to refer to the larger city when he wasn't in the Pacific Northwest. People would blank-eye Tacoma ("Like the truck?" Bea asked), but they would nod to Seattle, always making a bad joke about flannel or coffee or rain. Tag had left Tacoma after high school, enrolling at Arizona State University. He told most people he left because he loved the contrast between Washington and Arizona: pine versus piñon, mist versus mesa, shade versus sun. Once he moved away, though, Tag missed the green, dense moisture of Washington. He had to use body lotion by the handful, had to forgive himself for staying inside when it was sunny out because every day was sunny in Arizona. Regardless, he'd think back to Tacoma and feel vaguely disoriented, like he was trying on someone else's glasses, the world all blurry and sharp at the same time. Within a few days of being in Tempe, things felt righter, more even, the bleached-out lines of the buildings, the stucco and sandy dirt and fuzzy horizon. At least, that's what Tag told himself. In quieter moments, when his gut ached for the wet calm of drizzle on windows, Tag had to admit ASU was the only college he got into and thus his only choice.

Halfway through the first semester of his sophomore year a friend told Tag he was driving out to California to join an anti-GMO campaign and would Tag like to join? Tag wasn't too interested in environmental causes—he had to look up what GMO stood for on his thick, aging laptop—but it was a free ride to Santa Barbara. The friend was relaxed and eager, a new friend, one that Tag liked and wanted to hang out with more. Plus, Tag had never been to California and his classes were starting to feel pointless in the way that any mandatory thing feels pointless after a while. Tag thought, why not.

Tag left college one October morning and never went back. Grassroots organizing, he told his parents. In truth, there was a lot of grass and not much organizing. Tag canvassed door-to-door for the first few weeks he was there, a predetermined route printed out, flyers in hand, a small speech semimemorized. It was easy work, and this shouldn't have surprised Tag as much as it did. After all, it was Santa Barbara, and nearly everyone who answered the door was at least a little left of center. Even those near the naval base agreed that they wanted to know what was in their food and sure, they'd take a flyer. The work was unpaid, a detail Tag's friend had conveniently failed to mention. In lieu of cash, Tag and the other volunteers were given beer and pizza at the end of their shifts, the pizza always vegetarian and the beer always craft. Since it was free and his only reliable food of the day, Tag would inhale anywhere from three to five slices. He'd also gulp down a couple beers and pocket another four cans, determined to get his money's worth.

Tag's friend knew the surfers who let them crash on their crusty, weak-springed couches. The guys in the house worked as grocery butchers or bistro waiters, but all of them introduced themselves as surfers so, to Tag, that's what they were. After a week of knocking on doors, the friend drove back to Arizona. Tag stayed behind. He told the friend and his parents that he wanted to finish out the campaign. He was doing real, progressive work in California. Enacting change. Educating the populace. Truth was, Tag didn't want to go back to school. He'd begun to suspect it was school and not Washington that had made everything feel wrong as a teenager, and the feeling had followed him to Arizona. In California, though, Tag had yet to feel uneasy or out of place, even if he wasn't sure GMOs were that big of a deal. The surfers let Tag stay on their couch because he was tidy, didn't eat their food, and, more important, didn't drink their beer.

The campaign ended in November, inevitably successful, and Tag got a job at a fast-food restaurant within walking distance from the surfer house. He needed the money; he didn't have a car. In high school, he'd been on the grounds crew of the municipal golf course and between that and the canvassing, thought a service job would be easy, but it was much more physical than Tag expected. The way his feet swelled after standing so long, the heaving of baskets out of the fryers, the manic orchestration of orders. The heat. On his days off, Tag would go with his roommates to the beach. Once they gave Tag an impromptu surf lesson, but when it became clear that he couldn't do much more than a doggy paddle, Tag instead read the random self-help and entrepreneurship books he found scattered around the house on the beach. Occasionally he'd look up from his book to watch the surfers bob and stand and swim in the growing daylight, waves winking in shades of expanding blue, sky marbled and stained, and think, this is the fucking dream.

But there's only so long a guy can sleep on a couch. When one of

the bedrooms in the house opened up, Tag began selling weed to afford rent, buying ounces from the line cook who offered him a joint
after a particularly grueling Saturday lunch rush. Tag priced himself lower than the dispensaries, and though his roommates loyally
bought eighths, most customers still preferred their medicinal flower,
since it was always more potent than anything Tag could peddle, not
to mention legal. Unwilling to go back to burger-flipping full time,
and realizing the bud market was oversaturated, Tag decided to experiment with edibles. He had never been much of a stoner, but he'd
always had a knack for chemistry, so, after a few failed cannabutter
attempts, he was able to produce a somewhat palatable batch of pot
brownies. Tag gave them to his roommates, curious as to just how
baked his baked goods would get them. Two hours into couch-glued
bliss, the surfers began to crave the whimsical bright yellow shapes of
Kraft Macaroni and Cheese with a roaring, focused intensity. Tag,
ever the salesman, helpfully went out and bought a couple dozen microwavable cups, which were consumed in blissful mouthfuls. The
next day, newly inspired, Tag decided to experiment with cannabutter-
infused mac and cheese, and Dank and Cheese was born.

The instant popularity of Tag's new product, again, shouldn't
have surprised him as much as it did. It seemed like a good idea. It
was a good idea. And people from all walks of life scrambled for it. It
was, in a way, wholesome and nostalgic: Who couldn't think of macaroni and cheese without wistfully thinking of childhood, regardless
of its chemical potency? Business was so good Tag no longer had to
sling ninety-nine-cent fries. He could pay the guys in the house what
he back-owed for utilities. He could afford to buy a new mattress, a
fan, and luxury sheets. The cheese went from off-brand bulk cheddar

to high-end crumbled labels. Tag bought his small, used green pick-up truck. Expensive sunglasses.

At first, the notoriety that came with this new career—drug chef—was, as it always is, attractive. Tag started casually seeing one of the surfers' friends, Jules, though Tag was never entirely sure if Jules liked him or just the idea of him: a white college dropout drug dealer who lacked tattoos. She could introduce Tag to her WASPish family while scandalizing them with allusions to Tag's cash-laden, criminal profession. Tag never did meet Jules's family. Jules never offered, though she constantly complained about their "square, bourgeois hypocrisy," the mandala tattoo haloing her belly button pulsing in anger, blond dreads whipping his face in bed. In any case, Tag was too busy experimenting with different noodle and cheese combinations to pay her much attention (wagon wheel and Gruyère was an unexpected bestseller; he called it Swiss Pioneer).

As the months went by, Tag grew increasingly paranoid, keeping his shades drawn and not picking up his cell phone. At the time, Tag thought it was a reasonable precaution because of his legally questionable business, but in retrospect, it was more likely a side effect of his endless THC consumption. Regardless, one morning, desperate to feel the carefree awe of his first few weeks in California, Tag joined his roommates at the beach. Jules later found this decision enraging. She always demanded Tag lie with her until she woke up, the moment at which he was supposed to both kiss and smoke her out, her eyes winking open to the sound of the trance EDM playlist she used as her alarm, Tag blowing a heady shotgun between her lips. Jules was the closest thing he'd ever had to a girlfriend and he imagined these kinds of compromised routines were par for the relationship course. That morning, however, he slipped away from Jules, bringing along a tattered paperback he found buried behind wet suits and crunched beer cans.

Exhausted by his anxieties, as well as Jules's recent interest in deep tissue massage (received, never given), Tag yearned for Arizona for the first time, for the regimented class schedules and the dry expansiveness of the landscape. He grabbed the book off a random shelf because the cover reminded him of Tempe, though he soon discovered the book was about Utah, albeit southern Utah, which was more or less Arizona. The book's cover was a silhouette of a person leading two mules up a hill, a desert sunset stretched out behind them. It was the biography of a young man who, a hundred years ago, went out into the desert with two pack mules and was never seen again. The man had left mysterious graffiti scattered throughout the area's surrounding canyons, always of one Latin word: NEMO. No one.

Dank and Cheese was becoming uncontrollably popular, more and more unknown numbers texting and calling Tag's burner, more and more anonymous people showing up at the house asking for him. Tag had earned enough to buy the nicest stereo on the market. He decided what he did every day. He had Jules. But there on the beach, dawn freshly broken, Tag's cell phone already chirped with texts from eager clients and an angry girlfriend; becoming no one was an increasingly attractive option. Even after almost three years, Tag wasn't sure his roommates wouldn't eventually rat him out to the police or rival dealers, even in a weed-friendly state like California. Tag stared at the book in his hands. Utah? Who knew? All Tag knew of Utah was skiing and polygamy. And yet, this book talked about so much more. He was twenty-three years old and living a life that most guys would be deeply jealous of, he knew, but reading about a delusional adventurer wandering the canyons' boundless, unexplored wilderness: That, Tag thought. That sounded like freedom.

Tag sold down most of the rest of his stock and left three batches of Dank and Cheese in the fridge, all Swiss Pioneer, for his roommates and Jules. He left a note on the bed for Jules with the recipe, saying she was welcome to continue the business if she wanted, he'd left his burner for her with all the contacts and the number unchanged, and enough cash for rent for two months. He did not say goodbye. Instead, the paperback on the dash of his truck, he drove east.

"**D**o you still have the book?" Bea's cigarette had long gone out, but she held it as if it was lit.

"I reread it the other month, actually." Tag had been speaking straight out into the night, looking ahead or at the ground, but now he turned to Bea. "You know, it's pretty terrible. Really dense and scientific. I remember it being this amazing, revelatory thing. I'm not a fast reader, but I swear I read this book in, like, two days in California. It blew my mind. I've kept it on my dresser for the past six years and couldn't bring myself to open it. I didn't want to break the spell or something. But when I finally did, I couldn't even finish it." It was as if now that Tag started talking, he couldn't stop. He had one hand cupping his chin. Bea thought of mandala tattoos and blond dreads. "Isn't that crazy? I literally abandoned my life because of this book and it turns out it fucking sucks." He started to laugh.

"I don't think that's crazy," Bea said.

"Really? A shitty book isn't crazy?"

"Not at all. You want to know crazy? I lied at my job so badly the feds got involved and now I'll never be able to work on a trading desk again. My severance runs out in a week and I have one functional credit card. I can't pay my own rent. If I don't get this job, I won't be able to pay my mom's rent anymore, either. But you know what's crazier?"

"This treasure thing?" Tag asked, giggling.

"No." Now Bea was laughing. "Yes, but no. Get this—my mom has no idea! She thinks this is a fun weekend with her boyfriend! She has no idea what happened," Bea's hands were on her knees. "She just thinks she's getting evicted. That's it. Isn't that insane?"

Hank walked outside saying the toilet was fixed and people were singing again, but paused when he saw Bea doubled over, gasping. "Is she all right?" he asked.

"She's getting evicted," Tag explained, still laughing.

"Shit," Hank said. "Beer's on me, then."

They went back inside. Hank bought a round and then another. They sang Dolly Parton, Bea hitting most of the notes, while Linda danced around in wild circles. Hank forced Tag to join him for a Justin Bieber B-side. Tag mostly stood behind Hank, but mouthed enough of the song that it was clear he knew every word. Bea cheered. Her eyes felt wider, her feet lighter. She didn't feel drunk, but she had the same loose, giddy feeling she did after vomiting. Her phone had died, a relief. There was more beer. The room began to spin. Tag asked her if she was all right, brought her a glass of water. The bar did last call and while the guys settled up, Bea went outside. Leaning against the building, the brick still sun-warm, she closed her eyes. Her mother could have this, she decided. Her mother could have a fun weekend with this internet guy and once they were driving back to Salt Lake, Bea would tell her about Bob and New York and the derecho and her job. She'd do the questionnaire and the project to-morrow. She'd get an interview. She'd get the job. It'd be fine. She inhaled. She exhaled. She did the math. There was enough, for now, for this weekend. Just enough. It'd be fine.

"Hey, can I bum a smoke?"

It was the guy with the hat, the guy from the grill. He was pale, face and neck splotchy with ingrown hairs, and his eyes were an un-earthly blue. He hooked his thumbs through his belt loops. Behind him, a new, huge black pickup parked in front of the store. A large black dog barked from the passenger seat, its teeth flashing. Bea was abruptly sober. She handed over the pack. "You're not going to have one?" he asked, offering her one of her own cigarettes.

She wanted one, but something told her not to. She crossed her arms, looked back at the door. "I'm good."

He pulled out a lighter, an old-fashioned one, brass, and dramat-ically lit the cigarette. He leaned toward her as he inhaled. "I liked your Dolly," he said. His free hand brushed her hip.

Bea took a step away, pretending to adjust her sandal. "Thanks."

"I also like how you're not wearing makeup." The dog in the truck began to bark.

"Thanks," she said again, more slowly this time.

"You from around here?" He pointed his cigarette at her face. "Wait, don't tell me. I already know you are. It's the way you carry yourself. I noticed you while I was singing. And you smoke, like a real person."

Bea didn't respond, pretending to look something up on her phone. He came closer. She stepped away. "What? Do I smell? Sorry, I've been camping the last couple of days." The guy smiled wide enough that his lower teeth were exposed. "You know, if you were my girlfriend, I wouldn't let you out of the house in that dress, but you're not, so I'm not complaining."

"Good night," Bea said, walking down the road. There was no one else around. The night went on and on and on. The dog barked and barked and barked. The guy walked fast to catch up with her, put a hand on her lower back, and told her to hold on. "Don't touch me," she said. "Please."

"Don't be like that, I'm making sure you get home safe, no need to be a fucking princess about it." He was angry, viscerally so, his cheeks splotchy and getting redder. Bea began to apologize. He lifted the hand with the cigarette, but then the pizza parlor door opened, and Tag and Hank appeared. Bea waved. "Hey," she shouted.

"You know those assholes?" the guy asked. "It's rude to talk while someone's singing," the guy yelled. He grinned as if joking, but he wasn't, and they all knew it.

"Technically, you were rapping," Hank said. He and Tag joined them.

"Oh really, you're going to be like that?" the guy said, blowing smoke into Hank's face.

"You good?" Tag asked Bea. Bea crossed her arms and nodded. "Good," Tag said.

"It's karaoke," Hank said. "Chill out."

"It's basic respect," the guy spat.

"Your dog's upset," Tag said, pointing. The dog had started to alternate between yelping and howling. A long string of drool hung from its jaw. "You may want to calm it down."

"Don't tell me what the fuck to do with my dog, bro," the guy yelled.

"Hey, *bro*, don't lock your dog in your truck, *bro*," Hank sneered. The guy threw his cigarette to the ground and stepped toward Hank, adjusted his hat farther onto his head. The guy was shorter than Hank, but Hank was skinnier. Bea grabbed Tag's hand, squeezed it. "Let's go," she said, smiling at Tag. The guy noticed.

Tag looked down at her hand and then up at her, face slack and dumb. "Go where?" he asked slowly.

"I left my phone at the grill," Bea said.

"You're holding your fucking phone," the guy said in a low voice.

"Yeah, I meant my keys," Bea turned to Tag. He swayed slightly. He was drunk, she realized. She squeezed his hand harder and tried not to panic. "Remember?"

"Your keys. At the grill," he said slowly, eyes brightening as he caught on. He squeezed her hand back. "Hey, Hank, it's time to go."

Hank faked a lunge at the guy and when the guy flinched, Hank snorted. "Typical," he said. As they walked away, there was the slam of a truck door and the dog's whine. Bea wouldn't let herself look back.

Christy knew he had a gun. He showed it to her in their motel room. A heavy black pistol. When Christy admitted to having never touched one before, he told her to take it, and she put a hesitant pointer finger on the barrel. He told her to actually take it. She did and her ears began to buzz, as if clapped. Holding a gun while sitting on a hotel bed seemed like a great way for them to finally bridge the distance between their online personas and in-person bodies. The danger of it, the rush: Surely this would make him maintain eye contact, make him sit down next to her. Make him touch her. But it didn't. Bob stayed standing and Christy stayed sitting. After a few seconds, he gently took the gun back, his fingers not even brushing hers, and put it into its case, double-checking the lock. That morning, when he said that he brought it with him for their hike, how he liked to keep it under the passenger seat and he hoped she didn't mind, Christy flushed. She could feel the gun pulse under her seat. The possibility—no—the promise of it. There was still a chance of something happening. She pulled the sleeves of her sun shirt over her fists and refused to be nervous.

Bob had pursued *her*, if a few direct messages counted as flirtation. His posts were about treasure possibilities: you could climb this; if he hiked that; someone should drive there. All hypotheticals, no follow-through. Bob's private messages, however, were thoughtful and direct. He'd fact-check her research about alpine forestry or trout runs, ask what her favorite research methods were, compare best mapping practices. Frustrated by the fact that she had to log in to the Conversation to know if there were any new messages from him, Christy sent him her phone number. They started to text, though things didn't start to really heat up until she sent a flirty selfie of herself. About to head to the library to print off the data we discussed! He responded by asking more about what was on the table behind her than the buttons she left open on her blouse. Is that a map?

Christy had been disappointed. She was getting older, she reminded herself, though it wasn't much consolation. Regardless, they started talking on the phone almost every week, their conversations spanning hours. Bob mentioned an ex-wife, but nothing else. He never mentioned his age, or his current job, or even his last name. He never mentioned a lot of things, Christy was realizing as they drove toward their hike. For the past few months, Christy had talked to Bob more than anyone else in her life. She told him about Montreal, about the cancer treatments, about her daughter and how she worried about how to text her back. He would encourage her openness, ask follow-up questions and murmur support, but wouldn't share anything similar about his own life. She had seen him as the strong-and-silent type. Nothing like her ex-husband, nothing like herself, but that was part of the thrill. She spilled herself out toward him and hoped he got caught up in the current.

They passed a roadside burger stand with a tall neon sign. Bob said it reminded him of a place he brought dates growing up. "We'll grab lunch there," he said, "before we go to the town hall meeting." He winked. Christy's heart leapt into her throat. She said she always loved a good chocolate malt. He said he preferred vanilla. They turned off the highway. The morning brightened. Christy put on her sunglasses and texted her daughter not to wait up for them. Exciting things were happening.

➤

It was late morning and a headache ripped across Bea's skull. The cabin's pullout couch was stiff and creaky, its springs digging into her hip. She checked her phone. Christy had texted, saying she and Bob were going on an intel-gathering hike for most of the day. There was a town hall meeting tonight, too, but don't worry and don't wait up. EXCITING THINGS R HAPPENING!!! Multiple star emojis.

Bea fell back asleep and not because she meant to. She dreamt of being on an airplane headed somewhere filled with palm trees and fruit, but the wings had fallen off and the windows were blown out and everyone was screaming except the pilot, who happened to be a shaggy dog. She woke up an hour later and the headache was a hot snake curled behind both ears. Across the room, the bed was rumpled. She hadn't been able to bring herself to sleep in it last night, the sheets smelling too strongly of her mother's signature lavender and patchouli. Christy's luggage was gone, but the aspen tree was still there, the map tucked behind its yellow leaves. Whatever exciting things her mother and Bob had planned, they didn't involve Bea or the map and therefore only involved each other. Bea was too hungover to feel worried. Christy was an adult. Christy could figure it out. In fact, her mother may have already figured it out. She would reply to Christy later, Bea decided, after a shower and coffee.

Drying her hair, Bea considered herself in the mirror. She looked terrible. Her face was sallow and papery. She pulled at her cheeks, picked at a zit. The light, she told herself. The light in this bathroom is fucking awful. Her hair was ragged and too long, thinned at the ends and already curling in the bathroom's humidity. For years she had worn the same curtain of muddy brown draped just past her shoulders, the same style her mother would cut when Bea was a child. Bea had never deviated from the formula, never thought to. Her hair was at best an afterthought, at worst an inconvenience, something she needed to maintain for her professional life. But she didn't have professional life, at least not right now, and if she landed this job, it'd be an entirely different life than before. There were scissors in a drawer by the mini fridge.

It was too easy, the chunks of curls rapidly dotting the sink in dark parentheses. Bea cut until she became self-conscious enough to stop. The fresh ends tickled her earlobes. Short and uneven. If not better, different. Bea imagined her mother's shocked face and smirked.

The instant coffee in the kitchenette was horrific, grainy and burnt, and made Bea's hangover worse. Pulling on the same debate shirt and athletic shorts as the night before, Bea wandered outside. The weather was a relief. It was windy and the temperature was tolerable, almost mild. The street and sidewalk in front of the RV park were empty, Pat's Grill closed, the motel quiet. Bea walked, her feet still aching and swollen from the hike. The sidewalk went from concrete to dust to concrete. A large brown dog appeared and trotted next to her for a minute or so, never looking at her but keeping pace, close enough that Bea could smell its breath, sweet and loamy. Just as she worked up the nerve to pet it, it veered away toward an industrial garage. The main drag felt smaller and more barren than the night before. The karaoke-pizza-outdoor-outfitter's neon OPEN sign was lit, despite the place being closed. Next door was an empty storefront with a wooden wagon in its window display. Then a hardware store and a thrift store, also both closed. Across the street, the movie theater, its letter sign advertising TOWN HALL 7PM. Bea turned the corner. Across a wide, empty parking lot was a squat, single-story grocery store, its doors sliding open and closed on their own.

Bea wandered down the aisles. Steady rivers of cold poured from the overhead vents, stinging her sunburned arms and cheeks. The store was quiet aside from the hum of the overhead lights and the occasional beep of the register. In the freezer section a clean-shaven man in coveralls squinted at the frozen drumsticks. Seeing Bea he asked, after an apology, if she wouldn't mind telling him which was the low-sodium option. Down another aisle a German couple angrily muttered over granola bars. Bea circled the store twice and saw no hot coffee. A voice announced the store was doing a promotion on ice cream. Buy one, get one. She approached the register, but a woman hurried over and threw a six-pack of PBR onto the conveyor so carelessly one of the bottles fell out and rolled toward the scanner. The woman wore an oversized coat, too big and thick for the season. She could've been thirty-two or sixty-seven years old. "No wine here," the woman said sternly, looking up at Bea with giant brown eyes. "Only at the state store in Bluff." Bea had no idea why the woman thought she might want wine, but when she considered it, she would've bought a bottle if there had been some. Bea thanked her. The woman paid and gave Bea one of the beers before hurrying out of the store. The cashier said he'd couldn't let her keep the beer. State law, he said, his voice so exhausted and detached, Bea couldn't bring herself to ask where the coffee was, which is how she left with only that which was behind the till: Lucky Strikes and Skittles.

Bea sat on a bench in the parking lot and smoked. She poured Skittles into her mouth between puffs. She didn't swallow the Skittles, just sucked on the marbled mass until it congealed into a soft, chemical wad, like she used to as a kid. The combination of nicotine and sugar was revolting enough to make her forget about her hangover. Legs wide, sun in her eyes, candy clumped in her cheek, Bea wondered if this was how cowboys felt, wondered if she should spit, just to try it, but then the elderly drumstick man walked past, nodding hello, plastic bag hanging from his hand. Bea readjusted herself upright and tried to swallow. She gagged and spit the Skittles wad into the candy wrapper. Overhead, a hiss that sounded like a bird but was really a jet, and then nothing again.

She opened her email and downloaded the project directive. A dataset from a California wildfire a few years earlier, one of the worst in the state's history. Acres burned, length of burn, maximum and minimum temperatures, wind strength and direction. She was to provide a hypothetical analysis on possible meteorological impact across the West, specifically the Great Basin, with an eye toward energy demands. Easy. Too easy, Bea thought, until she read the closing paragraph about how *such reports will be a daily expectation for an entry-level research analyst*. She paused, but then thought it a good thing: she'd outshine all the other applicants and then negotiate the job title once she had the offer.

There was a map of the area in the included data. The fire had been close to Santa Barbara and Bea debated if she should text Tag.

It'd be around when he lived there, wouldn't it? She wasn't sure. She began to type up a report on her phone. A firm like this cared about facts, but not precision. Throw as much quantitatively necessary spaghetti against the wall and see which clients it stuck to. Data for data's sake. There was no grace, no art, only pure utility, but Bea could do that. She'd been doing that. Her thumbs flew. Hydrological dependency. Interstate infrastructure. Jet stream. Solar fields. She'd been doing this for years. She could do this in her sleep. A few cursory calculations, references to the relevant data, general recommendations. Upside. Arbitrage. It took her ten minutes, fifteen after she checked for grammar and punctuation. She wouldn't hit send yet, though, she decided. Better to sleep on it, come back with fresh eyes, and then submit. This wasn't the desk; it was a summer weekend. She finished her cigarette and lit another.

Carolyn hadn't posted anything since the other day. They were probably eating lobster rolls, ironically playing college drinking games, debating whether or not to do MDMA. Their entire weekend was predictable and enviable and empty. In a different life, Bea could've been there agonizing over her bikini line and cocktail choices, fake laughing along with someone's mundane college memories, ignoring how much the food cost. She would've done it, all of it, for the pictures and the inside jokes they'd rehash back in the city, for the memories, for the assurance that her place in this group of easy, glamorous, comfortable people was finally, fully realized. Bea looked at the photo and felt like she should be distraught, chest filled with some pang of longing, but instead there was nothing but a hollow distance. The weekend felt like thousands of miles away because it was. Grant and Carolyn cheersing, again and again and again, in her absence. They had no idea how much power she had, Bea thought. She could send Carolyn a message right now and ruin it all, the whole facade. But what if Carolyn already knew? What if Carolyn didn't care? Impossible. Of course she'd care. Who wouldn't? Bea dragged on her cigarette and started to understand the habit, how you could sit on a bench outside a grocery store and do nothing but think and stare and no one would find it concerning. She never liked lobster. Rubbery, like chewing earplugs.

The headache was back, faint but knocking, and there were no more Skittles. Every vein in Bea's body ached for caffeine. She pulled herself off the bench and headed toward the grill, but ducked away when she caught sight of Tag through the windows. She was about to turn back to the cabin when she remembered the motel. The dispensers in the lobby were Starbucks brand. The woman at the front desk asked if Bea was a guest and Bea smiled and refilled and said she was a guest of Bob's.

Back at the cabin, Bea wondered where her mother was, and whether she should call to check in. She opened Christy's contact in her phone, but then didn't dial, recalling her plan from last night. Better to wait until the end of the weekend to tell Christy she was with a man who was, at best, a pathological liar; let her have her fun. She sent the thumbs-up and cowboy emojis instead, but it wouldn't deliver. The wi-fi had slowed to a crawl. Email wouldn't load. Apps opened to spinning infinity. The karaoke spot had free internet, but it didn't open for another two hours. She finished her coffee and her stomach turned.

Bea opened all the windows in the cabin, paced between the kitchenette and pullout. A Book of Mormon in the nightstand, brochures for local air balloon tours perched atop the microwave. She sprawled out over the bed, the sheets still smelling like her mother. She pressed her face into a pillow, inhaled. This time the lavender actually calmed her, arms going loose and head lightening, just like Christy always claimed it would. She inhaled again and then turned to the side, wondering if she was tired enough for another nap, when she saw it again. The map. Careful and light-fingered, Bea unrolled it. It was too big for the kitchenette's narrow drop table, so she folded the pullout back into the couch and laid it across the floor, weighing down the corners with forks and cups.

The arrows to nowhere, the typed notes, the photos and drawings, the mismatched paper. Each a sliver of her mother's brain, pathways to places where Christy had wondered over the past year and a half. Bea crawled around the papers, following lines and deciphering handwriting. It became a game, trying to figure out what document referred to what part of the map. Bea could trace the earliest bits of Christy's search: receipts from the local Connecticut grocery store, printouts on thin yellowed paper with the dates and times stamped at the bottom of the pages. They were printed last winter, weeks after Gertie died, days after the dinner.

Bea had made the reservation several months in advance. Neon sign, red sauce, suited waitstaff, formalwear—everything her grandmother loved. The restaurant had been the buzz of the office when it opened a few years earlier, guys bragging about their dinners there in ways that were either underhanded ("best rigatoni in the city") or back-handed ("they're called captains, not waiters"). Rumor had it they didn't list prices on the menu, which would also tickle Gertie—so stately, so country club. A simple chicken parmesan would set you back sixty-five bucks, the rigatoni fifty. It was an absurd experience, spending hundreds of dollars on comfort food you could order in almost any neighborhood in the city, but that's what made it so glamorous. Michelin or no, a fifty-dollar rigatoni would seem delicious because it's fifty dollars.

Phil wasn't the kind of guy who would eat there. He brought an honest-to-god lunchbox to work, but he gave Bea generous holiday bonuses, enough for her to take an ice cream scoop out of her loans one December at a time. Her grandmother, meanwhile, wasn't getting any younger. Gertie fell down the stairs the week before Christmas and spent the holiday wrapped in an afghan in her favorite chair, huddled over presents and hot toddies. That year, Bea had originally bought her grandmother a pair of driving gloves, supple oxblood leather, but then the doctors said Gertie's eyes were going, nearly gone. Gertie getting behind the wheel was now forever off the table. This reservation, at the fanciest Italian restaurant in Manhattan, was the consolation prize. Her grandmother gasped and weakly squeezed Bea's wrist when she told her. "What will I wear?" Gertie asked, her voice high and girlish. Bea had been paying Christy's health insurance premiums ever since the bankruptcy filing the year before, arguably gift enough, but gave the driving gloves to her mother. "Someone has to get Gertie into the city, might as well do it in style." Christy kept the gloves in their box and said nothing.

The earliest reservation Bea could get was during the first week of February at 5:30 p.m., which was perfect: early enough for Gertie to eat and get back to Stamford, far enough into the future for Bea to start budgeting for both appetizers and dessert. But by New Year's, Gertie had become feeble and silent, hardly leaving the plaid chair in the living room. Soon, she was refusing food and doctors. By the end of January, she dozed off for an afternoon nap, TV murmuring, and never woke up.

A few days later, Bea sat down at the tableclothed two-top. The waiter—captain—asked if she was expecting someone else tonight, but Bea said no. It was just her. Scanning the dining room, she was the only one eating alone. Obvious and pitiful, like spinach between the teeth. If things had been different, she'd have taken a half day from work, gotten a blowout and a manicure, put on a new dress and maybe even heels. She would've met her grandmother at the curb, asked the maitre'd for a photo. Instead, she wore ChapStick and wrinkled slacks and didn't realize her ID tag was clipped to her cardigan until she was halfway through the breadbasket.

The restaurant was louder than she expected, filled with laughing businessmen and nasalized housewives and a disturbing number of children. People kept knocking the back of her chair as they passed, even when she pulled in close enough that the table pushed into her ribs. A boy on the other side of the room had an iPad in his lap and giant red headphones wrapped over his head. Bea had always considered these kinds of restaurants near-holy, atmospheric in attainability and price, a haven for the kind of wealth that was easy and unafraid. If you walked through those doors, if you sat down at this table, how bad could life be? There was over two hundred dollars of mediocre Italian food going cold in front of her and yet, instead of careless celebration, Bea was convinced everyone was staring at her, an interloper who didn't know how to use a spoon to wrap spaghetti, whose clothes were old and loose and not in the sophisticated way. A couple at the table next to hers left without finishing their bottle of wine, their plates piled half full with food. Bea assumed this meant the restaurant didn't allow to-go boxes, and she shoved forkfuls of lasagna into her mouth until the captain came back and asked if he should pack up the table for leftovers.

But Bea kept ordering. A fusilli drenched in vodka sauce, a mysterious dish called Chinese chicken, a pile of triangled fried mozzarella, more wine. The food was fine. It needed more salt, but Bea didn't dare ask for a shaker. Her grandmother would've adored it, all of it. Gertie would've asked if her lipstick was all right, she would've lightly flirted with the captain, she would've said she couldn't possibly eat more and then ordered the chocolate cake with extra frosting. She would've asked for salt.

Bea had just signed the check when she saw Carolyn weaving between the tables. Bea blocked her face with a hand. They hadn't seen each other since the gallery opening in October and she thought maybe Carolyn wouldn't recognize or acknowledge her, but she did, holding up a hand with a small smile. Martha turned to look and, when she saw Bea, squealed and waved with both hands. They came over to Bea's table, Martha saying how wild it was they were here at the same time, wasn't the ziti amazing? "Amazing," Bea agreed. The captain swooped in and asked if Bea would like her things packed to go. "Sure," Bea said. Carolyn winced as he skirted around them with the half-full plates and Bea fought the urge to apologize.

Carolyn asked who Bea was with. "My grandmother," Bea said.

Carolyn smiled. "My grandmother loved it here, too," she said. The captain reappeared. Bea accepted the takeout bag. "You know, my grandmother went outside to catch a cab for us. I should make sure she's okay." Bea went to hug each woman. Martha patted Bea's back. Carolyn, though, held Bea tightly. "We should really catch up sometime," Carolyn said, keeping Bea in the hug for a beat too long.

The invitation to their party would come later, but in that moment, bewildered, Bea mumbled a quick goodbye and rushed out of the restaurant. She paused at the curb, just long enough to remember Gertie wouldn't be there waiting, that there was no cab, no Gertie, and there never would be. Bea turned and went straight to the subway, then Metro-North, then a town taxi, and then to Gertie's front door, the takeaway bag torn and cold. Christy was at the kitchen table, the driving gloves still folded in their tissue in front of her. "I wanted to drive in and surprise you," Christy said. "I didn't want you to eat alone, but then—" Her mother started to weep. Bea slid the leftovers into the microwave, one after the other. They ate in silence, the food tasting better than it had at the restaurant, though Christy didn't believe Bea when she said so. Her mother said it was the best pasta she'd ever had and Gertie would've adored it. "What am I going to do?" she cried. Bea tried to comfort her, but Christy began to howl. "*What* am I going to *do*?"

Judging by the patchwork of papers, her mother's focus was a giant cross section from New Mexico to Idaho, though the map was hardly geographically accurate. Bea analyzed a printed Wikipedia list of various ancient Pueblo graffiti sites in Colorado connected by frantic arrows to a map of the Nevada high desert. Above both, Christy had written BLAZE, underlined four times. There was another BLAZE across Yellowstone National Park, Bea squinting to make out *trail markers* written in pencil nearby, though the note was faint and, judging by the white-worn cloud around it, Christy had erased and rewritten it several times. On the edge of the map there was a blue Post-it with scribbled calculations of how many chains equals an acre equals a mile.

Bea noticed her mother's math was wrong, found a pen in a drawer, and gently wrote in the correct conversion. A Target receipt was taped on top of a topographic map of the Rio Grande, blocky black letters spelling GULLY DROWN / HOUSE OF BROWN??? across the list of items purchased. Bea's throat hitched when she saw the receipt was for a tablet and its case, both on clearance. Every river system, underground aquifer, and dam was highlighted in Christy's wobbling lines of yellow, pink, and green. There was a significant number of notes on Mercy, the town retraced in a rainbow of circles, as if her mother had revisited and reevaluated the spot many times. Typed and cut out and pasted above it: *where weather and water meet*. The note had soft edges and weak glue, evidence of frequent moves. Next to it, in fresh ink, her mother had written a one-word question: BOB?

Bea typed the URL for the Conversation into her phone. Miraculously, the wi-fi worked again and the website loaded. She scrolled through OnlyBob's profile: nothing since the cliff photo. The latest from ChristineM52 was only a short diatribe about the widespread misuse of *where/were* in recent posts, the post concluding with a plea to maintain the quality of conversation!!!!!! It would've been funny if Bea hadn't noticed the time stamp: thirty minutes ago. Her mother was, or had recently been, online.

Bea's social media handles were a mundane assortment of her initials and birthday. She'd missed the craze of fake AIM profiles during her middle school years, no one telling her she could make up a username and troll chat rooms, despite the fact that she would have logged in as BeautifulM917 and no one, aside from her mother, would've been the wiser. It didn't take long for Bea to come up with a vague name—Pretty917, she was never one for creativity—and log in to the Conversation. The interface on the user end of the forum was the same as the public-facing side, white text boxes and pixelated animations. Bea clicked onto the thread and opened the reply box. Pretty917 responded to ChristineM52: where r u. She refreshed the thread a few times, hoping for her mother's typical all-caps response, but none came.

She started a new thread. Title: "where weather and water meet"??; text: hot springs? maybe in UT/AZ? Two minutes later, a response from a trailguy69: lol. She found OnlyBob's older posts. She replied to them with more like OnlyBoob and just call me EveryRobert. When heckling lost its charm, Bea begun to read the posts. Turns out, many had already posited that the warm waters were hot springs. The comments were smarter than Bea expected, nuanced and curious. There were questions of etymology and epistemology, semantics and syntax. Water could mean more than water, it could mean entire ecosystems. Meet: Is that an economic term, rather than a physical

one? Did you know that the first beaver trappers in the West mea-
sured by rope yards, instead of metric miles? That there was an ancient sea here that impacts evaporation rates to this day?

An hour slid by, maybe two. Bleary-eyed, Bea went out onto the
cabin's porch and lit a cigarette. She pulled up a picture Christy had
sent when she first moved to Salt Lake. Her mother had driven out
to a trailhead in the mountains and asked a stranger to take the
photo. Snowy peaks sprawled along the horizon in bruised blues and
purples, bare, skinny aspens quivering on all sides, the sky long and
unbroken. Christy posed with her signature double finger-guns. She
wore pink leggings and a pink sweatshirt and a giant blue visor. With
her cigarette-free hand, Bea pulled up the photo and edited it to
make the sky more brilliant, the leggings more pink, and then texted
it to Christy. in case you want a non-piss pic to give bob. She added an
exploding brain emoji. call me when you get this. Christy hadn't texted
since EXCITING THINGS, almost six hours ago. The quiet was
unusual. Bea thought of Bob, his squeak-laugh, the offers to pay, and
then sent a follow-up: dinner at the grill, just us? She made sure her
ringer volume was on its highest level and then sent a heart emoji for
good measure. She waited for the texts to be marked delivered, but
they never were.

One hundred million years ago, there was a vast sea filled with
spined and scaled things. Its beaches were surrounded by lush ferns

and towering trees, and flowers of every color, which were the favorite of a potbellied, squat creature that extended its beak to clamp off the long, sweet petals and chewed thoughtfully, slowly, before wandering to the next thicket of bushes, gobbling up a small rodent on the way, blood mixing with pollen. It avoided predators, though it didn't have many, being so large and leathery. It eventually died, like everything, and so did the flowers and ferns and trees and sea, like everything. Now, a dog carries half of one of the creature's fossilized ribs in its mouth, trotting toward the shade of the campsite nestled under some spindly cottonwoods at the edge of a canyon.

It finds a spot among some nearby grasses, walks in a circle to mat them down, digs a bit to get to the cooler sand, and then lies down. The bone doesn't taste much different than any other bone, maybe a bit less, since there's no flavor of recent muscle or marrow, but the dog doesn't care. It's something to gnaw. It hasn't properly eaten since the night before, when the two men argued in the tent, voices echoing off the pink canyon walls curving up above them. They were so loud, shouting about being late to dinner, that they scared off the birds and lizards the dog was eyeing. The owner said if anyone needed dinner, it was the dog, and made a scene of overfilling its camping bowl. The dog didn't mind, ate every last bit of kibble as the men continued to yell, but it hasn't eaten since. Bored and hungry, it wandered off that morning and eventually found a small bird. Then, while it lapped water from a nearby creek, washing down the feathers stuck to the back of its throat, it spotted a bone jutting out of the side of a ledge. Now, back at the camp, it gnaws the rib. It waits, though it doesn't know it's waiting. It doesn't know the difference between one hour from now and one hundred million years before.

The dog picks up the bone and ambles toward the cooler shade of the tent. Inside, a tangle of sleeping bags, on top of which its owner sits. The dog lies down again, back legs to one side, bone between its front paws, and chews a broken, brittle, ancient corner. The dog understands its owner is upset, feels how tense and still the air in the tent is, despite being cooler than outside. It understands how when the owner thrashes and yells, it has nothing to do with the dog, just like the dog understands eventually the owner will stop, sigh, and rub it behind its ears, the spot the owner knows it loves best. This time, though, the owner doesn't. Instead, he throws a phone across the tent, startling the dog to its feet, its brown-black haunches raised. It watches as the owner picks up a backpack and the phone and then leaves, the dog right behind him. It watches as its owner trots off through the grasses and reeds in the direction of where they hiked the day before. The dog sniffs the air, tracing its owner's scent as he moves farther away, and as it fades, settles down into the shade of the tent. The dog knows the owner will be back. The dog will gnaw the rib until then, or until it gets too hungry, whichever comes first.

Montreal. The divorce. The boyfriends. The girlfriends. The diagnosis. The doctors' appointments. Calling her daughter. Taking care of Gertie. Taking care of Gertie's estate. The Conversation. The map. Bob. Utah. There'd always been a next step, something to look forward to, to plan toward, for years. Christy's life had been a conveyor belt of responsibilities and hopes, her days short, her calendar

full. Ever since Gertie died, the treasure had captured her full attention, the conversations she'd have on the Conversation, the conversations she'd have about the Conversation with Bob, her conversations
with Bob. Suddenly, though, Bob was no longer willing to have a
conversation. Specifically, about why they were standing on a bluff in
the middle of the desert.

The morning had started so well. A gun, a promise of a milk-
shake. Christy didn't know why they didn't go straight to her areas of
interest. She had three main suspects, but Bob had said there was
something else they needed to do first, driving off through town and
pulling over seemingly at random. He told her to get out of the car,
and he'd been excited, jostling his truck keys in his fist. Christy
thought it might be a fun surprise, a picnic or a scenic overlook. Instead, it was a long hike to a bluff. She could feel sweat pooling in her
sports bra and she had forgotten her sunscreen. Bob mumbled and
she asked him to speak up.

"Any minute now," he said. He didn't look at his watch.

"Why don't we go get those milkshakes? We can always come
back. It'd be beautiful at sunset, don't you think? After the town hall
meeting?"

"We're not going anywhere," Bob said forcefully. He put his hand
over his eyes and squinted.

"We're just going to stand here?"

"Just be patient."

"Can we at least sit down while we're being patient? My back is
killing me." Bob softened and said sure. There was a gnarled tree
nearby and Bob said they'd still have a good vantage point against its
trunk. Christy didn't question what he was looking for. Maybe he

meant analyzing the geography, maybe he meant watching the wind patterns. Once they found a shaded spot under the tree, Christy made sure to sit in such a way that their legs touched. Bob didn't seem to notice, glancing between his phone and the horizon. She pressed her hip into his. She tossed her curls back and put a hand on his shoulder. He looked at her. She looked at him. She asked, "Isn't it gorgeous out here?"

"Sure," he grunted.

"Hot, too. Very hot," Christy said, grinning, but he didn't seem to understand. She changed her approach. "You want to tell me why you brought me all the way out here? Something you want to tell me?"

"Nope," Bob said, his bottom lip jutting out.

"You sure?" Christy traced his shoulder with her fingernail. A bright bloodred, going in circles and circles. "Nothing?"

Bob turned back to her, his mustache slanting up as he watched her nail go round and round. "I'm not sure what you mean," he said.

She'd have to do this herself, she guessed. Christy swallowed a sigh and brought her nail to his chin. "I think you know," she said softly. "I think you know exactly what I mean." She brought his chin close to hers, and then her lips close to his, and then—

"What the hell—" Bob yelped and pushed himself away. "What the hell are you trying to do?" He was flustered, so flustered he patted his back pockets for his wallet and phone. "We're here on business," he said, walking out of the shade. "This is an important stop. We can't be distracted."

"But we can have some fun," Christy laughed, still thinking they were in the game. Perhaps he hadn't been with anyone since his ex, perhaps he was shy. She didn't anticipate this, but she knew how to handle it, too. She could wait. She leaned back against the tree. There was no cell phone service. She crossed her arms and considered the horizon, how it hazed and curled in the growing heat of the afternoon. Bob turned to her, as if to say something. Christy winked and he blanched, turning back around. Christy smirked, closed her eyes. They waited in silence.

"Finally," he said.

The figure was small, dark, and hunched, emerging slowly from a distant canyon. Head, shoulders, torso, legs. Christy could tell by the walk that it was a young man, and as he got closer, could see he had on an oversized backpack and a green hat. Bob shifted from foot to foot. Christy stood up and waved. The boy did not say hello and neither did Bob. Christy said hello.

"You have it?" Bob asked the boy, nodding at the backpack.

"My name's Christy." She held out her hand.

"Why would *I* have it? You're the one with her," the boy said, ignoring Christy. "You were supposed to give it to *me*, remember, old man?"

"That wasn't the plan," Bob hissed.

"What was the plan?" Christy was smiling.

The boy rolled his eyes, turned to Bob. "You'll be at the meeting tonight?"

"Obviously," Bob said. "You?"

"Yeah," the boy said. He hooked his thumb into a belt loop. His other thumb went into his mouth and picked at something in his molars.

"Well, isn't that great," Christy chirped. "I'll be there, too. It'll be a party."

The boy looked at her. His eyes were disorientingly blue, icy and blank. "You should wear a hat with that skin," he said flatly.

"Next time I will," Christy said, refusing to break eye contact. She held her hand out again. "I'm Christy."

The boy's palm was soft and wet. "You said that," he said.

Christy put on her sweetest smile. "How do you know Bob?"

They were still pumping their hands, up and down, up and down. "Same way you do," the boy said.

She turned to Bob. "Why didn't you tell me we were meeting up with another hunter?"

"He's not," he said, mostly to the boy. The boy grinned, but didn't explain.

There was a long pause. "That's a fun hat." Christy said, using her free hand to point at the boy's head. "'Best cluckin' breasts'?"

"Do you ever shut up?" Bob barked. The boy snorted.

"I'm trying to get to know to our new friend," Christy said.

"This is ridiculous," Bob said, and began to walk away.

"Don't you want the backpack?" the boy yelled, but Bob didn't turn around.

Christy made a move to let go of the boy's hand, but he wouldn't let her. He held on and licked his front teeth. Christy's smile faltered. "I guess we'll see you at the town hall," she said.

The boy dropped her hand. "You will," he said slowly. "You most certainly will."

Christy slung the backpack over one shoulder. "See you soon!" she said, but the boy didn't respond. Christy walked away and the boy stayed on the bluff, hands on his hips, sun overhead. After a minute, she looked back and he was still there, the desert stretching out behind him, and Christy, unable to not acknowledge someone, waved. The boy did nothing.

Diamondbacks versus the Dodgers, bottom of the sixth and neither team had a run. Bea was buzzed enough that the baseball was soothing. Earlier, while she was chain-smoking and reading the Conversation, the men from the RV asked if she wanted to join them for the game. Bea pulled the rocking chair over. The men motioned at a cooler and said Bea could take whatever she wanted, just as long as she promised to be a Diamondbacks fan for the afternoon. Bea pulled a can out of the watery ice as the first hitter came to bat. "That's a good one," one of the men said solemnly, and it took Bea a minute to realize he meant the beer and not the game. Neither man had said more than five words since.

Bea called her mother periodically, but each time it went straight to voicemail, which was fine, Bea decided. Cell service was spotty out here and, if anything, there was only one road through town and she was facing it. She'd see Bob's truck, she told herself, though she wasn't sure what truck he was driving, only confident Bob was the type of man who would drive nothing less than Ford's latest hauler. The afternoon heat strengthened and, sitting under the weak shade of the RV canopy, Bea opened another beer, telling herself she wanted something cold to hold, but the alcohol softened both her hangover and anxiety. The men grunted occasionally, one audibly farted. The Diamondbacks hit a home run and Bea cheered with them, opening another beer. Her thoughts went slippery.

She tried her mother again. Voicemail. She went to her feeds. Carolyn had posted a new photo. A manicured hand—a new color this time, a pale gray—lay limp beside cocktail glasses, heavy with multiple rings of varying vintage and thickness, though none on that finger. It could've been taken anywhere, at any restaurant or patio or terrace. There was no caption, but there was a location: *cheers*.

Bea opened her project report, reread it. It was good. She knew it was good, because she knew she was good at her job, or at least, she'd be good at this job. She copied it into an email. Sending it to the recruiter felt routine, uninteresting. She rocked her chair back and forth and finished the beer. The afternoon ticked by and then, at the bottom of the eighth, the game went on a lightning delay. The men were going to start dinner. Did she want to join? Bea didn't. She stood up. Her legs were loose, unsteady, and she had to pause a few times before she got back to the cabin. She stumbled into the bathroom, turned the shower to the coldest temperature, and sat in the tub under the water. She sat there for a long time, arms around her knees and spine going numb. She occasionally opened her mouth to the water. She got out when she heard her phone chime. It was Tag. Bea didn't remember giving him her number. hey we're closing up early bc of the town hall and headed to our house if you want to hang. Bea sat on the bed in a towel and read the text again, examining it for any subtext, but it was just a text. Earnest, friendly, gameless.

Christy's number went to voicemail again. "Hey, hey, heyyyyy," Bea said, but then stopped. This was her mother, she reminded her-

self. She cleared her throat. "I don't know where you are. Oh, wait—"
A new text. Tag had sent the hang ten emoji and the fish emoji.
Hang ten and a fish. She responded with a question mark. He sent
an address, a six-minute walk away. Bea looked to the ceiling and
then looked to the floor, and when she didn't get the spins, decided
she was steady enough to go. Her phone was still connected to her
mother's voicemail. "Yeah, so, call me? Okay. Great. I'll be with Tag,
by the way. Okay, bye."

She pulled on the most respectable outfit she could find: jean
shorts and a plain black T-shirt. No chance of makeup, having left it
all in Salt Lake, but Bea told herself the zits along her chin weren't
that noticeable, especially considering the bright flush of sunburn
across her nose and cheeks, though that could be from the beer. She
was only here for the weekend, she reminded herself. She'd never see
Tag or Hank again, so why care. Ringlets were forming along her
hairline, tight like pasta. She never thought she had curly hair like
her mother, but then Bea had never had hair this short. She licked
her hand and pulled and patted but nothing tamed them. At least she
was showered. She stepped into her mother's bright pink flip-flops,
the only shoes that didn't bother her still-raw blisters, and headed out.

The house was a couple hundred yards behind the RV park, which
disoriented her. The cabins overlooked the desert, and the view
evoked a feeling of being on the edge of empty wilderness, but just
out of view were blocks of homes and cars, more inhabited than she
expected. Bea recognized Tag's green truck under a rusted metal car-

port. Up the front steps there was a potted cactus with a brightly colored WELCOME TO OUR HOME sign stabbed into its thorny base, a white crust oozing from the puncture. Bea stood next to the cactus and knocked on the door. There were noises from the other side of the door, hushed laughing and the squeal of tires, but no answer. Bea pulled at her quickly drying hair, using the black screen of her phone as a mirror. A mistake, she thought. It got too curly when it was this short. Another round of laughs and squeals, and then the loud, low throat clearing of an older man. Bea chewed the dried skin off her lower lip. I'm here, she texted. Tag responded immediately. in the back!

The backyard was dead grass and a yellowed camper trailer. In the middle of the yard, Tag tended to a small fire in a burned-out feed trough, a charred log in one hand. He raised the log. "You found us," he said haltingly.

"Nice place," Bea said. She shoved her hands into her armpits.

"It's my dad's." Hank arranged camp chairs around the fire. One of the chairs wasn't unfolding and he shook it angrily. "And mine, I guess. I grew up here."

Bea nodded. Tag did, too, holding the log in the air. Hank looked between them and then loudly inhaled through his nose. "Do you, uh, want a drink?"

She was woozy from the RV beers and the buzz had tapered off into a sluggish haze. She didn't want more, but saying no felt rude. She gave an exaggerated shrug.

"I have some home-brewed IPA in the trailer, too," Tag offered. "Just tapped, so it's fresh. Or you can have one of his beers." He tossed the log onto the fire. "Whatever."

"I don't think I've ever had homemade beer," Bea said.

"Home brewed," Hank corrected, raising a coy eyebrow at Bea. "It's Tag's passion project."

"You don't have to," Tag said.

"I'll try one," Bea said. "Why not."

"Brave," Hank said. "I'm going to grab some more wood and make sure my dad's all set with his dinner before he leaves for the town hall. You need any help in there, Tag?"

Tag walked into the trailer. "Nope, it'll only take a minute."

Hank turned to Bea. "He usually needs help. You should go help him."

"Really?" Bea swallowed. "I mean, if you think he needs it."

"Oh, he needs it," Hank said. "Trust me."

The inside of the trailer was neat and sparsely furnished. A blue corduroy couch, a small wooden crate improvising as a coffee table. There was a banquette, some cabinets, and a tightly made bed. The crash pad from the hike sat on one side of the door, a bundle of fishing poles clustered on the other. It smelled like chalk and lemons. It smelled, Bea realized, remembering the drive, like Tag's truck.

"You need any help?" Bea called out.

There was a crash, the sound of broken glass. Tag stepped out of a narrow door. Behind him, a toilet with its lid up. "You okay?" Bea asked.

"Yeah, fine, totally fine." Tag rubbed the back of his head, gave a weak laugh. "You surprised me, is all."

"Hank said you needed help."

"Of course he did."

"From what it sounds like, you might."

"It's just a bottle, it's fine, I'll clean it up." He grabbed a broom from next to the couch. He tried to laugh again, but it was half-hearted, humiliated. "Hank," he said, but didn't finish his thought.

Bea pointed at the bathroom. "Have you been doing this for a while? The beer?"

"Yeah, yeah. It's great. A little tricky sometimes, it's surprisingly harder than the cannabutter, but I think I've figured it out. Just a matter of some chemistry and engineering."

"Casual."

Tag bent into the bathroom and swept up the glass. When he stood, Bea took the dustpan from him. He gave her a grateful smile and pointed her to the cabinet under the sink. There were three different bins, each carefully organized by trash, compost, and recycling. Bea threw the shards into the trash and then immediately regretted it. Should it have been recycled? She went to ask Tag, but he was back in the bathroom, where there was some splashing.

There was a newspaper clipping taped to one of the upper cabinets above the sink. It was an obituary. *Mercy Local, Mercy Legend. Beloved restaurateur and notorious outdoorsman Pat Brown passed away surrounded by family and friends at home. He's survived by his wife, Vera Brown, and the many friends he considered kin . . .*

"Do you prefer a glass or a bottle?" Tag asked.

"Either." There was a photo of the man, white bearded with a small knob of a nose, laughing and wearing a fishing vest. Like a granola Santa Claus, Bea thought. From the bathroom, a flush. She turned. "Why do you brew it in the bathroom?"

"There's a spigot in here, well, technically it's the shower. You need water. It's sanitary, I promise."

"Nothing like a shower beer."

"I shower in the house," he said, not catching the joke. "Better water pressure. Are you okay drinking out of a bottle? They're disinfected." A disembodied hand held out an empty Coke bottle. Bea came closer and watched as Tag grabbed a long tube and pointed it into a utility tub. There was a splash and then the room went malty. Bea's stomach turned. Tag cursed. "Sorry, this is going to take a minute."

"You sure you don't need any help?"

He didn't respond, too absorbed in the process, and not wanting to interrupt him any further, Bea said she'd meet him outside. The fire was at a roar, black smoke huffing up into the sunset. The sky behind the smoke was its brightest blue, the sunset close. Hank smirked as she sat down in a chair across from him. He held up an open Coors and lightly shook it. "There's plenty more in here," he said, kicking a cooler at his feet. "Tag's a pretty clean guy, but it's still bathroom beer."

The booze made her body heavy, slow. She fought the urge to close her eyes. "I'll wait for one of the home brews."

"You sure?"

"He's going through all the effort, it feels rude not to."

Hank let out a loud sigh that could've been a burp. "Tag's like a puppy, you know? Sometimes I have to rein him in, tell him to ease off, but that's him. Can't talk him out of anything. You know he wants to stay here? Buy a house or something? Which is nuts. Everyone I grew up with has left. Dad says the town's emptying out like a hole in a bucket. You see the McMullin ranch? The one on the edge of town with the super-tall fencing? No? Okay, listen to this, it's crazy. The McMullins have been in Mercy for four generations or something. Maybe five. Probably as long as my family has. I don't know if I told you, but I'm a true local around here." Hank shoved his neck into his chest and gave Bea a big-eyed look of importance. Bea smiled until he kept talking.

"Anyway, the McMullins have been ranchers out here for forever. They had a crazy number of cows at one point. Booming business until it wasn't, which happened like fifteen years ago, around when I started high school. No one really knew it was happening, you know, because McMullin was always bragging about being this big football booster, but then all of a sudden he sold off all his stock. You know what he has now? Ostriches." Hank smacked his knee, beer sloshing. "Can you believe it? Likes to say the birds are his retirement plan. Bought a half dozen of them, thinks they're going to be big with the tourists, pictures and stuff. You know what it really is? They couldn't keep the cows anymore. Feds drove them off, had helicopters scouting them and everything. Cited them for trespassing. Trespassing! They've had their stock out in the country for almost a century and suddenly they're trespassing? But then cattle prices dropped too low. It's also why my dad's out of a job. Used to be a herder, even did a few seasons with McMullin, but got into this accident and now he has bad arthritis and is on disability. Could've found something if the economy stayed all right, but what do I know, I mean, I'm sure he's listening to us right now and will come out hollering any second, right, Dad? Anyway, after the ranch shut down, Mrs. McMullin divorced him for an old hippie in Moab. All their kids live in Idaho or something nowadays, who knows, but they want nothing to do with Mercy so McMullin sold off his stock. Told me and Tag all about it. He was at the grill after word about his divorce got around town.

Steak with a sunny-side egg on top, extra horseradish. Ate that every night. And now he has all these ostriches. No one even knows where he found the damn things. He names them after old movies, Dirty Dancing and Grease and Erin Brockovich. I'll see those birds bobbing around the old corrals and have to remind myself it's not an acid flashback. No idea why he thinks tourists would like them, you couldn't pay me to get near those things. They're mean and they're fast. Crazy fast. They can crack open your skull with one kick. It's a miracle the old man is still alive. Cows may be big, but at least they're dumb, sweet, and slow."

The trailer door slammed. "I really need to figure out a new way to drain things in there." Tag sat in the chair next to Bea and handed her a glass of murky brown liquid. "It's a double IPA. I've been working on it for a month or so, calling it Double Trouble. I might have been too heavy on the hops, but let me know what you think."

It tasted like sour dirt. "Tastes great," Bea said.

"Really?" Tag said, surprised.

"Yeah." Bea took another sip. She nodded. "Great."

Hank laughed. "It's shit, isn't it? Taggart tries, but he's still figuring it out, if his dumbass names aren't proof enough."

Bea took another drink, a large gulp this time. "It's great."

"You don't have to say that," Tag said.

"He's got grand plans to turn the grill into a microbrewery one day," Hank said, sipping his Coors. "I think it's just about as dumb as the ostriches." Tag got into explaining the laws about canning and bottling, but it was the water demands that really hindered things. "I'd need a billion water rights to break even," he said.

"Dude, the answer is sitting right in front of us. Hell, you're practically the owner of them." Hank crumpled his can under the heel of his sandal.

"That's never going to happen," Tag said. "Never."

"We should go to the town hall meeting and ask those old guys for the permits. I mean, it's just water waiting to be used." Hank cracked another beer. "I'm sure Vera would be down."

Tag motioned at Bea's beer, which was hardly touched. "Want to try the pilsner? It's lighter than the IPA, easier to drink. I can get you one. You know what, I'm going to get you one. I'll be right back. Hank, don't bother her. Be chill."

Hank shook his head. "I should be telling you that."

Bea pulled out her phone to check her email. Hank squatted next to her chair and held out a Coors. "If you drink it quickly, I won't tell him."

Condensation from the can dripped onto her arm, cold enough that it almost stung. "His beer isn't that bad."

Hank sucked his teeth, his tongue sliding around under his cheek. He gave a quick nod and then drank the Coors, even though there was another one in the cup holder of his chair. "You're too nice," he said as he gazed into the fire. Bea looked at her phone. No response from the recruiter. She clicked over to her texts and noticed Hank watching her. He smirked. "You waiting to hear from someone?"

"My mom," Bea said.

Tag ambled out of the trailer, three bottles aloft. "All right, everyone's trying this one. It's good, I swear. I think I nailed it."

"Like you nail anything," Hank said, winking at Bea.

"Damn it, Hank, cut it out." Tag handed Bea a beer and glared at Hank. Hank walked back to his chair, hands up.

"Sorry," Tag said in a low voice. The two guys exchanged a look, but Bea couldn't parse it, her brain slow and foggy. Instead, she sipped the beer. It was light and tart. "This is good," she said.

Tag smiled at her, appreciative. "That sounded like you actually meant it."

"I do," Bea laughed. "I really do."

The sun dipped lower. Tag settled into a chair and Hank lit a spliff and they passed it around. They let the fire spark and spit and the night settled in around them like dust, gray and hazy. Tag reminisced about the islands off the Washington coast, how as a kid he'd camp out in the damp forests with his parents. Bea mentioned track practice during Connecticut winters, how she'd hide in the bathrooms complaining of period cramps while the rest of the team shoveled snow off the track. Hank said he was never into sports, but he used to sing the anthem before basketball games. They all stood up, hands to hearts as Hank belted out the first verse of "The Star-Spangled Banner." Hank's father came out then, telling them not to get up to any trouble while he was gone. "And Hank, you know me and my buddies get the firepit after the meeting. Tradition." Hank and Tag exchanged a look as the old man climbed into a truck idling in the driveway.

As he drove away, Hank asked Tag if it was time and Tag said better now than never. Hank whooped and pumped his fist. The guys left, Tag into the trailer and Hank into the house, without any more explanation. Bea sat in the chair, two barely touched bottles of beer next to her. The spliff, though, was enough to make her admire the settling sunset, the shadows all lavender. She waited a moment, and then, without much thought or planning, walked around to the back of the trailer. There was nothing but desert, truly this time. She could see far into the horizon, the mesas dark and looming. The sky was a cup spilling red and purple, the clouds both immediate and infinite. She opened her email and reread her report. It was good. She was good. It would be good. She clicked the screen off and stood in the growing dusk, entranced, until Tag pulled up beside her in an ATV and asked if she wanted to go on an adventure.

They are angry about road signs. In the 1860s, the blood of the Civil War not yet dry, there was a law passed about the states and their roads. You make them, you mark them. A hundred and fifty years later, in a historic movie theater in the middle of the desert, they reference this law, spit flying, pointer fingers rigid. One side wears hats, the other lanyards. They are separated by a rope down the middle. The county commissioner and city council are on the stage seated at two metal folding tables, faces grim, hands fisted. There are no microphones and so no one pays any attention when the commission asks for people to settle down. People keep yelling. They hold up their signs about signs, their signs about no signs, their signs about wild turkeys. Christy goes up to the man with the sign about wild turkeys. He says people—he points at the lanyard lovers—keep coming to his house to ask about the Russian olive trees on his property. These people say they're invasive, but turkeys love those trees, and this man loves those turkeys. "A God-given Thanksgiving," he keeps saying. "Just like He intended." His hands have a light tremor. He isn't wearing a hat, but a younger, bigger man next to him is. The turkey man asks if she's from the country, and when Christy says yes, she lives in Salt Lake, the younger man shakes his head. The turkey man drops his sign, squints, and asks why she's here. "You media?" he asks, low and slow.

Christy was never one for civic engagement. She didn't like to read newspapers, preferring to learn about the issues of the day by eavesdropping at the nail salon or farmers' market. She voted when she remembered to and when she did, she voted Green Party, because her ex-husband hated them. Bob had described the town hall as a local meeting, something that happened regularly at the movie theater, nothing special, but it'd be an excellent opportunity to gather crucial information about the landscape and local history. "These people know things you can't find on the internet," he said. "Good people, you know?"

Christy imagined the coffee socials after church services of her childhood, when Gertie would lead her to the church's gymnasium and there would be tables full of pastries and people wore their nice clothes to talk about nice things, kids playing and priests mingling. Casual, local community. When they pulled up at the theater, a line of people already snaked down the sidewalk. Bob tucked in his T-shirt and holstered his gun. He assured Christy that packing heat was normal for this kind of thing. He described it like that, too: packing heat. The way he said it made her pause. The phrase was too affectedly casual, almost scripted, but Christy was not a gun owner and would never be one, thank you very much, so she didn't question it. Instead, she asked if it was okay that she had her hiking clothes on. Bob gave her an exasperated look. "No one's going to pay any attention to you," he said briskly.

"The boy we saw earlier seemed very confident he'd see me," she said, but Bob just muttered about how ridiculous she was being. Still, Christy applied lipstick in the truck's rearview mirror. People were more likely to talk to you if you were put together, she knew. Bob slammed the driver-side door and Christy smudged pink past her cupid's bow. Cursing, she opened the glove compartment for something to wipe it off, Bob hitching his pants up. There was nothing but receipts and the car registration. She checked the backpack she took from the boy. It was empty aside from protein bar wrappers, dozens of them, but at the bottom of a front pocket she pulled out a heavy brass lighter engraved with the initials C.W. She flicked it open, but Bob yelled at her to get a move on before she could see if it worked. She slid it into her pocket and hurried out of the truck.

They got into line. Bob started up a conversation with the white-haired men in front of them, asking them how they were doing, saying how he was looking forward to the vote. Christy noticed how Bob made an exaggerated effort to stand with his hands on his hips, one hand above his holster, giving him the posture of a squat, mustachioed rooster. The men grunted amiably and asked Bob where he was from, and Christy was surprised when Bob said Utah. She tried to say she was, too, but Bob was right, no one paid any attention to her. The line moved slowly. A harried, scowling woman at the door told Bob and Christy to choose a side, pointing at two separate lines in the lobby. Bob hitched up his pants and kept a light hand on his gun. He pointed at the line with the hats. The woman said if they wanted to speak, they had to be assigned a number, but Bob waved her off. "Just here to support," he said, his voice so unnaturally loud it even made Christy stare.

They waited along the wall of the lobby. Christy kept making eye contact with a woman in the other line. The woman was thin and tall like a leggy, stooped bird. She had gray hair with a streak of blue behind one ear. They made eye contact again and, figuring she should try to talk to someone, Christy waved. The woman flinched and whispered with someone next to her, their eyes cutting over at Christy. Bob asked what Christy thought she was doing. "Being friendly," she said. "Don't," Bob hissed. Christy rolled her eyes but kept to herself. More people arrived, gripping handwritten signs or thumbing their belt loops.

When they were let into the theater, Bob told Christy they should stay in the back and let the locals take the seats. "Easier to talk back here, too," he added. People filed into the rows, but almost no one sat. Christy dropped her hand so it could graze Bob's, but he didn't take the hint. Christy tried again and her elbow hit his gun holster. She crossed her arms. Bored, she turned and said hello to the turkey man, but Bob pulled her away just as the man started to explain mainstream media to her. "Don't," he hissed again, squeezing her forearm as he said it. It was the first time Bob touched her with any real intent or force and Christy rubbed the soft flesh of her bicep as if it hurt, though she only felt triumph. Something, finally. The commissioner stood on the stage and announced the agenda. Public comment on signage designation for within the national monument, as well as the proposal to pave the Dell Trail, followed by council vote. The room hadn't been quiet since.

They are supposed to follow a system. People are given numbers and come up to the front and say their piece, but only if they have a number. They'll try to alternate, one side followed by the other, depending on how many people want to speak. Everyone wants to speak. Almost none have a number. The side with the crew cuts and the turkey sign yells the loudest. The other side, the side with the tote bags and blue-streaked hair, starts to yell, too. The commissioner reads aloud a printout about how and where they'd put road signs. Someone yells about the new maps that the government made, the ones that eliminate private property. Someone yells about overgrazing and bee populations and extinct grass species. Someone yells about the yelling. Everyone is shaking their signs in the air, and if they don't have a sign, it's a fist or a hat or a baby. The commissioner continues to read aloud. There are eight council members, all above the age of sixty, all white, all glowering. One side starts a chant about saving our lands, the other side starts to chant about saving our rights. The chants curdle into a block of noise, overwhelming and deafening. A baby starts to cry. The commissioner rubs his eyes under his glasses. He looks to the lady who was managing the door and makes a signal with his hand. She nods and pulls out a laptop. The council members shift, sit up straight. The crowd has not noticed, still yelling, but Christy has. She pokes Bob in the side, tries to get his attention, but he's absorbed in a conversation with someone just out of view. Christy can't hear what Bob is saying over the crowd's noise, but he gestures wildly with one hand. His other hand grips the top of his gun. Christy pokes Bob again. This time, he looks at her. The person next to him does, too. It's the boy from the desert and his blue eyes are glittering with excitement. He licks his lips. She points at the stage. The council members are raising their hands one by one. The side of the room with the lanyards quiets. The hat side quiets, too. The last council member raises his hand and the lady with the laptop nods at the commissioner. The commissioner announces the motion has passed. Dell Trail will be paved. Christy and Bob's side erupts into cheers. Someone even throws their hat. The lanyards have their mouths open, but mostly stay quiet. The baby is still crying.

The meeting ends and they leave. Bob suggests getting food, but not to Christy. He tells the boy they should go to a spot down the road. It has great burgers. It isn't the spot with the neon sign Bob pointed out, it's a small, one-window drive-in down the road, but it serves milkshakes. "Nothing like some milkshakes after a lively round of civic service," Christy says, trying to be playful, but neither man responds. Christy asks for a chocolate malt and then saves a picnic table while the men order. At the table next to her are three white-haired men shaking hands and smiling. Christy overhears them say it's a great day. Christy senses these men are powerful, influential. The sort of people she and Bob should talk to. She leans over and nods even though she isn't exactly sure what she's agreeing with.

"What do you think's better here, the single or double cheeseburger?" she asks. Double, they all say, looking over, and ask what she got. "A chocolate malt," she says. They say there's none better in the whole county. There's a lot of smiling. "A great day," she says, and they nod. Christy shifts in her seat and then makes a serious face. "But who wants a paved trail? Won't that just get really hot with all this sun? I have to imagine the cows wouldn't like it, either. Think of their hooves." The men look at each other and look back at her.

"You from outside?" they ask politely. "Outside of where?" Christy asks. The men exchange dark looks and then turn around, no longer friendly. Bob shows up with her shake. It's vanilla, not chocolate. Christy ignores the shake and lets it melt out of principle. The boy and Bob start to talk in a sort of shorthand, all one-word questions and replies, until Christy catches on that they're talking about the hunt.

"You're on the Conversation?" she asks the boy. The boy gives an exaggerated smile, his lips disappearing into his gums. "You tell me, ChristineM." Christy doesn't let herself look surprised. Instead, she busies herself with the straw of her melted malt and asks the boy for his username. "Since you already know mine," she says, keeping her voice light. The boy tells her to guess, but then Bob says, with a noticeable edge of worry, that it's not important. "We have a lot to talk about," he says. "We shouldn't waste any time." Bob begins to discuss the Conversation, what they should post, if anything, about the town hall. The boy asks clarifying questions and nods along, and it becomes clear he doesn't know much about the hunt. Christy chimes in to correct how Bob isn't a personal friend of MadMax, but otherwise stays quiet. Bob always needs help, she reminds herself. It isn't like she can climb cliff faces.

The boy doesn't seem like a climber, soft and pale, but maybe he has other skills. If anything, she's bothered how Bob never mentioned the boy, never asked her if they should involve him in their hunt. But they had hardly hunted that weekend, only walking out to meet the boy, and in any case, Bob said he couldn't do anything without Christy's map, and the map was in the cabin. Bob could use a friend, she thinks. He practically giggles while explaining his interpretation of the poem's second stanza. He seems happy. That's all she wants, right? Bob to be happy. Bob and the boy begin to show each other things on their phones, Christy clearly forgotten, so she tries to eavesdrop on the old men at the other table in order to, as Bob said, gain information. They're in a serious discussion about some sort of appearance. There's a congressman on the phone. Their heads are so close the brims of their hats touch. Something about the upcoming presidential election, but Christy can't make out the specifics.

She turns her attention to the table behind her. It's the tall, lanky woman with the blue streak. There are two other women with her, all in hiking clothes. Christy waves again. This time the woman gives her a small nod and a smile. Christy throws both legs over the bench of the picnic table and fully faces the woman. "What a meeting!" Christy says. The bird woman agrees. Her friends turn to look at Christy. "I'm Christy," Christy says. "I live in Salt Lake." This seems to soften them. They all say hello. "What brings you down to the country?" the woman asks. "I've always wanted to visit," Christy says. "It's just such a beautiful place, don't you think?" They murmur, agree. They ask if she's gone out on a hike, if she's seen a canyon or a slot or a sunset yet. Yes, Christy says. Yes, yes, yes.

Bob and the boy are deep in conversation. The boy has his fingers in his mouth and Bob won't stop talking. Neither of them have touched their food, but they're speaking loud enough that the other tables are giving them looks. Christy clears her throat. Her phone is in the truck and she needs to get in touch with her daughter. They should go back to the hotel. The boy snorts and jerks a dirty, chewed thumb at her. He tells Bob he doesn't have all night, says Bob needs to figure this shit out. Christy asks what he means by *this shit*, though she already knows. The boy doesn't acknowledge her, just says he doesn't have time for *this shit* and to call him when things are good to go. Bob tells him they're not done, this isn't over, but the boy is already up and walking away.

Bob watches the boy leave, who quickly disappears down the road. Bob's face is open and full of need. It's a look Christy has never seen on him. Vulnerable, almost desperate.

"Is he yours?" Christy asks.

"What?" Bob snaps.

"That kid. Is he your son?"

Bob laughs, genuinely, full of squeaks. "Of course not," he says, and doesn't explain more.

Christy remembers the lighter in her pocket. She'll keep it, she decides. "I didn't think we were bringing anyone on board until we found the exact spot. Until we knew the solve."

Bob scowls. "Well, if you showed me that damn map of yours, maybe I—we—wouldn't need other people."

"We need someone to help with mountaineering. That kid didn't seem very flexible at all, let alone strong enough to climb a cliff. Tag and Hank are much better. I've seen them climb myself. In fact, they helped me climb! It was hilarious, listen to this, my daughter and I—"

"Do you ever shut up?" Bob snaps. Christy quiets, as do some of the surrounding tables. The moment is long and tense. Christy dry swallows and begins to quietly apologize, but Bob stalks away, almost jogging. He leaves behind his burger, still wrapped in its wax paper.

It wasn't supposed to be this way. It was supposed to be fun, lighthearted, giddy. A flutter in the chest, a tender handhold. There was supposed to be one bed in the hotel room, not two. There was supposed to be research and debates, a meeting of minds, a romance. The burger is better than Christy expected, thick and greasy, and she's finished half of it by the time the bird woman asks if Christy's all right. The entire table is looking at her with large, flat eyes. They wait for her to swallow. Christy forces a grin, rolls her eyes. "Men are idiots," she laughs. They don't. They ask if she has a place to go. "My daughter is staying just down the road," Christy says, suddenly awkward. They nod, eyes still wide. She stands and waves and is halfway down the sidewalk when she remembers Bob has her phone.

This was supposed to be their big moment, how they were going to find it together. The two of them, together. That was the whole point of coming here. Together. But now she's alone. Would she have come to Mercy alone, gone to the town hall meeting alone, gone to the spot alone? A catch in her throat: No, probably not. She is not an alone person, never has been, and never will be. Christy throws the remains of Bob's burger into the street. She almost throws the lighter, but then a car honks. She flicks them off and turns back toward the burger stand and the table of blue-haired bird women.

Hank's headlamp bobbed a dozen yards ahead from where they stood, the white beam whipping back and forth through the dark. He shouted for them to hurry up. Bea and Tag stood on either side of the broken irrigation pipe, the ATVs parked behind them and the water pooling around their sandals.

"Is this part of the plan?" Bea whispered.

"We can turn around whenever you want," Tag said, not whispering, but not speaking at a full volume, either. Tag followed Hank toward the house, which wasn't as big as Bea had imagined. She expected something huge and ostentatious, a McMansion with multiple stories and columns out front, but it was a single-level ranch and there wasn't even a garage. If anyone was home they would hear the hoots and splashing, but neither Hank nor Tag seemed too worried. There was a lamp lit in a window of the house, revealing an austere room with a low-level couch and a tapestry hung on the wall. It looked nice, Bea thought. Minimalist and neutral, like a place you would rent for a long weekend.

The couple moved to Mercy a year ago. Californians, they bought a dozen acres outside of town and built a yoga studio. Which was fine, Hank had assured Bea as they got ready to ride out. He was totally fine with that, Hank loved yoga, it was great for climbing. It would've been chill if they had just kept to themselves, but these new people started coming into town and lecturing people about recycling and water conservation, even putting flyers into people's mailboxes. "They had a point," Tag said. "But we're not idiots," Hank added. There were plans for a new reservoir west of town. Farmers needed the extra irrigation and it would open up new residential pipelines. More water access, more development. "It was a big deal," Hank said as he finished his beer and started up the ATV. But this couple wouldn't hear of it. Apparently damming one of the streams was a total affront to their idea of what Mercy should be. "These people must've had some government connections, because now the whole thing is over. Kaput," Hank spat. Locals didn't have any say over the matter, which enraged him. No Californian was going to come to his town and tell him what to do.

"Didn't Tag move here from Santa Barbara?" Bea asked. "Most of us aren't really *from* here," Tag said sheepishly. Hank rolled his eyes and jumped onto the ATV, its engine clicking. After the reservoir plan was scrapped, Hank decided to do a little investigating. "And guess what? They have a fucking koi pond in their backyard. A koi pond! It's the size of a small swimming pool, for fuck's sake." Even Tag thought it was pretty fucked up. The couple wanted to start a retreat where people could commune and disconnect. Refresh and recharge. To each their own, but, as Hank put it, "What the fuck does that have to do with fish?" They had been planning to do something about it for a while. Operation Sushi, they called it. The couple were definitely at the town hall meeting, they'd never missed one, and now they had Bea to keep watch while they seized their chance.

"Tomorrow we'll anonymously notify the county of a burst pipe and the commission will come out and it'll seem like negligence. These folks will be looking at a few thousand dollars in fines and no more fucking fish," Hank said.

The pond was not a pond, though. It was no bigger than a kiddie pool, an ink-black puddle with a dim, algae-filmed light and a water pump. A pair of lily pads with a bright yellow flower floated in the middle, but it wasn't until Hank kicked the water that it became obvious they were fake, stiffly tossing like tankers at sea, and Bea couldn't help but think of her mother. She checked her phone for texts again, but Hank demanded she put it away. "The light," he hissed, his headlamp blinding her. They stood around the koi pond and Bea wondered if this was it, that all Hank needed to do was to see the fish and pond and, vindicated by their existence, they'd leave.

But then he and Tag hacked through a water pipe. She was rattled by the broken pipe, convinced she could hear the rushing water over the sound of the pond pump's soft bubbling and thus someone from the road would be able to hear it, too. The derecho had been a verbal estimation built on years of economic and meteorological experience, pitched as a hedge against future agricultural deliveries that neither Bea nor the bank would ever physically handle, and despite HR describing it as "possible securities fraud," Bea never believed there was any true danger. Standing close enough to a stranger's hobby pond that she could smell the fishes' oily musk, after watching Hank and Tag hack through a water pipe, felt entirely different. This, she thought, was real.

Also real was the loaf of sandwich bread Tag pulled out of his backpack. For a second, Bea thought the guys were going to have some sort of deranged picnic, and the thought of staying any longer made her panic. "I'm not hungry," she stammered. "That's too bad," Hank cried, grabbing a slice from Tag. "Because I hear there's a fish fry tonight!" Tag and Hank threw bread into the pond. The water thrashed with flashes of white and orange, mouths sucking up from the depths in quivering, translucent ovals. Hank crouched down and plunged his arms into the water. Tag did the same, though he only went finger-deep.

Bea kneaded the bread into tiny balls. She did not want to touch the water or the fish. She wanted to be inside the house, sitting on the couch and watching a show where every episode was the same.

She wanted a sweatshirt and some tea and for her mother to call her back. There was a large splash and a koi launched out of the pond, flying right past Bea's ankles. She shrieked. "Grab him!" Hank shouted. The koi flopped and croaked, eyes bulging, dust clumping onto its gills. "I'm not really into fish," Bea said, which was true, she really didn't like anything other than tuna and even then only with mayo and cheddar and a slice of really good rye. With a fish in each hand, Hank gave a wobbly-knees dance. "Check out at these fat motherfuckers!" he yelled, smacking the fish together like tambourines. The koi heaved and twitched in the dirt next to Bea. Tag picked it off the ground and shook it at Hank. Hank shook his fish back. The koi all gasped in unison, mouths flexing in silent screams. Bea tried not to look at them, horrified.

After Hank pulled the plug on the pond's pump and couldn't find another pipeline to hack through, he visibly deflated. Sensing a pause, Bea said she thought she saw a light turn on in the house. Tag anxiously looked around and said they should get out of here. The wind picked up. Hank held the three fish in one hand, their gills occasionally fluttering. When they got back to the ATVs, Tag pulled open his backpack and Hank threw the fish in.

"What are you going to do with them?" Bea asked.

Hank shrugged. "Think they taste any good?"

"I don't think they're edible," Tag said.

"We're just going to let them die?" Bea began to shiver. "Like, that's it?"

"You're worried about the fucking fish?" Hank laughed, but then quieted when he saw the expression on Bea's face. "You know what?

I know a good spot for them, especially if you need to get warm, but I'm not sure those are the clothes you want to wear. In fact, I'd venture to say you wouldn't want to wear any—"

"Hank." Tag's voice was a low warning. "Not tonight."

"What? Where else are we going to go? She's cold, it's late, the stars are out." Hank turned to Bea. "If I went back into town and grabbed some bourbon, would you be down for a swim?" They were close to the road, close enough to feel the air of passing trucks. Neither Tag nor Hank seemed concerned about being seen. Bea bit back a thrum of panic. "I'd like to do something with these fish," she said.

"The fish are going to love this place, tons of places for them to swim, trust me." Hank started his engine up. "I'll see you both there?"

"Sure," Bea said, not knowing where.

"All right," Tag sighed. Hank cheered and sped off toward the road. Tag handed her the backpack. "I'm sorry, you're going to have to wear this, unless you want a face full of koi."

Earlier, when they had first headed out, Bea was loose and warm from the beer and the spliffs, and when Tag asked if she wanted to ride with him, she didn't hesitate to get on behind him. She laughed as they had driven out to the pond, whooped whenever Tag did. That ride had been endless, all giddy nerves, the first drop of a roller coaster. But now, whenever the ATV bounced over a rock, there was only a dank, wet smell and an occasional faint thrashing against Bea's lower back. The deli near the south entrance of the Broad Street subway station had the best tuna melt in the entire city. Their sandwiches were the size of dinner plates, the bread perfectly toasted, the cheese perfectly melted, and the tuna salad stacked two inches high. At the bank, she'd order it for lunch a few times a month. Flying through the dry dark desert, arms around Tag's waist, koi kissing death-gasps against her back, she knew clearly, unquestionably, she'd never order another one again.

⊲━━▶

The chef chopped onions too quickly, annoyed how, once again, he was left to deal with close alone. That crazy girl and her crazier mother: ever since they started showing up, he was stuck with a half-assed manager and busser, both disappearing at random times, both taking too many breaks. He liked Tag and he liked Hank and he liked his job, more than he thought he would, but he liked routine and structure more. Anytime Tag ran off and left him hanging, he wanted to shout how he had a family, kids, but you didn't see him running out of here at the first sign of a stuffy nose. But he didn't and he wouldn't. Instead, he chopped faster, singing along to the radio, until he sliced his fingertip against the cutting board, red staining the purple papery skins. There were bandages in the back office. No more onions, he decided. Let Tag do the onions. He was in the office, wrapping his finger in gauze, cursing against the sting, when he heard a knock at the front. The lights were on, but the grill was closed. He had flipped the sign when Tag left, locked the doors after the last customer paid, which was about an hour ago. He knew there was a town hall meeting that night. He hated working the late shifts during meetings. If he stayed in the back, they wouldn't know he was there. He pressed a bandage against his split finger, pulse in the wound. More knocking. A dog started barking. The finger throbbed. The knocking became angry, fast, pounding, and then shouts, hey, let me in, is anyone there, I just want some fucking food, but there was no reply. The chef had slipped out the back door, left the lights on, radio on, apron on the floor, knife bloody on the board.

PART THREE

Mercy Is a Place

that blessing which you hunted, hunted too;
what you were seeking, is what found you.

—EDWARD ABBEY

There was music. There was dancing. There were only six of them in the cabin, but it was a party, a real party, the first party she'd been to in years, Christy realized, exhilarated. She sat on the bed and talked with the blue-haired bird woman— Laura? Laurel? she couldn't remember—about their favorite brand of baking flour. They held juice glasses filled with cheap red wine, they compared manicures, they laughed. It'd been easy, so easy, to walk up to the picnic table and ask if the women had seen a cell phone, no, oh it must be back at my cabin, oh you're also at the cabins, what a coincidence! After being forced to a schedule and a plan she didn't agree to, after hoping for a chocolate shake or a moment alone and then getting the opposite, finally something went Christy's way. Finally, some kindness. The women finished their food and mentioned a box of wine, a portable speaker, maybe even some tequila. Christy walked with them and, as they approached the cabins, said she should check on her daughter. They said they were in the cabin just across the way and Christy smiled, nodded.

She expected Bea's cabin to be locked, but the cabin door swung open. She called out her daughter's name, but no one was there. The cabin was a mess, clothes everywhere. Typical, Christy thought, before realizing she wasn't sure if it was. Would her daughter leave dishes scattered across the floor, towels heaped on the bed? A small metal trash can near the door was tipped over in a way that it was clear to Christy it had been kicked. Her stomach fluttered. She hadn't lived with her daughter in nearly two decades. This could be Bea, or this could be Bea on vacation. How would she know? Christy scanned the room for the map, but it was such a mess, and she could hear laughter and music start up from the other cabin. She kept the light on as she closed the door. She'd check periodically to see if the light was still on as proof her daughter came home, she promised herself, and then headed to the party.

And oh, the party. It'd been so long. It'd been screens and phone calls and the television until midnight. It'd been long walks around the block hoping the Zs would come outside. It'd been wandering the aisles of some big-box store filling her bag with lipsticks, screwdrivers, a fleece jacket, wondering what it would take for someone to notice or care enough to say something. But here, now, Christy was surrounded by music and people and laughter, the room humid and dense with the bubbling, hazing thrall of a good time. She could talk about anything, she remembered. This had always been her saving grace: her ability to talk to anyone. Gertie used to say that if Christy were left alone she would try to become best friends with the wall. Despite her ex-husband's suffocating charm, she held her own at parties as his date, people loved her jokes, their hands at their breastbones, a stitch of soft surprise between their eyebrows. She never turned down an invitation, especially when she knew there'd be music, but the invitations had disappeared. She couldn't remember when it happened, only that it had, her Fridays and Saturdays barren aside from doctors' appointments or cooking dinner for herself and Gertie. How long had it been since she had a cocktail among strangers? How long since she introduced herself, since she waited for the perfect song to dance to, since she truly laughed?

Maybe it was years ago, when she first got back from Montreal and thought a party would be a good opportunity to reconnect with everyone in Connecticut. It'd been around Halloween and she sent out invitations to everyone she knew, even Gertie's friends, telling them costumes were mandatory. Maybe it was because it was her big homecoming, maybe because it was one of the last few years Gertie and her friends were still living independently, or maybe it was because she personalized each invitation, but people actually came, actually dressed up. There were fairies and cowboys and presidents and wizards. Gertie was an orchid, clad in her favorite pink silk pajamas with an orchid brooch on each lapel, white hair sprayed and rolled in three thick, high wads. Christy was a fairy-tale princess, her pointed, ribboned hat knocking against the tops of the doorframes and her long, draping sleeves damp from other people's cocktails. Someone's brother's boyfriend brought a saxophone and an amp and played unintelligible jazz music, loud and manic, and no one could hear each other and no one cared. There was so much laughter, so much dancing, so much music, that Christy almost stopped looking for her daughter, and despite checking her phone and asking Gertie if she'd heard from her, Bea never came. But still, the laughter. That's what Christy remembered the most.

And look at her laugh now, look at all of them laughing. People's bodies were limp and long with music and drinking, everyone more beautiful inside the room than they were on the walk over. The cabin felt huge and small at the same time. Christy noticed how there were no men present and immediately her laughs became louder and her posture worse. She knew none of the women's names and it didn't matter. Christy accepted every refill of wine. They asked if she had any requests and Christy mentioned Otis Redding, T. Rex. They didn't have either but they had the Dead, would that work? Christy danced. Her hips felt good. The blue-haired woman laughed and joined her in the small space between the couch and the bed. They didn't touch, but Christy felt like if they did, it would be all right. The night went on. People disappeared one by one, but Christy didn't ask where or why. The music changed to poppier, happier songs. She and the blue-haired woman danced, long enough for Christy to forget about Bob. She forgot about the boy with the hat. And then she forgot to check the light in her daughter's cabin. One of the women fell asleep in a chair, her head bobbing against her chest, arms hanging at her sides. The music was turned down. Another woman had a joint and the blue-haired woman followed her outside. Christy sat on the couch. Her shirt was slick with sweat, her neck stiff. The room was hot from the party, the air buzzing. Christy closed her eyes, and leaned back into the shallow cushions, a little stiff but content. She hummed along to a song she almost knew, but couldn't place, the music becoming softer and softer and softer.

If you were flying overhead, perhaps in a 747 on the LAX–DFW route, it would look like dozens of shallow-bowled craters, placid and foggy, interrupted every so often by a snarl of juniper or the shimmer of sandstone. They went on and on, dot after dot, each an eye of a different dilation. Get closer, though, and they pulsed with heat and gas, sulfuric parts, steam smoking off them in languid whips. Tag aimed the ATV toward the largest, closest pool and cut the engine. He rubbed the back of his neck and turned to face Bea. "Cool, huh?" he asked shyly. Perched on the back of the ATV, hands tucked under her thighs, Bea suppressed a shiver. She still had the backpack on. It was slumped and damp on her hips. The fish had long since stopped moving. But the water was gorgeous, each pool skimmed with the reflection of the night sky. "Have you ever been in one?" Tag asked, climbing off the ATV.

The pool closest to them burped, a huge bubble bursting on its surface like a wet, black zit. "Never," Bea said.

Tag dipped his hand in. "You have to be careful about some of these, the rocks can shift, especially after big storms, but I think this one should be all right." He took off his shirt and shoes. Steam ribboned into the air, acrid and gray, as he pulled his hair back into a knot. He smiled with half of his mouth and climbed into the pool. "You coming?"

"How deep is it?" Bea asked, delaying, as it was clear the pool was shallow enough for Tag to stand, his torso exposed. He had an outie belly button. It was like a worm cut in half and Bea couldn't stop staring at it. "Are there fish?"

"Nope, nothing but some slime at the bottom. It's a little slippery but not that bad." He crouched into the water, belly button and shoulders disappearing. He fanned his arms out and threw his head back, torso buoyed in a dead float. He closed his eyes. "Temperature's perfect."

Bea did a mental check: an old pair of full-coverage bottoms and a thick, sweat-stained bra. A bikini would've shown more, but she hesitated. Tag's eyes were still closed, long enough for Bea to know he was being polite. She flushed and turned around, fingers on the hem of her T-shirt. She could be this person, she told herself, but she also knew for every second she delayed, she was revealing more and more her prudishness, a trait Bea had once taken pride in—Christy had always bragged how she was no prude and thus Bea had insisted on the virtues of modesty since before puberty—but after her near-celibate twenties, Bea had lost confidence in the idea, quietly convinced her loyalty to the concept was less of a defense of her body than her ego: it wasn't a matter of deferring advances, but being the one to control why there weren't any advances to begin with.

But here, now, maybe she could be the person who took her clothes off without overthinking, could be free and easygoing and in the moment. It was something that Grant had told her to do: relax. "You need to relax," he murmured when he tried to position her naked body toward his floor-to-ceiling living room windows, or when she asked him if he thought Martha and Carolyn would invite her to their annual Christmas party. *Relax.* Which was the problem, wasn't it? She was an analyst, hyperfixated on every movement and word, always trying to predict what other people may think or do, so she could respond appropriately. It was probably why she never was invited to parties, or why Grant never texted her back. The inability to just relax. It wasn't like she was getting naked, she chided herself, and it'd be rude not to join Tag. Despite the heat of the day, the night air was sharp and chilled, and her arms had nipped into hard goose bumps. She could do this, Bea told herself. No, she *should* do this, and before she could change her mind, she pulled off her T-shirt and shorts and she slipped into the water. It felt like climbing into an egg yolk. Tag turned around and Bea threw an arm across her clavicle as if to scratch a shoulder. "Isn't it great?" he asked.

"Yeah," Bea said. "Definitely." The bottom was felted in something slick and thick, and she flinched as her toes skimmed it. She held on to the edge and pulled her feet toward her stomach. Tubs, hot or otherwise, were not something Bea enjoyed. The efficiency of a shower, something you could turn on and off, seemed much more reasonable than soaking in your own filth, unable to do much of anything until the water went cold or your hands pruned, whatever came first. The hot spring didn't seem much different. Bea's shoulder began to ache and so she let go, a tentative foot hooking on to a submerged rock. She adjusted a too-loose bra strap. The air was cold and humid in alternating moments, her scalp prickling, her breath evening out. Bea ducked her shoulders beneath the surface and realized Tag was staring at her, a smile playing on his lips. "You'll get used to the smell, everyone does." Their eyes met and he held her gaze with an expectant look. She had no idea what to say. She said, "Do you come here a lot?"

"All the time. I feel like it's the only place I can really breathe." He snorted, shaking his head. "Sorry, wow, that must be the spliff talking. But seriously, this place is the reason I stopped here. When I first drove through, I was planning on camping closer to Powell before heading up to Moab. I thought I was going to stay in Mercy for a couple of days to climb. I heard about these hot springs from a guy at a campground near Vegas, drove out, and parked here until Pat found me. I was expecting him to call the cops, but he asked if I was okay, quizzed me about where I was headed, why I was living out of my car. He owned this place. At the funeral, Vera told me I reminded him of himself when he was younger. Pat's the one who offered me a job at the grill. Told me about Hank's dad and the trailer. Set me up. It was only a few days after I left California, I didn't have a lot going on and I didn't really have a plan. I figured I'd stick around Mercy for a bit and save money while I figured out my next steps. That was six years ago.

"Vera still owns this land, but she asks me to keep an eye on it. She lives in St. George nowadays and doesn't visit often, but she talks about turning this into some kind of resort. Build a few cabins, line the pools with concrete, have people make reservations, the whole thing. She says Pat would want someplace where families could come and make memories, which I get, but there's also something special about it being this way, you know? Untouched." He cleared his throat and shifted his position in the water. "But I think she needs the money."

Maybe it was how gently he spoke about Pat, or maybe it was because she was in her underwear, or maybe because when he shifted, he shifted close enough for her to feel his thigh near hers—Bea felt a wild, skipping lurch in her chest. "You're, like, the property manager?" Her voice was high and childish.

Tag answered her seriously. "Something like that. I make sure everything is kept clean and people aren't camping, things like that." He motioned with his hand and water dripped from it onto Bea's shoulder. She ducked her face under the water and opened her mouth. The water was a chalky, warm sharpness that made her teeth ache.

She came back up. Her thoughts were bouncing and manic. Was this the spliff, too? Maybe it was the spliff. Water dribbled out from her lips. The moon came out from behind the clouds and Tag's face became blue-white and full of shadows, which somehow made his mouth wider, softer. He noticed her cheeks full. "I mean, I keep it clean, but wouldn't drink it," he said. Bea raised her eyebrows and then dramatically swallowed. There was a tight, short moment, Tag's face frozen in amused shock, and Bea didn't dare move. But then Hank roared up in the ATV, the vehicle's headlights blinding them. He whooped and Tag whooped and Bea wiped her mouth with the back of her hand, her teeth aching.

"Look at what I found," Hank shouted. He held up a short, branching object, dotted and fluttering, and as his silhouette came into focus behind the moonlight, a cold coil shot up the back of Bea's throat. It was the aspen. "I found it on the side of the road near the grill." Hank held it by its trunk as he walked up to the pool. "Guess what it is?"

Bea sank down into the water, no longer caring about slime and smell. "It's a Virgo," Bea said quietly, mostly to herself.

"A what?" Tag asked, turning to her.

"It's an aspen! And it's a fucking fake aspen tree!" Hank shook it hard enough a leaf fluttered off. He laughed. Bea wanted to get out of the water and grab it from him, but the way Hank held it, fisted and tight, was the same way he held the koi earlier, and his face was tight with something dark and desperate. Another leaf dropped off and fell into the water. The thin yellow fabric swirled around Bea's shoulders. Tag pulled himself out of the pool and walked up to the ATV. "Did you bring whiskey or just a random fake tree?"

When Bea was sure they weren't looking, she caught the leaf, pulling it underwater in her fist. Maybe Christy wanted to show the aspen to Bob and she dropped it on the way back to her hotel room with him, too busy in an embrace or a joke to notice it gone; maybe they put it in the back of his truck and it fell out, bouncing along the road as they headed toward a romantic dinner in the neighboring town; or maybe Christy left it at the cabin dumpsters, discarded and unneeded, as she went to meet Bob at the town hall.

Bob, with the piss. Bob, with the steak. Bea was used to her mother's distractions and whims. They had always been childish, shortsighted. But her mother never abandoned her plants, not in all the moves and upheavals they'd been through. Christy was careful and meticulous with them, and though her mother never named her plants, she talked to them enough as if they were friends or children or both. It had made Bea jealous when she was younger, Christy's cooing over her latest cactus or peace lily, but now, noticing the unnatural bend to the aspen's trunk, Bea was filled with dull panic. The aspen shouldn't be in the middle of the desert, neglected and damaged. Her mother wouldn't let it happen, wouldn't forgive Bea if she let it happen. When both guys were busy arguing over a Vegas hockey team, she put the leaf into her mouth. It was thin and silky and tasted like nothing. She climbed out of the pool. She took the whiskey bottle from Tag and, drinking from it, swallowed, the leaf slipping down her throat. Bea started to cough, hard and violent. Tag stopped arguing with Hank. "You good?" he asked.

She grabbed a towel and wrapped it around herself. "I'm fine, just cold," she said.

"If you're cold, you know, we could burn this thing," Hank said.

He plucked a leaf off one of the branches and inspected it. "It's basi-cally trash."

"It's not trash," Bea said too quickly.

"Okay," Hank said, drawing out the word with a sideways look. He took off everything but his boxers and climbed into the pool, leaving the aspen behind. Bea grabbed it. She held the tree against her stomach. It smelled faintly of burnt grease.

"You really like that tree, huh?" Hank laughed from the pool.

"Yeah, I mean . . ." Bea tried to appear relaxed. "You know what? I'm going to plant it."

"It's fake," Tag said. His mouth was parted, worried. Bea shook the tree. "It's a plant, right? It should be planted!" Neither of the guys laughed.

Bea chose a spot far from the water, toward the bluff and close to a large juniper bush, somewhere hidden but memorable. She didn't have a shovel and her nails bent against the dry ground as she dug, sulfuric steam wafting over her, warming her fingers, small droplets gathering on the edges of the tree's leaves. After a while she was able to dig a hole deep enough to keep the tree somewhat upright. She clustered rocks around the base of the trunk and then wiped her hands on her thighs. She stepped back. Surrounded by the desert, the aspen looked even more fake, but she was satisfied. If her mother wanted the aspen, then Christy could come back tomorrow and get it, Bea decided. And if Christy didn't, well, better here than on the side of the road.

Bea walked back to the pool. As she approached, the guys made a show of clapping and told her she did a great job. "You really saved that tree," Hank said. "We should take a picture," Bea joked, but no one made a move to do so. The wind picked up and Bea remembered she was in her underwear, her nipples hard stones against her bra, but she didn't want to get back into the water. Shivering, she pulled on her shirt and shorts. Tag noticed and was already climbing out of the pool. He went into the ATV's storage compartment and held out a sweatshirt. "You'll want this," he said. The sweatshirt was a worn, faded red, with SUN DEVILS written across the chest and a small, sunny demon underneath. He started up the engine.

"You're leaving? But we just got here," Hank whined. "We were starting to have some fun."

"We don't have to leave," Bea said. "I'm fine."

"I'm happy to tell Linda you're out here all alone," Tag said, putting on his shirt. "I'm sure the two of you could have even more fun."

"Don't be an asshole," Hank slapped the water. "You know I don't have her number and I know you don't either."

"We really don't have to leave," Bea said.

"I'm tired, and you're shaking." He was right, she was.

Hank drank from the whiskey and then, as if remembering it, motioned toward the aspen. "Hey, what about the trash tree, huh? Leave no trace?"

"Don't worry about it." Tag helped Bea onto the seat. "We'll get it tomorrow."

───◆───

Mercy wasn't a stranger to treasure. Depending on who you asked, the entire Southwest was filled with it: land, antiquities, water, dinosaurs, tortoises, pottery, coal. But who owned what? Who kept what? Who lost what? Who?

This was once the most populated place on the continent, humans everywhere, tens of thousands of them. Elsewhere, there were crusades and gunpowder; here, a sprawling palace, bigger than Buckingham, the beating heart of a forested empire filled with art and agriculture, science and commerce. They had many names, Anasazi, Ancient Puebloans, Hisatsinom. They hauled lumber and limestone hundreds of miles south, traded them with a people called the Aztecs, people who wanted to build a city of their own one day. But here they didn't need to build; they had more than enough. They had complex calendars, widespread water systems, and a sprawling network of highways. They had life, they had wealth, they had knowledge. There were people, so many people, and then, as tends to happen, there were too many people. And then only the land knows. They disappeared in less than a generation, maybe fleeing south, to the water and the Aztecs, or maybe not. Their buildings crumbled. Their land wilted. The few who remained returned to the old ways. Wandering, gathering, and they never spoke of what happened.

It could happen again. If you ask Mercy, it probably will.

More time, more people. This time settlers from the east, bringing new gods and new deaths. They drove off the last of the wanderers, literally, in Model Ts, screaming about divine right. Soon after, they brought in more new people, this time immigrants from California, and corralled them in the desert. Safety, they said. Patriotism, they said. The prisoners left behind pets and houses and businesses. Here in the desert, they had nothing, couldn't have anything. And still, they published magazines and formed bands and wrote poetry. They became a new city, the fourth largest in the state. A few miles north the guards tested a new poison, one they'd use on the prisoners' relatives across the ocean, entire cities blistering and burning and blinded, after which the guards declared victory and sent the prisoners back to California, because they couldn't stay, not here, not anymore.

Their buildings crumbled. The land wilted. The poison stayed.

Meanwhile, lily-white and lovers of their own special heavens, the remaining people built and built and built. The hearing aid, Kentucky Fried Chicken, the electric guitar, TVs, the Zamboni. Millions around the lake, then more, and then more, every mouth and hand consuming, needing, taking. Water, trees, fire, birds, elk, cows. They spread asphalt on top of the old highways. They put up stadiums, they built temples. More and more, up and up. Life, elevated. Small highway towns became small highway cities, dotted with swimming pools and golf courses. Desert became lawns, ranches became parks. In the middle of the summer, they opened a new park, where people could fling themselves down a giant toilet bowl, flushed in a million gallons of water, squealing with joy. More people came. They heard how the grass was always green, the sun always shined, and nothing was too expensive.

Look, Mercy knows. It's always known. It's seen it before and it'll see it again. It's the way things are, the way things have always been.

Philosophical mumbo jumbo, the Poet would spit, chew bulging in his cheek. That doesn't change anything, the koi would say, their skeletons skid marks on the asphalt. Some would say God was the only law, some would say they were here before laws, and Vera would roll her eyes about the kombucha on the grill's drink menu. But everyone would agree that things were changing. Mercy wasn't the same Mercy. Remember when the grass was so tall you'd lose your sheep in it? Remember when there were thousands of cows, herds so dense you couldn't run a dog through them? Remember when there were actually kids in town? A school, too. The dust, though. The dust stole this town and it's been dying ever since.

But Mercy didn't think it was dying. In fact, Mercy thought itself very much alive. It was on the precipice of puberty. A reawakening, a discovery. No, Mercy wasn't dead. Not yet, not yet.

Every cabin is dark except for one. Pulling up, Bea wonders why the lights are on. Did she leave the lights on? The door swings open with a gust of wind. Clothes are scattered, the bed rumpled. Bea's toiletries bag is overturned, her sneakers tossed to one side. Her chest seizes and she reflexively clutches Tag's waist tighter, and even though she doesn't notice, he does. He asks if she was expecting anyone else that night. Maybe her mom? No, Bea says. No, her mom was with Bob. Her mom wouldn't, she motions at the door, the mess, she says, but can't continue. Right, Tag says. Okay. The night is cold and long and there's no one else around. The campground office is closed until morning. The police are two towns away. I have to tell you something, Bea says, her voice cracking. The aspen tree? It's mine.

The tree? Tag asks, confusedly. The one Hank found, Bea says. My mom gave it to me, we brought it from Salt Lake. I had it with me in the cabin, it was here when I left. Hank wouldn't, Tag says, and by the way he says it, Bea believes him. But someone took it out of the cabin, she says. Your mom? Maybe, Bea says, yeah, but she's scared, unconvinced.

Tag gets off the ATV. He goes up the steps and surveys the room. No one is there, but someone was, recently, and even though he doesn't know her well, Tag doesn't believe Christy would make the mess. Too violent, too pointed. He gives Bea a grim nod, then gets back on the ATV and drives them to the trailer, dark and locked and safe. They trade sips from one of the homemade IPAs, both trembling and doing a poor job of hiding it. She'll take his bed, they decide; he'll take the couch. She borrows a phone charger. Neither of them sleep, both alert to the other's tossing and turning. They hear when Hank comes back and parks the ATV next to the trailer, how he shuffles drunkenly across the backyard, how the back door of the house opens and closes. They stare at the ceiling, they adjust their blankets, they roll over. They hear a coyote howl. Bea thinks about Christy, about the car keys on the cabin side table, about the rocking chair knocked over on the porch. Her mother wasn't there. Her mother was gone. Bob. A stranger from the internet. Anger flares, the familiar feeling she's always had, old and worn, but as the seconds tick by, it becomes something colder and sharper. Her mother harmonizing with the radio while doing the dishes, her mother holding Bea's hand across the center console before school, her palm clammy and warm and safe. Bea waits for her phone to have enough battery to turn on and when it does, she sends a frantic text to her mother begging for updates. The text is marked delivered, but there's no reply. It's late, she tells herself, and this will have to be enough for now. Across the trailer, Tag hears Bea tap on her phone, hold her breath, and then let out a long, worried sigh. Separately, silently, they vow to leave at dawn. Bea, to find Christy. Tag, to help Bea. They'll wait until then, listening to each other's breathing while staring out of the trailer's small, smudged windows. Beyond them, the desert night stretches on and on, alive and indifferent.

Christy awakes to someone lightly shaking her shoulder. It's the bird woman, the one with the hair. The woman clears her throat and haltingly asks if Christy wants any coffee. The woman's voice has an edge of embarrassment, hesitant in a way where Christy knows the woman has forgotten her name. No matter, Christy doesn't remember the woman's name, either. Another woman, just as tall as the bird woman but blonder, stands at the kitchenette making said coffee. Christy doesn't recognize her, though the woman makes a half-hearted joke about the dancing from the night before. Bowie, the woman says, shaking her head. It's always Bowie. The joke seems to be for Christy, but it's lost on her.

She desperately needs to pee, the feeling coming instantly and forcefully, but the bathroom door is closed and there's the sound of a shower running. How are there three women here? Christy wonders. Where did they all sleep? The bed is unmade. Aside from the couch Christy sits on, there's no other soft surface. Coffee? The bird woman asks again, this time holding up the coffeepot. Unfortunately, we don't have any clean mugs left, she adds in a false apology. They have plenty of mugs, Christy can see a clean one on one of the shelves above the sink, but she understands the hint. She thanks them for the offer, for the night before, for everything. It was wonderful, Christy says, standing slowly, so fun. So fun, the women echo. Christy opens the door and gestures across the way. I should get back to my daughter. The other women nod and wave and tell Christy to take care.

She knocks on the cabin door. When there's no answer, she tries the doorknob. It's unlocked, which makes Christy shake her head. She'd have to tell Bea to be more careful, she thinks. The cabin is dark. Remembering how she left the light on, she's relieved her daughter came back, then shamed that she never checked during the party. She calls out her daughter's name, full name. There's no answer. It only takes one step into the darkness for Christy to know her daughter isn't there. No one's there. The cabin is still a mess, maybe even messier. She picks up a sock from off the ground. It's stiff and crusted with dirt and sweat, red and brown, and must be from the hike the day before. Or was it the day before that? Christy goes to check her phone for the date but remembers, yet again, that she doesn't have it. She has spent the majority of her life without a cell phone, never needing one until ten or so years ago, and even then, she never thought she needed it. But now, seeing her daughter's belongings without her daughter, she needs it, desperately. There's no landline in the cabin. She'll go to the office and ask to use their phone, and does, but as she holds the receiver, she realizes she doesn't have Bea's number memorized. Gertie's doctor's office, the main office of her ex-husband's old job, her favorite bakery in Montreal: she knows all these numbers by heart. Bea's, though, is a mystery. Gertie had been the one to save the number on Christy's phone, right before Bea's college graduation, telling Christy that it was time for her to be the parent and stop waiting for her daughter to call. She never had to memorize it. It was always there, in her favorites list, waiting for her.

Christy hesitates. Should she call the police? It seems melodramatic, too much, and yet a prickle of panic spreads across her chest. But what would she say? She doesn't know where her daughter is. She's worried about the mess her daughter left in her cabin. But maybe Bea texted her where she was, maybe it's just a matter of finding her phone. She should do that before taking drastic measures, she decides. She should go to the motel and confront Bob. She hands the receiver back to the man behind the desk, thanks him, turns to leave, and realizes she still has the dirty sock in her hand. She holds it up. "My daughter," she says. "If you see her, tell her I have her sock." The man is confused, but nods. Of course, he says.

The motel room is empty. Two twin beds, both unmade. He'd brought a large canvas tote, green and blue with white stitching, like something you'd bring to the gym, which Christy had found charming. It's gone. His boots are gone, too, a shadow of clay and dust on the carpet next to the door. Her phone is nowhere to be seen, and her tablet's missing, but her suitcase lies untouched on the floor. She sits at the edge of his bed and picks a single curled, black hair from the sheets. She sat in this same spot their first night together, only thirty-six hours earlier. Bob under the sheets in his giant white underwear, her in a borrowed T-shirt and shorts. They were back from dinner at the grill, Christy having just showered, and discussed the upcoming town hall and its implications for the hunt, what paving could mean for their search area, if they thought the ordinance would pass or not. Were geologists investigating the area? Were there geologists on the Conversation? They browsed the forum on their respective devices, wondering, and then Bob asked if he could see her map. It was the first time Bob had mentioned the map, how it would be useful to have around to reference, but Christy avoided the question. Instead, she playfully swatted at his hip and asked what does that have to do with geologists? They kept chatting and Christy kept joking until she swatted his hip again and didn't move her hand. It'd been so long since she'd been hugged, since any gentle touch, that sitting next to Bob with her hand on his hip, nothing but a thin sheet between her skin and his, made Christy's entire body thrum. When she suggested it'd be a lot more comfortable if he moved over a little, don't you think this bed can fit two, she didn't think he'd pull the sheet up to his chin and shake his head. Not until I see that map, he said. She didn't think he was serious. Maybe this is the game he likes, Christy thought, and she slid her fingers up the back of his T-shirt, clawing ever so lightly. He squealed and recoiled as if burned. He stared at her and she stared at him until her smile faltered. She went to the other, still-made bed and got under the sheets. He turned off the lights. She whispered that they could look at the map tomorrow. Her voice had lost its teasing edge, but her body desperately thrummed. She whispered good night. He didn't respond.

She counted his breaths, willing him to get up and come to her, comfort her, assure it was all a joke, come here, but he never did. It was after midnight when she woke to the bathroom light on and the sound of slapping flesh. She didn't fall back asleep after that. He eventually climbed back into his bed and quickly fell into long, phlegmy snores. She spent the rest of the night on her tablet, reading the Conversation, trying to convince herself she wasn't upset. The next morning, as they got ready for their hike, he asked her again about the map. They couldn't do anything without the map, he said. Which wasn't true, the map was just an extension of Christy's brain. She said something like *wouldn't you like to know*, thinking she was flirting, thinking she should hold back at least one part of herself from him, thinking there was still a chance it was a game. He scowled and she said she'd already gone on a hike without it once, which made his eyes light up and demand to know who with. Her daughter, she said. Who else? He laughed at that, visibly relieved, and even held open the door for her as they left the room. She decided she'd give him the map after the town hall. They were going to spend the night drinking wine and discussing the map's brilliance—Christy's brilliance—and then, and then!

Christy had been so pleased with her plan. She thought it clever, fail-safe. She had thought so many things. Now, as she sits on the motel bed, she nearly laughs at how obvious it's all been. She's been so full of need and hope and it's blinded her, but it always blinded her, even in its most threadbare and desperate forms, even when everything else was proving the opposite. Idiots and optimists, Gertie had often warned her, are usually the same. This whole time, Christy thought what she had with Bob was something fun, something easy, something mutual. She never thought it was love. No, he was someone to commiserate with and confess to, words on a screen and a voice through the phone. He always picked up, he always responded. Reliability becoming, as it so often does, an intimacy. He was the only person Christy told about her ex-husband's son in Montreal, he was the first person to suggest moving to Utah. Like so many before her, Christy went west for a fresh start and new chances. The old Stamford Victorian sold for enough to give Christy time. By then her relationship with Bob had bloomed into regular phone calls. He found the furnished house in Salt Lake City on a rental website and told her it was a good deal. Christy sent the link to Bea, who agreed it was a good price, enough that she could cover the rent each month. It'd been years since Christy moved anywhere, not since she left her ex-husband, and she'd never moved anywhere alone. Utah was exciting, all the space and sky, all time and choices. But it quickly became overwhelming. Without the demands and distractions of motherhood or marriage or daughterhood, there was only the wide, sprawling expanse of the next hour. In that vacuum, there was Bob and the treasure, and Christy flung herself at both, having nothing else to do or lose.

"And now," Christy says to herself, flicking the pube off her thumb. "He's gone."

She goes to the only other place she can think Bea might be: Pat's Grill. It isn't open yet, but she knocks on the door. Hank appears and says they don't open for another twenty minutes. "Any chance you know where my daughter is?"

"She's not with you?"

Christy shakes her head. "And she wasn't in her cabin this morning."

Hank rubs his mouth. "I knew it."

"Knew what?"

"Ask Tag."

"Oh," Christy says, both shocked and relieved. Good for her, she thinks. One of us should have fun on this trip. "I lost my phone and got worried," she says.

Hank pulls out his cell. "I can call him, if you want?" Christy nods and he begins to type. "You know, Tag's, like, a half hour late for work. And he's never late," he says with a sincerity that surprises Christy.

"Then it must be for a good reason," Christy says.

Hank smiles. "Yeah," he says. "It is good, isn't it?"

He Wasn't Just a Poet; in Fact, He Would Say He Wasn't

Born in Pittsburgh, but the family had moved to Michigan by the time he could make memories. The fifth child and third son of a secretary and an actuary. He was the youngest son and therefore his mother's favorite. His mother loved to tell him he was too handsome for all this nonsense, failing to understand that the handsomeness was how he was able to get away with nonsense to begin with. His father barely talked to him at all, which was how they both preferred it.

Slingshot champion of Ann Arbor, Michigan, as judged by Boy Scout Troops 4, 5, and 7 in a multiround tournament at Shady Pines

Camp, beating out Tommy Crossley, his runny-nose older brother, who wouldn't stop crying even after the troop leaders confirmed the bull's–eye from sixty-three yards, the wimp.

A caddy at Ann Arbor Country Club. Only for one summer, but long enough to have both his first smoke and kiss, on the same night.

Intermittent steady to Betty, Connie, and Rita. Betty always knew where the best parties were, though Connie was the better kisser and Rita from the better family. None of them let him do more than hold their hands, but he made enough suggestive comments that none of his buddies were ever sure.

Four tours of Vietnam, honorably discharged for his unofficial extra jumps during Junction City, a mostly failed campaign that nonetheless was his favorite time in the jungle; he'd sing the national anthem as he dropped into the treetops, the men around him eventually joining along, and when they did, he never felt more invincible, the bullets in his hip and shoulder notwithstanding.

Forest ranger at Isle Royale for two years, long enough to convince Rita to marry him and to never live through an Upper Peninsula winter ever again, ice and cold be damned.

Forest ranger at Mesa Verde, freshly listed on the National Registry of Historic Places, and teeming with scrawny, sunburned archaeologists who needed federal supervision. He was more than happy to oblige, and soon began to join them, digging and cataloging in his signature black ten-gallon hat. Rita, however, stayed only six weeks before fleeing back to Michigan, lonely and miserable and convinced her lungs were half filled with dust, and he didn't stop her, didn't even say goodbye.

Explorer. The place was a paradise, and he was more than happy to enjoy it. He'd follow researchers out to remote spots for digs, eventually learning enough of the area to guide people out himself, scrambling and climbing for as long as his bullet-filled hip would let him. After particularly successful trips, the sunburned PhDs would give him a few pieces of pottery, an occasional arrowhead, and once the chipped-off edge of a rock painting. He revered these objects, he'd later insist, creating a shrine in the corner of his park-issued cabin, labeling and dating each one.

Friend of the locals, most of whom were of Native descent, and they would drink and gamble and hike and goof off together. He'd win some pieces off someone's bad deal, or they'd go out to old ruins to shoot and then poke around. It was harmless. After all, if they were actually worth anything, why would they be lying around? They were precious to him, though, older than anything he'd seen in Michigan, and he felt as if he were a protector by possessing them, important and noble, almost powerful.

Boyfriend of Margot. He'd never been a real boyfriend, but he'd also never met a girl like Margot. She was a schoolteacher in Durango, brought some kids to Mesa Verde and they hit it off. She'd drive out to see him on weekends and they'd climb cliffs and swim in creeks and then head back to his cabin, sweat-slick and giggling, where they wouldn't leave until morning. She didn't want anything serious, and he wanted as much as she would give him. Sunday would come and she'd head back to Durango, and he'd spend his weeknights scribbling in a journal, desperate to understand it, this wild, loose joy, so deep and fast he felt like it could drown him. He didn't stop keeping journals, not even when Margot showed up one day engaged to some other man, weepy and apologetic. He bit his lip, refused to cry. Instead, he gave her a turquoise necklace he won in a poker game, told her to wear it and remember him. She came back a few weeks later with her new husband, the husband who asked where he got the necklace and if he had any more. His mother wanted one, the husband explained, and a few of Margot's friends did, too.

Shopkeeper never felt right; *trader* too slimy. He considered himself more of a connoisseur. He got paid, sure, but the people he got the necklaces and rings and buckles from always got paid, too. Everyone got paid and everyone wanted in on it. The bosses didn't like him doing business out of the park cabins, so he rented a place in town, a small yellow bungalow with a picket fence. He never slept there unless it was to sleep with one of the customers, usually married women whose husbands were off playing cowboy at nearby ranches, which suited him just fine. He bought more hats, still black but of better quality, and a car.

Fly-fisher. Margot's husband kept returning, each time asking if he had anything new. He'd see the husband pull up in his flashy car and wonder if Margot had come this time, but she never did. One weekend the husband arrived with a younger brother and some friends from Boulder for a fishing trip and asked if he could guide them to the best river spots. He knew some spots, but didn't ever fish, didn't think he'd like it—being cold and wet was never something he enjoyed, thanks to those icy winters in Isle Royale—and he didn't. He loved it. The art of the cast, the awe of the first pull on his line, the respect for the fish he scooped out of the water. It was what he was supposed to feel in the Lutheran church of his childhood, what all the books and hymns always spoke of. The quiet, the patience, the routine. Fish would humble you and then reward you and then humble you again, all in one afternoon. He started going out every morning before his ranger shifts. It was during those solo fishing expeditions that he found his most prized treasures: the clay snake with its polished onyx eyes, the jar filled with precious stones, the jawbone, the black-and-red platter. The skulls. He'd haul them back to the bungalow and put them up in the front room for display only. He wouldn't sell them to anyone, not even Margot's husband, and the archaeologists didn't seem interested in them.

Meanwhile, he was becoming interested in Elise, an art school grad who'd come to town to paint the sunsets and could hold her whiskey better than most men. She stayed in the bungalow long enough for him to give her a room to paint in and, in turn, she gave him a son. Margot's husband visited with a man who wanted six human skulls, and offered a price big enough that it felt foolish to say no. He quit the ranger job. He married Elise. They started a gallery to showcase Elise's paintings and his treasures. He went out every day to fish and find more pottery. His friends in town still consigned jewelry with him and he still sold to Margot's husband, but once the park became a National Park, there were more visitors, more customers.

Years passed. Elise had a gallery opening in Santa Fe and never returned. Fine with him; they'd both become mean and then bored, so indifferent toward one another they didn't even bother to divorce in the end. Their son was a teenager by then and wanted to stay in Mesa Verde. Fine by Elise. She was busy enough. The boy joined his father fishing and trekking, helping to haul the precious pottery and stones back to the bungalow. He wanted to become a ranger, but his father told him not to. No money in it, he said. No glory.

More consignments, more treasures. By then he had his pilot's license, owned his own plane. Toyed with the idea of opening a sky-diving outfitter, but couldn't trust anyone to fly a plane he'd jump out of. He'd pilot himself to antiquities road shows in Denver and Albuquerque and Sonoma, leaving his son behind to manage the shop. It was during one of these trips that the men showed up, demanding to buy the prized clay snake. The son refused. They grabbed him by the collar, asked him if his father knew who they were, and when the room filled with the smell of piss, the men laughed and let him go. They left a business card with a Vegas address. The son was terrified. The father, when he returned, curious.

He'd say it happened quickly, but everything remembered seems to happen quickly. The father would bring back bigger, more exotic treasures from the road shows. The father and son would fly to Vegas, Los Angeles, New York. They'd go to a nondescript shopping mall, the father disappearing into a back room and then returning with bags of cash. The customers would take them out, show these cowboys the big city. The son had his first taste of sushi, his first lap dance, his father cheering him on, laughing from under his signature black hat. The father bought an old ranch outside of town, dozens of acres. He demolished the farmhouse and built a one-level of concrete and glass. "Sinatra in Palm Springs," he said. There was a pool and a sauna and a tiki bar. The son didn't have the heart to tell his father no one did tiki anymore, but it wasn't like he'd care anyway. No college for the son, but the father never went, and look how he turned out. More trips, more jewelry, more pottery. The son lived in the bungalow and mostly stayed there, other than occasional trips to Santa Fe to see his mother. He liked movies, especially older action series from the '80s. The big hair, the big explosions, the big loves, the big muscles. He especially loved the ease of the stories, good guys versus bad guys, everyone neatly categorized. He bought a computer, played Pong and messaged with other lonely men around the country.

There were feds, there always were. But the father was good at playing the veteran card, even better at being charming. Most of the time they'd have a beer on the pool deck and laugh about the latest football scores, or the president and his intern, and soon the father was dealing out cards. It'd get late, and the suits would be flushed and full, telling the father to stay careful, thanking him for another good time. But then new suits started to come, suits straight from DC, and that was when the gold bars started to appear in Elise's old painting room. "Your inheritance," the father said as explanation, covering them with painter's cloth and installing a dead bolt on the door.

They didn't speak of it, not until the father slipped on a fishing trip, breaking his bum hip. There were surgeries and therapies and more surgeries. The old bullet lodged there had been tipped with lead, the area poisoned and weak. He might be wheelchair-bound for the rest of his life, the doctors said. There were dark months after this, the father bedridden and steeped in tequila. The son would change the bedpan and avoid calls from any big cities. Instead, he researched doctors and specialists, new methods and approaches. He flew someone in from Chicago, a young guy who spent summers up at Isle Royale and was the first person to get the father out of bed.

A few months on crutches, then a cane. It was a triumph, but not enough for the father to go to his favorite fishing holes or hiking trails. He tried to get the son to go for him, to take pictures and hook fish and camp out, but the son wouldn't do it. They didn't speak for a while. The son began an online course. He was the best in the class, mostly because he already knew how to do it, coding, just hadn't known what it was called.

The idea. His father was so alive when he spoke of it, showing up at the bungalow full of energy and looseness. He hadn't seen his father like this in years, maybe ever. The father already had the chest picked out, but he needed help with the clues. There was a new librarian in town, the son mentioned. About the father's age. Divorced. It didn't take long, it never did. The father and librarian spent most days together, huddled together on the bungalow's porch, choosing words and arranging phrases. It was the librarian who did most of the writing, the son noticed, but he would never mention this to anyone, not ever.

A programming job with a defense contractor in Colorado Springs. The son would have to move there at the end of the month. The father panicked. The son was the one who had to bring the chest out to the spot; he couldn't, not with the cane. Why not the librarian? She can't hike in water! No, it had to be the son. Your inheritance, the father insisted. The son bristled, said most inheritances are kept, not given away to strangers. They were never really mine to begin with, the father said solemnly. I found them, looked after them, but now it's someone else's turn.

At first, the son planned to keep it, pretend as if he'd hiked it out to the burial spot. It was his turn, he thought bitterly. But the longer the box stayed in his room, the more wrong it felt. He was leaving for a steady job with a great salary. He had no interest in wilderness or antiquities. It was a good story, too, the son had to admit. A real ad-

venture. Would a good guy hold on to it for himself? Betray his father's wishes? The weekend before he was to leave, the son hid it. He
took pictures of the location, just in case. He came back, successful,
and the father asked the son to help set up a website. The son did, and
then moved away the next morning. Later, when his father got arrested, the son pulled strings at his job to get him a lenient sentence.
An old man, he said. Different times, he said. When his father's website crashed, the father panicked, convinced his legacy was gone for
good, and so the son created a message board. They were surprised
by how many people joined. The users were petty and invested, and
the son would call his father to read various posts aloud. His father
loved it and the son soon realized he did, too. Father and son had
never spoken more, had never laughed together more. The father
didn't want to be active in the forum, but the son was. Careful, the
father warned. We don't want anyone to suspect anything. But the
son wasn't worried. His username was his favorite movie. He only
posted when he felt it necessary, which was only when things got out
of hand, threads unspooling in a way that he knew would upset his
father. He had the power to lock those down, and did, out of respect
for the Conversation.

---

been boots on the ground for a week or so now and starting to
get confident it's going to be the big solve. everyone's been
obsessed with parks and geysers, and that's amateur
thinking. no one's thinking about the numbers. it's all

numbers, people. the Poet's a fisherman, right, but he's also a pilot. that's what his ex-wife said in the court disposition, how he spent his insurance settlement on a new plane (EDIT: pdf of disposition transcript here & here, but thought that was already available on the site?). whoever is going to find it needs to think like a pilot. heavy burden—cargo. no longer walking—air travel. obvious. good news for me is, my dad was a pilot. so i know pilots don't use internet maps. they use actual maps, usually their own. i have a map and now i have a where and it's nowhere close to everyones recent wheres. numbers, people. pay attention to the numbers. can't wait to be a millionaire lol

hey **@NCGuy** if it's all about numbers why don't you post a few and share what you're thinking? :)

@NCGuy shut up and show us your map lol **@arnold578** this guy always posts vague stuff like this there's no reasoning with him. flag for **@MadMax**. EDIT: recent transcript edit isn't enough. more proof or imma keep flagging **@MadMax** **@MadMax** **@MadMax**

ALL I'M SAYING IS the Poet was a pilot and anyone who's serious about this needs to follow the numbers. Why should I share my proof and let someone else find the treasure before me??? Here's a hint: IT'S NOT IN COLORADO!!!!!!!

@CoolJake The guy found his spot. We all have a spot, right? I'll go out to mine every time I can until I find the treasure or someone else does. Too bad my spot is a 1900mi round trip ha ha ha anyway I had a lot of hot air and confidence when I was young too. Got to be careful though, **@NCGuy**, no room for ego in the desert. Make sure you pack some water and post some more photos for us, alright? Some details about your map

won't hurt with making friends around here. That's how this
will get found, through community and Conversation. We can
help! We want to. I want to, at least until I earn enough PTO to
drive 1900mi again ha ha ha

@arnold578 dude can go look up literally any other
forum post on numbers don't give him any more oxygen.
@MadMax @MadMax @MadMax

@CoolJake STOP FUCKIN FLAGGING ME. look ok fine i'm in
the desert in UT. everyone thinking geysers or some shit is
obviously a fuckin idiot.

lol you wish @MadMax @MadMax @MadMax @MadMax
@MadMax @MadMax

FUCK YOU flagging @MadMax on YOU

@NCGuy Utah, huh? Didn't Bob also think Utah? Also Christy
They were very loud about that but haven't heard from them
in awhile. @Jazzy, have you? Aren't you a Utah person, too?

hi Arnie! yup I'm a desert gal too. @NCGuy whereabouts are
you right now? I'm in St George, you're welcome to come by for
a beer and compare notes/maps. always happy to have some
searchers come through. Haven't heard from Bob and Christy
in forever though . . .

your all so fucking dumb I'm with Bob right now lmao old guy
wouldn't be here without me @Jazzy @arnold578

You're with Bob? Wow! I thought he was a lone wolf. You both
should come to St. George! Would love to meet the infamous
Bob! And you, too, @NCGuy. I've known Bob for ages. He's one
of the OGs around here.

pics or gtfo

@**Jazzy** yeah bob is here he says hi he's liked your research, thinks your train depot theory is pretty smart but he knows i'm right about the pilot lol @**CoolJake** you would wish you could have a pic, you sick fuck!!!! FUCK YOU!!!!!

ok then how tf did you meet up with bob huh

it's been two hours and still nothing @**NCGuy** @**MadMax**??? I thought cursing was prohibited????

LOL FUCK YOU @**CoolJake**!!! More like PUSSY JAKE!!!!!!!

Chiming in to say this seems like a giant waste of time y'all. Don't believe the Bob thing for a second either.

alright, @**NCGuy** most of the people here have been doing this for years, kid. you showed up 2 months ago and haven't stopped talking nonsense. no one who is close to solving would have cellphone service, let alone enough data to post dumb rants about how everyone else is blind and stupid. guy's username is the same on every social media platform. he posted a picture of his dog yesterday on one of his feeds. he's in the desert, maybe even utah, but you can't bring animals on any fed lands, so he's clearly either trespassing, nowhere close, an idiot, or all the above. most likely he's posting this from a dennys hoping for attention and we're giving it to him, so, @**CoolJake** I agree with @**krazykourt**, this is a total waste of time, unless @**NCGuy** you want to start sharing details, which is the whole point of the Conversation. respect the conversation, right @**MadMax**? and i even agree with him, it's not in CO, but don't disrespect the searchers who think it is

You think i'm trespassing? TRESPASS THIS, **@arnold578** !!!!!!

☒

Oh my god!

WTF!!!!!

lmao OMG IS THAT WHAT I THINK IT IS?

not that impressive tbh . . .

I'm at work and can get fired for this. This is entirely unacceptable. **@MadMax**

wow, convo's first dick pic

I can't stop laughing holy sh**!!!!!!!!!!

@MadMax URGENT this is an EMERGENCY

I don't understand why he's holding a water bottle next to it?

LOLOLOLOLOL

wait omfg I love Cluckin Breasts. Winston-Salem, ya?
Best fried chicken in the Triangle!!!

lmaoooooooooo

this is utterly inappropriate **@MadMax**

Ok but also . . . is that Bob in the background? Does anyone know if Bob is on a search right now? Because there's

> definitely a guy standing in the background and he definitely looks like Bob . . .
>
> ---
>
> hey **@arnold578** and **@krazykourt** think me flagging this idiot was a waste of time NOW?????
>
> ---
>
> ENDING THIS THREAD OUT OF RESPECT FOR THE CONVERSATION. USER BLOCKED FOR VIOLATION OF THE TERMS OF THE FORUM. PICTURE HAS BEEN DELETED AND THREAD IS ARCHIVED.

It was late, almost midmorning, and the sun blinded everything inside the trailer. There was a long, wobbling moment of disorientation, almost as if Bea were in a dream, though she was awake enough to know she wasn't. She pulled at a thin wool blanket and then remembered, sitting up suddenly, the entire night coming back to her: Tag, the trailer, the cabin, Christy. Bea fumbled for her phone. No calls from her mother, her texts still unanswered. She dialed her mother's number and it went straight to voicemail. Her gut seized. From across the trailer, Tag snored, soft and deep. She started to quietly gather her things, but couldn't remember where her shirt ended up. The backpack, she remembered, and then, the fish. Forget the shirt (forget the fish). It didn't matter, she'd take the sweatshirt. But where would she go? The cabin was off-limits. Whoever was there the night before could come back. She checked the time. Almost ten a.m. The grill? No, the motel. She'd go to the motel and confront Bob herself. They should've gone last night, should've gone straight to the room and banged on the door and gotten her mother out of there. If only Christy would answer her phone. Bea dialed again. Nothing.

Tag was asleep, one arm thrown over his face, the other outstretched into the space between the couch and cabinets. Bea tried to step over him when his phone went off, buzzing on the ground, startling her. She fell backward against the sink full of dirty beer bottles, waking Tag, who quickly pulling his legs into his chest. "Are you all right?" they both asked, embarrassed.

"Your phone," Bea said, pointing at the ground. It was still ringing.

Tag answered it with a thick, groggy hello and then immediately stood up. "Fuck, dude, I'm sorry, I'll be there in a minute, just give me a minute, okay? I overslept, yeah, okay, yeah, I told you, shut up, listen, I'll be there. Fuck, I'm sorry, all right?" He hung up and pulled on a shirt. "Hey, I gotta go, I'm, like, two hours late for work. Hank's called me a million times and it's apparently so slammed your mom is helping out." He lifted couch cushions, ripped away the blanket. "Where the fuck is my wallet." He pulled open the backpack and the smell—thick and sour and wet—made them both gag. He took her shirt out of the bag. It was streaked with glistening iridescent slime. A thin black wallet tumbled out of it. "Shit, you can use the laundry in Hank's house—"

"My mom's at the grill?" Bea asked, her voice catching.

"Oh, right," Tag said. "I'm sorry, I should've said that first. She's pouring drinks there." He reached out to her, but stopped himself and put his hand on his hip instead. "She's fine. She's okay."

Bea nodded and waved a hand in front of her face, acting as if the smell was making her eyes water. "I should go see her."

"I'll give you a ride." Tag took off his shirt and handed it to her. "Here, it's going to be a billion degrees today, you're not going to want that sweatshirt. It's clean, too." Bea took the shirt and Tag went into the bedroom. It was a white and green ringer tee, PAT'S GRILL MERCY UTAH EST. 1988 emblazoned across the back. It was soft with wear, the neck and sleeves stretched and loose, and when she put it on, it was still warm.

Tag reappeared, fully clothed, and Bea handed him the sweatshirt. Tag took it and opened the trailer door, letting her go first. She stepped out into the white light of the day. It was already bracingly, pantingly hot. Tag was right, a sweatshirt would've been suffocating. Bea went to thank him, turning just in time to see him surreptitiously press the sweatshirt to his face. It was quick, no more than a half second, though long enough for Bea to consider doing something to interrupt, a cough or a laugh or a question, but then she realized she didn't want to. She let herself watch him, his eyes closed, hands balled into the fabric. After a moment, he dropped the sweatshirt, jangled his keys in his front pocket, and then, looking up, made eye contact. He blanched, tried to say something about laundry, apologizing, but Bea stopped him. She pulled the green collar of the T-shirt over her nose. "Smells good, too," she said, and when she smiled, he did, too.

◁▶

The grill was a storm of screaming children, screaming parents, and scowling seniors, almost all of them drinking juice, so much juice, orange and apple and an occasional cranberry, spilling and slurping and demanding refills. Christy tried to stay out of the way as Hank swam against the bar's sticky, multicolored tide. After a long, hectic thirty minutes, the chef came out and wordlessly delivered her food, plate clattering as it hit the bar top. Christy's cheeseburger was unhealthily raw, the fries limp and cold. Christy didn't care, luxuriating in the fact that she'd eat the fries regardless of temperature because she was hungover, and when was the last time she was hungover? She nibbled at the bun, peeled the cheese off the meat, but nothing helped, and Christy would've laughed if her acid reflux wasn't so bad.

As the crowd grew, Hank shouted Christy could eat and drink free, as long as she handled the bar. "Where's Tag?" Christy asked, but Hank was already rushing to another table.

She fell into the rhythm of the bar easily, deftly tipping each pint glass as it filled, popping bottle caps off in one smooth movement. When one of the tap lines coughed and she was forced to fill a foamy pint, Hank said to forget it, told Christy to drink it herself, he'd tell the people they were out. The beer softened the hangover lurking at the base of her skull. She sipped the beer and nodded as Hank called out orders. She poured beers and, eventually, poured herself one, too. After a while, Christy fell into the cool, forgiving blank of methodical concentration, opening endless juice containers, starting a new brew of coffee, and wiping down each of the taps. Then, from the entryway, the sound of her daughter's voice.

"Where have you been?" Bea's hair was ragged and, to Christy's surprise, very short. It suited her.

Tag hurried past them into the kitchen, where, despite effusive apologies, he was met with a loud string of Spanish curse words. "What happened to your hair?" Christy asked.

Bea touched the closest curl. "I cut it. But—you're okay?"

"I'm fine. Hungover, but fine."

"Why didn't you text me back?" Bea asked. "I was trying to reach you all day yesterday." She was exhausted, deep bags under her eyes and dirt in her hair. She seemed small and lost, suddenly a child again. Christy pulled Bea into a hug. Her daughter's hair still smelled the same. Bea tried to pull away, but Christy wouldn't let her, and after a moment of shuffling, she felt Bea accept the embrace and lean into her. Christy's heart seized. "I'm sorry, honey, I lost my phone. You know I would've called if I had it," Christy said into her daughter's neck. Bea nodded. Hank had come up to them and asked, with clear desperation, if Bea had ever waited tables. Her daughter immediately said yes, which surprised Christy. Had her daughter waited tables? But Christy kept quiet as Bea took Hank's order book. "Don't worry, you can keep the tips," Hank said. "Christy, can you grab some more orange juice from the walk-in? Try to avoid Chef if you can, he might think you're Tag and try to kill you. And Bea, table two has been trying to order for ages. No specials today, all right? And remember to smile. Shit, looks like table five is snapping. Let's go." Christy watched as Bea followed him to the table, where a pair of scowling geriatrics pointed at their empty water glasses. Christy, already anticipating Hank, began to fill a pitcher with ice.

Eventually the grill began to empty out. The last group was a rowdy group of Swiss hikers, their cheeks chapped and red, table littered with empty pint glasses. They chattered and laughed among themselves, unaware of Tag wiping down tables and Hank organizing the register, until the chef came out from the back and flipped the sign to CLOSED. Service was over, he announced. They were out of onions. He stood with his hands on his hips and stared at the Swiss until they got the hint and left. Chef followed them out, still wearing his apron as he got into his truck and drove off. Tag and Hank were unfazed. They began to mop and wash down the tables. Christy busied herself behind the bar, organizing and cleaning, a headache growing stronger. Bea had been drying the same pint glass for nearly ten minutes. Christy took the glass out of Bea's hands and put it away. "I went by your cabin last night to check on you and you weren't there," Christy said, elbowing her daughter. "The door was unlocked when I went in, by the way. Sure seemed like you were in a rush to go hang out with someone last night."

"You went to the cabin last night?" Bea asked, eyes wide. "When?"

"After the town hall."

"So, dinner time?"

"If I had to guess, yes, it was around then."

"Of course it was you," Her daughter sighed. "What were you looking for?"

"You," Christy said. "What else?"

"Why you'd make such a mess?"

"I didn't make any mess," Christy laughed. "That was all you, honey."

"And why'd you take the aspen?"

"The aspen? Why would I need the aspen?"

"You didn't take the aspen out of the cabin?"

"I didn't do anything with the aspen, you're the one who said we should bring it with us." Christy rubbed her temples. "Any chance you have some Tylenol? My head's killing me."

"Where's Bob?"

Christy hadn't thought of Bob since the hotel, the brunch rush having wiped the morning from her memory. Her headache roared. She did not want to think about Bob. She poured herself a beer. "What about him?"

"You two have been attached to the hip all weekend. Why isn't he here?"

Christy hesitated and her daughter noticed. She drank the beer slowly, deciding how honest to be. "We got into a disagreement. I haven't seen him since last night. Not that it's any of your business."

A flicker of panic passed over her daughter's face. "You don't know where he is?"

"No," Christy admitted. "Since when do you care about Bob?"

Bea called out for Tag. Tag hurried over, rag over one shoulder. "She didn't take the aspen," Bea said to Tag, voice pinched. "And she doesn't know where Bob is." Tag nodded. He turned to Christy. "Hey, Christy, any chance you could call Bob? We should clear some things up."

Christy finished the rest of the beer. They were managing her, she knew. They were treating her like an idiot, and maybe she was, but even hungover, she knew calling Bob would be a mistake. The call would be so irregular, so outside of their typical communication, that he'd never pick up, and if he did pick up then Christy would have to casually ask where he was, and if he'd seen an aspen, an aspen he had never heard of, but if he knew where it was it meant he knew where her daughter was staying, it meant he went, uninvited, in the middle of the night, to the cabin where her daughter slept, to get it. No, Bob would never do such a thing. Bob wasn't capable of such a thing. In fact, maybe he wasn't even gone. He could be just down the street, maybe picking up some materials at the information center or getting better wi-fi at the pizza parlor or maybe even buying her apologetic flowers from the grocery store. He took her phone and tablet with him because he wanted to make sure she had them when they met back up. Christy shook her head. "I can't."

Her daughter's face morphed from fear to rage. "Are you fucking kidding me?"

"He'll be back for dinner, we'll ask him when he's here."

"Someone broke into Bea's cabin last night," Tag said evenly. "We haven't called the cops yet, but maybe we should."

"I told you, I didn't make that mess," Bea said. "Someone did that while I was gone. I stayed at Tag's last night because it wasn't safe."

Christy's brain snapped into a cold, sharp focus, the nausea disappearing. She turned to her daughter. "Give me your phone." Bea handed it over warily. Christy pretended to type a number as she walked out the grill doors. She brought the phone to her ear, hands shaking, and then ducked behind Tag's truck, out of view.

Christy scrolled through the recent posts. After a few days away from the forum, the Conversation felt foreign and distant, like a hip bar she used to frequent, everyone loud and young and overeager. Christy checked her private messages. There were plenty of notes from her various online friends: how's it going???? Send A Pic When You Can XOXO! did you go down to the desert finally???? Good luck out there mama! Nothing from Bob, but there was a post from early that morning that made her pause, finger hovering over the screen: if ur w/Bob tell him that kid is bad news. neither one of them will respond to messages after the post and MM is pissed. The post was at the top of the forum, the most popular thread in the past twenty-four hours. Christy hadn't given it much thought when she first opened the Conversation because the post's title—GETTING CLOSE!!!!!!—wasn't unusual. A lot of people were perpetually getting close. They wouldn't be part of the Conversation if they didn't think they were close or could be close eventually.

She didn't recognize the username, but there'd been an influx of college-aged men in the Conversation lately, boisterous and braggadocious and exceedingly annoying to everyone, including the other college-aged men, and Christy usually skipped their comments and posts. This one seemed no different, that is, until Christy scrolled down to the comment: I'm with Bob right now lmao old guy wouldn't be here without me

> *wouldn't be here without me*

> *without me*

The photo had been posted the night before and had since been replaced with a faint gray box with an *X* in the middle. OnlyBob hadn't posted since he peed on the crystals, but this user, NCGuy, was still active. She thumbed to his profile. There were dozens of posts and comments, one as recent as an hour and a half earlier. It was a comment under a thread started by CoolJake, who was asking about research into Yosemite logging trails. Most of the users were replying with relevant information, but NCGuy had said, U WANT AN ENEMY YOU GOT ONE, ASSHOLE. Someone tagged MadMax to report the profanity, but neither MadMax nor NCGuy had replied yet.

She wouldn't run, she decided. He didn't deserve her hurry.

The door was still unlocked, the mess now familiar. Christy's eyes went to the corner of the room where the map had been. It was empty. Christy looked under the bed, behind the pullout couch, in the fridge. She checked Bea's suitcase, craned her neck to peer into the cabin rafters. She moved to the bathroom. The toilet seat was up and the bowl filled with rank, yellow piss. Christy stepped back as if slapped. It was him. He did this. He stole her map. He, or that boy, or the two of them together, broke into her daughter's room and stole Christy's map. They left her at the drive-in and abandoned the motel and came here. What would they have done to Bea if she had been in the room when they got there? She thought of the boy. She thought of the gun. Christy retched once, twice, but nothing came. She slid to the ground, fist at her mouth, closed her eyes, and screamed, stomach roiling with wine and fury.

And then they were there, Tag and Bea, reaching for her, Christy, Mom, talk to us, hey.

It took Christy a minute to catch her breath. The nausea and rage receded, but didn't disappear, the sour clutch of it lingering in her chest. "Beautiful?" she asked.

"Mom?"

"I think it's time to go home."

No police, her mother said. It wasn't worth explaining how a collage of napkins and papers was valuable, let alone what the map was for. The supposed contents of the treasure could be illegal, after all. Tag offered to drive them back to the trailhead to get the Chrysler. He went to get his truck, telling Bea and Christy to be careful, to keep an eye out. Christy left to pack her things at the motel, insisting on being alone. Bea gathered her things. The only thing she couldn't find was a pair of her underwear—an old pair, huge and cotton and ragged—which set the hair on the back of her neck on end. But her mother was already humiliated enough, Bea figured; she wouldn't mention it. Better to leave it all behind. By the time Bea met her mother in the motel lobby, the sun was beginning to set, and Christy was in a face-off with the woman behind the front desk. Both women were grinning at each other with lipless passive aggression.

"I don't understand why I can't just pay for the late checkout fee and be on my way." Christy pushed a crumpled pair of twenties across the desk. "You can keep the change."

The woman pushed the cash back toward Christy. "Ma'am, I already told you, you need to pay for the length of stay *and* late checkout. The total for the weekend is two hundred and fifty-eight dollars and twenty-three cents. We take Visa, American Express, and Mastercard. We can do ten percent off with cash. No checks, hotel policy."

Christy pushed the twenties back across the vinyl desktop. "What do you not understand about 'I am only paying the late fee'?" she hissed.

"Hi, sorry, Mom? Let's get you some coffee. Okay, here, take a sip for me. There you go. Are we feeling better? Maybe we should get some fresh air, huh?" Bea steered her mother out the door, Christy muttering under her breath, and then reapproached the desk.

"Okay, hi, I think there must be a misunderstanding because, uh, Bob? Or Robert? He paid for everything," The woman stared at Bea blankly. Bea put on her biggest smile. "If you call him, I'm sure he'll tell you that. Why don't we call him?"

"I'm not going to call him, ma'am."

Bea was starving, hadn't eaten all day, and the hunger was curdling into something worse, something angrier. The woman was younger than her, face thick with makeup, and she couldn't stop blinking. "Why not?" Bea asked, trying to use her mildest tone, but failing.

"Because he's gone," Christy said from the doorway. Bea hadn't noticed her mother reopening the door and, judging by her bulging eyes, the woman behind the desk hadn't, either. "Bob's gone. He's run off with that boy and my map and also, apparently, your aspen. It's all on the Conversation, you can read it yourself. Everyone can read it, even she can read it." Christy motioned to the woman behind the desk as she walked over. "What's your name, honey?"

"Tammy."

Christy took a deep breath and folded her hands in front of her. "Tammy, I'm going to tell you what, Bob promised me he paid for this hotel room, but obviously he didn't. You said he's a friend of yours?"

"Of the hotel."

"Which means you have his information on file?"

Tammy nodded. Bea started to speak, but her mother cut her off. "Does that information happen to include a credit card number?"

Tammy shot a look at the security camera in the corner. "I'm not sure—"

Bea's phone chimed. An email from the recruiter. *They loved your project . . . interview this week, preferably Tuesday or Wednesday . . . final rounds already . . . let me know ASAP, would love to get on the phone beforehand . . .* She reread the email. *They loved it.* Of course they did, she thought. She was good at her job. She'd always been good at her job. The hundreds of reports written without credit, the late nights at the desk without thanks. *They loved it.* Recognition, finally. And yet, all she felt was a deep, hollow exhaustion. Soon, she wouldn't have to do the math anymore. Back at a desk, back in the math, back in the city. The spreadsheets, the caffeine, the reports, the late-night car rides back to Brooklyn. She could see it all, everything ahead, and it made her want to crawl into the corner and fall asleep. She closed her eyes. "I'll pay," Bea said.

"Great," Tammy said, clearly relieved.

Bea pulled out her wallet. Christy stopped her. "No."

"It's fine," Bea insisted. "I'll handle it." She'd have to fly back to New York tomorrow, which meant they needed to leave for Salt Lake as soon as possible. She rubbed her jaw. The drive would be endless, terrible, and the plane worse. Maybe she'd splurge on a business class ticket, but even lay-flat luxury didn't spark excitement.

"He promised to pay!" her mother screamed. Bea and Tammy froze. Christy sniffed, coming back to herself, and apologized. "Tammy, look, Bob was my boyfriend. He left without telling me, and now I don't know where he is. Men, am I right?" Christy gave a fake laugh. "He took my phone and tablet with him, too. You could say he stole them."

"Forget him," Bea said forcefully. Always the hysterics, always the drama. "I said I would pay. I'll get you a new phone, too."

Her mother ignored her. "Tammy, do understand what I'm saying? Why I might be upset?"

Tammy looked between Bea and Christy. "Bob left this morning.

He was in a big rush. Said it was nice getting to know me and told me to take care but wasn't sure if he'd be back. You're—you're his girlfriend?"

"Was," Christy said with a long exhale. "Or I thought I was."

"Mr. Reynolds has been a loyal guest for a few months now, but he never had a double room until this weekend." Tammy paused and looked Christy square in the eyes. "You should know, he left with a man this morning." She cleared her throat. "It was very early."

"Did the guy have blue eyes? Maybe a backpack?"

"I'm not sure," Tammy said. "He was young."

Christy motioned at her head. "Did he have a hat? Something about chickens and boobs?"

"Hold on." Bea had only been half listening, but this made her stop browsing flights on her phone. "Do you mean Cluckin' Breasts?"

"Yes!" Tammy snapped her fingers and pointed at Bea. "Breasts!"

Bea gaped at her mother. "*That guy* was with Bob? You know that creep?"

"I don't, but Bob certainly does," her mother said with disgust. "How the hell do you know him?"

"He wasn't very nice," Tammy said carefully. "The younger man said they'd never stay in the hotel again. Something about it not being fancy enough, but they were about to win the lottery or something? He was really rude, to be honest."

Bea pushed a credit card across the desk. "Forget them, they don't matter anymore. I'll pay and then we need get out of here."

Tammy typed into a computer. Without looking up, she asked, "Do you happen to be a member of our armed services?"

"Of what?" Bea asked, confused.

"And do you happen to be a student?"

"Yes, she is," Christy said, perking up. "In fact, she's both. Cadet at the Naval Academy. Tennis scholarship. The family is very proud."

Tammy smiled. "We love our country here, so I'm happy to offer you a thirty percent discount, along with a ten percent student discount. And we'll just take off that late fee, because of all the—" Tammy hesitated.

"Misunderstandings," Christy finished. "With the other guest."

"Yes," Tammy said, typing. "Your total comes to, let's see, one hundred and forty-four dollars."

As Bea signed the receipt, Christy slid a brochure across the reception desk. "I found this on the floor over there," she said, tapping the brochure. "I wanted to make sure you had it, because this is a *great* brochure. Have you read it?"

"'Canyon Balloon Rides'? No, I don't think so—"

"You *must*," Christy said slowly, tapping hard with every word, enough that the top flap slid forward to reveal the corner of a thin wad of twenty-dollar bills. "Promise me?"

Tammy shyly smiled. "Of course."

Bea waved as they pushed through the doors. "Thanks for everything, Tammy!" her mother said, blowing a kiss.

The four of them—Christy, Bea, Tag, Hank—rode out of town toward the Chrysler in a sticky, stale silence. The only talking came from the radio, where there was a discussion of an amphibian once thought to be extinct, some lizard in Southeast Asia. Black, blue, and green. Magnificent, the scientist kept saying. No bigger than a pencil. It was stunningly iridescent, almost glittering, and its young were born with claws on their bellies and backs, for protection against not only predators, but also their parents, who were known to happily eat their young.

Tag switched the radio to a jazzy pop song, lizards gone, and Hank bounced his knee to the beat. Bea rested her forehead against the back of Christy's headrest, the car hot and the radio loud. It'd been almost an hour, and they were still on the access road. Her mother shifted in the passenger seat and her hair fell into Bea's face. Bea sat back and watched the desert go by. The horizon was dappled with giant white clouds, each sprouting upward in perfect, cottony blooms, the sky beyond them a deep, dark violet. Bad news, Bea knew. She looked for wind direction, but none of the shrubs moved. West, eventually, she guessed, and held up her phone to take a picture. "These clouds are pretty wild," she said.

"Monsoon season," Hank grunted.

"It almost doesn't look real," Christy said.

Bea agreed. The city could make you feel small in a million ways, but it was mostly because of other people, because of things they did and demanded. Here, you were dwarfed by something much bigger and more powerful, intangible and merciless. She took a picture. It looked nothing like what was outside the window. She'd never be able to capture this. She'd go back to the city and try to explain and no one would really understand, no one aside from her mother, and even then, she knew they'd remember it differently. The wind picked up. West, of course.

————

The Chrysler was where they left it, blanketed in a thick coat of red dust. The engine started after a few attempts, gurgling and popping. Tag and Hank helped put the bags into the trunk. "You're good kids," Christy said, giving each of the guys a quick hug, before sliding into the Chrysler's passenger seat. "I'm too hungover to drive," she announced. Alone with Tag and Hank, Bea hesitated, unsure where to look or what to do. She wasn't ready for a goodbye, hadn't realized it was time. She tried to put her hands into her pockets, but remembered her shorts didn't have any. She gripped her hands in front of her. "Well—" she started.

Hank pulled her into a hug. "Come back and see us sometime," he said with an earnestness that made Bea's chest clutch. He patted her back, twice, and then walked back to the truck.

"Yeah, you should, uh, come back sometime," Tag said quietly.

The wind was, in fact, coming in from the west, faint but consistent. A hot wind, too. "It's a long drive," Bea said. "But, yeah, sure. Definitely." Tag nodded, kicked the ground. "Hug," Hank yelled from the truck.

They did, quickly, before Bea pulled away, her neck hot. "You have my number," he said. "If you ever, you know."

Bea knew she wouldn't text Tag back if he ever reached out—knew, without a doubt, she was never going to come back and visit. The weekend was over, just like this interminable period of unemployment was about to be over. This would all become a story she'd giggle through one day over a glass of wine, the story of her wild trip to the desert with her even wilder mother. The subletter! Eviction!

A treasure hunt! Bea could imagine every part of the scene except the person sitting across the table—if she was honest, there was no one in the city who she wanted to tell. Tag bit his lip, waiting. "Take care," she said, turning away.

The Chrysler seemed smaller, more delicate than the car they had driven through the access road just three days earlier. Every bounce and buck was met with worrying creaks and hisses. The radio was staticky, loud, while both Macon women remained quiet. Tag said he'd follow them back to the main road, but when Bea glanced into the rearview mirror, she saw nothing except dust. The road swerved to the left and lurched over a steep ridge. Bea pumped the gas. The Chrysler let out a long, rattling croak and then careened down the other side. There were one, two, three hard bumps, each met with a terrible metal crunch. Bea revved the engine. She drove. It began to rain. By the time they passed over the cattle bars marking the end of the access road, it'd become a thick curtain, dark and heavy. "That was terrible," Christy said. "I might be sick."

"You're more than welcome to drive."

"I've been drinking."

"Hours ago."

"I don't think they care about that when they arrest you."

"Since when are you worried about being arrested?"

"Don't be ridiculous."

Bea glared. "Oh, so now *I'm* the ridiculous one? After everything?" Her mother stared out the window.

The rain was a downpour, thick and angry. Bea found the lever for windshield wipers and put them at full speed. They scraped across the glass in loud, dragging squawks. Bea tightened her grip on the wheel and accelerated. Maybe, if she drove fast enough, they could outrun the storm, but the rain didn't let up. "Speed demon, huh?" her mother muttered, which only made Bea lay on the gas. The wind rocked the Chrysler every so often, its gusts whistling. Bea remembered the road as mostly straight, but there wasn't any cell service to check. Just keep going, she told herself. Through the sweeps of the windshield wipers, she could see the sign approaching, one arrow pointing toward Mercy, the other toward the interstate. Bea began to breathe. It was fine. It was only some rain.

Then: a glorious, horrible crack of lightning, huge and blinding. Bea swerved, sending her mother keeling into the dash, the old seat belt loose around her waist. Christy screeched, which made Bea swerve again. "What are you doing?" her mother yelled, hands over her face.

"I can barely see the fucking road!" Bea screamed.

"I think I broke my nose."

Sure enough, her mother's face was streaked in blood, but by turning she also turned the wheel, and the ground went from asphalt to rocks. Bea couldn't see where the dirt ended and the road began, the dark rain too thick. She clung to the steering wheel and started to curse.

"No need to panic," her mother said evenly, voice muffled by her hands over her face.

"Thanks, Christine, sure, this car's fucking forty-year-old suspension is definitely capable of off-roading and it's not like it's absolutely fucking pouring out. Extremely relaxing advice, Mom, I really appreciate it, please let me know if you have more, it's extraordinarily fucking helpful."

A bright white-blue snap of light, then a roar low and deep and close enough that it shook the Chrysler from wheels to hood in a long, terrible shudder. Bea stopped the car.

"Why did you stop?"

"I'm not driving in this," Bea said.

"Have you never driven in a thunderstorm? You can't stop, I'm bleeding!"

"I can barely see out the window!"

"The road is right there!"

"Where?" Bea gestured around them, arms flailing.

"There!" Christy yelled, though she didn't point, both her hands covering her face. "Jesus, Beautiful, it's right there!"

Bea ripped the keys out of the ignition and threw them into her mother's lap. "Then why don't you fucking drive!"

"I would, but in case you haven't noticed, I've broken my fucking nose," Christy yelled. When Bea didn't respond, her mother reclined the passenger seat. Blood dribbled across Christy's lips and chin. There was, Bea had to admit, a lot of blood. "Are there any tissues?" her mother asked. "Or napkins? Goddamn, this hurts like a real you-know-what."

Bea rummaged in the glove compartment, which had nothing but a loose bag of ancient, crumbling Cheez-Its. The back seat was covered in trash and takeout bags from the drive down from Salt Lake. "I might have something in my bag. It's in the trunk."

"No." Christy pressed her fingers against the bridge of her nose, the blood seeping between her knuckles. "Don't go outside." The storm churned around them, the thunder loud and low. Bea reminded herself that a car is the safest place for them to be in a thunderstorm, something about the rubber tires. Wasn't that true? She wasn't sure, had no idea where she heard it, but she repeated it to herself. They were safe. Bea rubbed her neck, the skin tender and sore from the seat belt. Her mother turned in her seat. "Someone's here," she said.

A low green truck pulled up next to them and honked. It was Tag. Hank hung out a window and made a cranking motion. Bea cracked her window, the rain ripping its way inside. "You can't stop here," Hank yelled between rolls of thunder.

"We're going to wait out the storm!" Christy yelled.

"You can't stop here," Hank shouted again. He turned and then, after a moment, reappeared. "There are going to be floods."

"What?" Bea could barely hear him.

"Floods!" Hank shouted, making waves with his hands. "It's not safe, you gotta keep driving."

Another crack of lightning, this time close, the air bright and tight and burning, and both Christy and Bea gasped.

"Follow us!" Hank shouted before disappearing back into the truck.

"Can't we come with you? In the truck?" Christy yelled, leaning over Bea's lap. Rain soaked her mother's face, making the dried blood watery and bright again. Christy waved her hand, desperate, but Tag had already pulled out in front of the Chrysler. Bea cranked the driver's window up and Christy collapsed into the passenger seat. Bea shifted the car into drive and pushed the gas, but the car didn't go, its back wheels spinning. She tried again. Another crack of lightning. Another. The wheels spun. Bea closed her eyes. Six in, eight out. All she had to do was get back to Salt Lake and then she'd never have to drive again. Six in, eight out. Another crack of thunder. Six, eight, six. Six, six, six, six, six. The sound of a door opening, the roar of the rain, and then after a minute or two, the door slamming closed. There was a quick poke of a fingernail into her stomach. Bea ignored it. It'd be fine. It was fine. Six, six, six. Another poke, and then another. "What?" Bea shrieked.

"I put rocks under the tires, it should help, but be light on the gas," her mother said.

Bea began to shift into drive, but then her mother put a trembling hand on Bea's knee. "Put on your seat belt," her mother said quietly. Ahead, Tag's taillights were two blurry, bloody suns.

The ride back was slow through the mud. The rain never let up, the thunder booming. When they got back to the main road, Tag put on his hazards and, relieved to have the guidance, so did Bea. Body humming with adrenaline, Bea chattered about how crazy the storm was, I thought this was the desert, but Christy was silent and, soon enough, Bea fell silent, too.

They pulled up to Hank's house, eventually, and Bea let go of a long, jagged breath. Christy rested her forehead against the dash. The rain pattered against the car. Bea's phone binged. Both women jolted, having not heard the sound in hours. It was a text from Tag, telling them they should come inside and warm up. *Do you like pancakes?*

To live without it is worse than the deepest itch. It's a pain that spiders from your gut and steals away every soft part of you. *That great and terrible wilderness.* That desire. The first swallow will push down your throat like a fist and you'll throb in thanks for it, lips open to it like a lover, chest aching.

Have you ever cried tears of pure salt?

Remember: more than half of you is made up of rain and in that way you are no more than a breathing sponge, and when you die, you'll weep water back into the ground like it was never yours to begin with, because it wasn't.

Only a few know how to find it beyond the rivers, how to read dirt and shadow, crawl up ledge and canyon as the day grows long and burnt, until finally: crystal spouts vomiting from red-clayed walls; glassine mirrors yawning under cliff edges; slow, sacred drips between stones; the hole dug beneath the cottonwood, filling with clear, pure life.

But the desert doesn't kill with thirst. Not always, not most often. Most often, the desert kills by drowning.

It begins silently. Perhaps the hush of twigs brushing up against one another, or a faint trickle as it pours onto bedrock, but this would be lucky, luckier than the brush mouse engulfed in its burrow, than the Mormon tea torn from its roots, than the squirrel battered into a pulp. Within minutes, it gathers momentum, desire. It throttles itself against the ground in a dark slurry of mulched debris, churning against the dirt and air, and begins to foam. It begins to accumulate. It begins to roar. A wave crests, black and horrible. Trees burst, boulders float, canyons fall. Less water than liquified earth, filled with every leaf and beetle and pebble from where it began, a combination as individual as a fingerprint. Put your hand in it and it'll rip the rings from your fingers; keep your hand in and it'll shed the skin from your bones. Knotted willow branches, rusted oil drums, foam coolers, backpacks, tents, beer cans. The frogs will navigate it, pushing along between the sticks. The fish, too. Don't worry about them. Worry about the way the flood will find any path it wants, through towns and homes, downhill or uphill. Its power does not care about your rules or theories, your laws or hope. The desert is flood and the flood is desert and there is nothing and no one that can stop it.

➤

Hank's dad, Jim, threw open every cabinet looking for the griddle. The storm sheeted itself against the windows, the panes buckling and rattling. Bea leaned against the fridge while the men wondered if skim milk was an appropriate substitute for buttermilk. Bea asked if Hank's dad needed any help. He said they needed syrup and when Bea offered to go get some from the store, the men all laughed. As if you're going anywhere, they said. As if it's not shitting rain out there. Her thumbnail was already destroyed to a jagged, raw edge, so Bea began on her cuticles, teeth gnawing at the skin until it became satisfyingly pulpy. Ever since she walked into the house, her thoughts were static, burnt from the drive. She was somehow still in Mercy, standing in this kitchen, watching as Hank's father mistook the salt for sugar. Her teeth moved to her pinkie nail. Tag shot her a few tentative glances, but she didn't meet them, preferring instead to stare into the middle distance, as if stunned. Since their arrival, the men seemed to have assumed there had been some dramatic confrontation between Christy and Bea, especially considering the broken nose, and all of them—Jim, especially—repeatedly asked if either woman was all right. Christy laughed them off, while Bea remained silent. She desperately wished she could smoke, but the men were right, the rain was relentless. Hank's dad whipped a batter, the tapping of the fork against the bowl like a second hand clicking forward, forward, forward.

Christy walked into the kitchen. The hollows under her mother's eyes had turned purple, her nose swollen and red, but Christy wore bright pink lipstick. She sang hello to them, shaking out her wet hair, and said she felt oodles better already. "You have incredible water pressure," Christy said. Jim's neck blotched and he asked if Christy liked blueberries. She didn't, which was good, he said, because they didn't have any. "I would die for a beer, though," Christy said. Jim quickly popped a Coors and nearly dropped the can as he handed it to her, Christy giving him her biggest smile, which made Bea sigh loudly enough for them to look over. "You want one, too?" Jim offered another can. Bea asked where the bathroom was. "Just around the corner," Tag responded, too quickly.

The bathroom was still damp from her mother's shower, the air heavy with Old Spice and industrial cleaner. There was no shower curtain and water was puddled around a matted gray towel on the floor. Bea stepped into the tub and pushed on the narrow window, but it was painted closed, rain and wind thrashing its thin, greasy pane. Bea sat down on the edge of the tub, water soaking her shorts.

The job interview was in less than thirty-six hours and across the country. The closest major airport was five and a half hours away. There was a flight leaving Salt Lake at eight the next morning that would get her to New York by the afternoon. The ticket was expensive, too expensive, but it would give her almost a full day in the city to prepare. More than enough time. Bea rubbed the crook of her neck, the burn from the seat belt raw and stinging. If only she could have a cigarette. From the other side of the door was laughter and talking and cooking. Bea was tired. Tired of appeasing her mother's every whim and idea, tired of doing the math, tired of it all. The weekend was over. This, all of this, was over. She'll never be back here, she told herself. She'll never do this again. She lit a cigarette, took a drag, waited, and when nothing happened, exhaled, letting it all go, eyes closed. She crawled into the tub and leaned back, savoring the sharp relief of the nicotine. From the other room, more laughing. The room quickly became thick with smoke and Bea didn't let herself care. Instead, she thought of her phone. She hadn't checked it since taking the photo of the storm clouds, hours ago, and out of pure, thoughtless habit, opened the app, which was how she saw the photo, the photo that made her choke, cigarette still in her mouth, which made her cough, and then she couldn't stop coughing.

Engaged. The man who could hardly bring himself to respond to a text message, to commit to a takeout order or position in bed, was suddenly committing himself for life to another person, a person he hadn't even posted about until this very announcement, an announcement that was identical to the one Carolyn posted, an act of embarrassing but respectable teamsmanship, proof of how they were both personally and publicly in sync. It was a surprisingly clichéd photo. They stood on the beach, perfectly backlit by a brackish, milky sunset. She covered her mouth with her hand while he knelt. The picture was taken too far away to see the ring, but it was no doubt huge and heirloom. There were dozens of comments under the post. The top one was from Grant, who posted a simple red heart. No caption. The location tag: *FOREVER*. The ocean, the sunset, the hand over the mouth. Bea put her fingertips to her lips, imagining, still coughing, and then burst into hoarse, crazed laughter.

A light knock on the bathroom door, the sound of Tag's voice, annoyed and serious. "Hey, Bea, no worries, Jim smokes, it wouldn't be a big deal if you went out back, but I guess the weather—what I'm saying is you really shouldn't—" Tag stammered. Bea threw the cigarette into the sink and turned on the tap. She swallowed a cough as she opened the door.

"What—are you okay?"

"Me?" Bea pointed at herself, hand gripping her phone. "Never been better."

"Really? Because you're, well, you're crying."

"Oh," Bea said. She touched her cheeks. They were wet.

"You sure you're okay?"

Bea tried to smile, but instead fell into a series of deep coughs. Snot poured from her nose. The sunset, the heart emoji. She wiped her nose with the back of her hand. "You know, I could use a beer."

"Okay." Tag nodded. "Sure." They walked back to the kitchen. Bea sat down next to her mother. Tag handed Bea a beer. Christy glanced at her, but Bea avoided the look, taking a long swig from the beer.

Hank suggested they try to find Bob that night, but Christy

didn't think they could. Not without her phone. "And I can't message him if he's banned."

"Banned?" Jim asked. "What does that mean?"

"There's a post," Hank said, holding up his phone. "On the Conversation."

"My nose is killing me," Christy said, an ice pack pressed to her face. "Read it aloud for us, Hank?"

Hank held up his phone for dramatic effect. The thread was short, written by MadMax, explaining why he was forced to ban NCGuy and OnlyBob. They had violated multiple Conversation policies so egregiously that the Poet himself specifically requested the ban, effective immediately. "I don't know why he would mention the Poet. Max knows that'll spark crazy conspiracy theories," Christy muttered, adjusting the ice pack. "Marshall's already saying NCGuy is the Poet. I'm sure KerriDigs is going to swoop in any minute and claim the treasure is a hoax like she always does."

Martha was the first comment after Grant, *ABOUT TIME,* followed by a dozen exclamation points. *BEEN WAITING FOR THIS DAY FOR YEARS.* Years. How long had she been going over to Grant's apartment? All the nights she asked him to join her out, but he'd never respond? Bea put her head in her hands. It was so obvious, it had always been so obvious. She laughed softly.

Christy shot her a scornful look. "It's not funny, the Conversation is going to be unusable for a week, maybe longer."

"For the best, don't you think," Bea said. She finished her beer and then took Christy's. *FOREVER. YEARS.* It would be an incredible wedding. Lavish, but tasteful. The photos would be everywhere. Christy would relish the news, would lecture about blood diamonds and how she always said Grant sounded like a total loser, which was true, her mother had always said that, but Bea couldn't let Christy win. Not like this, not here. Her mother's beer was warm. Bea didn't care. She drank.

"I didn't know people were poets these days," Jim said. He tried flipping a pancake, but half of it fell out of the skillet. He cursed.

"It's the treasure guy," Hank said. He pulled himself up to sit on the counter and scrolled his phone. "The one I told you about."

Jim grunted. "Met a few people who've come through town talking about things like that. Never seem to have any idea what they're doing."

"I think I know what I'm doing," Christy said coolly.

"I didn't mean any offense," Jim said. The skillet sizzled as he poured more batter into it, the kitchen filling with a yeasty warmth. "You seem smarter than most of those folks."

Bea opened her texts. She scrolled her contacts but realized, with hollow certainty, there was only one person who'd understand, and she was sitting next to her, explaining the origins of the Conversation.

"I've got a map and everything," her mother said.

Bea put down her phone. "Not anymore."

"Thanks for the reminder, honey." Christy turned toward Jim and with a wink said, "You know, I was pretty close to finding it, too."

"You were?" Jim asked.

"You saw the map," Christy said, squeezing Bea's forearm. "Tell him how close I was."

She pitied her mother sometimes, she really did. She could be, it was true, a real loser. "You weren't close at all."

"Yes, I was," her mother said, shoving Bea playfully.

Bea finished the beer and belched softly. "No, you have no idea where the treasure is. If you did, you'd have it by now, but you don't." Christy tried to interrupt, but Bea kept talking, her voice rising. "You know why? Because you didn't come here for treasure. You came here because you wanted to have a romantic weekend with your internet boyfriend, but he was just using you for a free hotel room and your research and now he's running around with some creepy asshole and your map. This was never about the treasure. Not that it matters, because there isn't a treasure out there to find. It's probably all some elaborate internet hoax started by some attention-starved guy, which, fine, it could be a fun game. But that's all it is. A game."

"Oh, honey," her mother sighed, "I knew you'd never understand."

That old feeling boiled in her gut, the same feeling she got when Gertie would call out to her, say how her mother was on the phone and Bea should be a good daughter and say hello, and when Bea refused, how Gertie would look at Bea, direct and cold, and tell Bea she'd regret it one day. "What exactly would I not understand? Do you understand you wouldn't be able to do any of this if I weren't paying your bills? If you had a job? Would I not understand that?" Bea was yelling now, standing. "How about, when are *you* going to understand that none of this is fucking real?" The room went quiet. Bea stared down at her mother, furious and waiting, while Christy pressed the ice pack at her nose, face blank.

Jim cleared his throat and slid a plate of lumpen pancakes onto the table between Bea and Christy. "Dinner's served," he said, a little too loudly. "Hank, be a gentleman and get the butter out of the fridge. You ladies prefer to eat them with forks or with your hands? Me, I like to grab and gobble." He demonstrated, using both hands to shove a pancake into his mouth.

Tag stood at the window. The rain was nearly gone, its pattering now faint. There was lightning, but it was farther away. "You know, these storms usually head north. If you left now, you'd be following it the entire way back to Salt Lake," he said. "We have plenty of room here, right, Jim?"

"Oh, you ladies are welcome to stay and ride out the storm," Jim said quickly. "I can get the inflatable mattress all set up."

Christy's face softened into a smile. "You know what? That would be lovely," she said, her tone cheerful. Seeing the way that Jim brightened when Christy said this, clearly thrilled, Bea knew he'd let her mother overstay her welcome, let her do whatever she wanted, and expect nothing in return. Bea's scalp prickled with fury. Yet again, her mother would move through life without any care or need for things like rent or bills or responsibility. Christy didn't even ask Bea before saying yes, she probably didn't even care if Bea stayed. Bea opened her phone browser and scrolled to the most expensive option, first class leaving in twelve hours, and clicked Purchase. "I can't," Bea said. "I have a flight in the morning."

Christy picked up a pancake and began to eat it. "You're leaving?" she said evenly.

"Tomorrow's Monday," Bea sneered. "I have to get back to work."

Her mother began to butter the pancake, smearing a thick slab of butter across its golden crust. She turned to the men. "Do you know

Bea used to answer emails on Christmas morning? Her grandmother and I would be making hot chocolate and she'd be on her laptop yelling, Five more minutes! That's all I need! Just give me five more minutes!" Christy held up her hand and wiggled her fingers. "On Christmas morning. Can you imagine?" Hank's dad chuckled along politely, but he was the only one. Christy bit into the limp, wet cake and chewed slowly. She turned to Bea. "You've been with me for nearly a month and I've barely seen your laptop. I don't think you even brought it here, did you?" Bea didn't respond. Christy sniffed. "You know, I was beginning to think you didn't have a job anymore."

Hank pointed his beer at Bea. "Didn't you say you were fired?" he asked.

"I wasn't fired," Bea said quickly. Her mother watched her, chewing slowly. Bea swallowed, set her jaw. "I quit."

At this, her mother laughed, mean and loud and long. "Honey, I love you, but you'd never quit."

Bea pushed away from the table. She didn't have to be here. She shouldn't be here. "Thank you for dinner, Jim, but I should get going." When her mother didn't immediately move, Bea added, not unkindly, "I'm leaving."

"Oh yeah?" Christy asked lightly. She held up the car keys. "Don't know where you're going without these." Bea leaned over to take them, but her mother balled them in her fist. "You've drank an entire beer and most of mine and the weather's terrible."

"I—" Bea started.

"Sit down," Christy said quietly but firmly. "You'll make your flight. I'll drive. But I'm not going anywhere until I finish these pancakes."

Outside, the desert was quiet, waterlogged and bloated. The good-byes were cursory and quick, though Jim insisted on hugs, which meant Tag's arms were around Bea again. The moment was awkward, the two of them shuffling and halting, and Christy smirked as she watched. They had no idea how obvious they were, but wasn't that how it always was. "You got everything?" Jim asked.

"Missing a few things, but nothing we can't live without," she said.

"And your nose?" he asked.

"Just a dull throb." He was a nice man, Christy thought. Pity to have to leave so soon.

"We'll let you know if we see Bob in town," Tag said, but Christy shook her head.

"Don't bother. Good riddance."

"You let us know when you get home safe!" Jim yelled. The men waved as Christy pulled out of the driveway and Christy waved back. Bea silently stared ahead. Christy drove quietly for a bit, sticking to the speed limit, drifting the car around the lakes of rainwater that had formed in the road. The air was muggy, almost foggy, and the Chrysler's headlights were two weak beams into the night. She didn't regret confronting her daughter at the table and pointing out the obvious, but if her daughter was truly leaving, Christy didn't want these last hours to be tense and combative. Better to swallow her pride, treasure the time they had left. Who knew when Bea would be back, if ever. "I'm sorry about your job," she said.

"It's fine," Bea said. And then after a moment, added, "I have a job interview on Tuesday."

"That's great. Do you think you'll get it?"

Bea shifted her weight and the passenger seat squeaked. "I do," she said quietly.

"Good for you," Christy said, and meant it.

"If you really think you know . . ." her daughter began, though the thought tapered off, not fully formed. Christy stopped for longer than necessary at an intersection, not wanting to interrupt. Bea sniffed and then continued. "Why didn't we go try to find it on our hike on Friday? Why waste all this time with Bob?"

The question surprised Christy, but she hid this. "Because I'm not sure exactly where it is. That's why I needed him. He knows the desert better than me, how to read the land and such. At least, that's what he claimed." Christy thought of the boy, how he walked out from the canyons with arrogance and ease. He probably knew the land, young enough to hike for hours, happy to camp and climb. Bob didn't just need Christy, she realized, he needed the boy, too. But she wasn't going to admit this to her daughter, not yet.

"Were you going to split the treasure with him?"

"That was the plan. Though I guess we didn't really talk about it in specifics. Had to find it first, you know? But he seemed like a fair guy."

"He's a thief and a liar."

"True," Christy said. And then, with a chuckle, "But aren't we all?" She drove through town, the grocery and grill both dark. There was no light on in the hotel lobby. "They're good guys, Tag and

Hank. I hope you keep in touch." Christy lightened her tone. "And if Hank's father ever accepts how he's gone bald, he wouldn't be half bad, don't you think? A little rough around the edges, a little shy in a weird way, but a good guy. But I swear to god, I've never had such salty pancakes before. They were so salty! Completely inedible. Why are you laughing? I'm serious."

Bea pointed out the window. "Turn here," she said.

"Here?"

"Just trust me."

Christy turned. She drove past industrial garages until they got to a fence. "Are we supposed to be here?"

"Since when do you care?"

Christy killed the engine. "I thought you had a plane to catch."

"We have to get the aspen," Bea said simply. Christy didn't totally understand, but she didn't question it. They parked in front of a gate, and Christy got out of the car and followed Bea into the dark.

Don't blame yourself. Everyone believes it. You thought numbers were absolute, objective, real. You thought quantifiable meant actual. You thought laws were facts. You thought you could know what happened next. You thought a lot of things, but mostly, you thought there was such a thing as control.

Sure, the clues were all there: the southerly wind shift, the approaching high-pressure system, a moisture surge after a long, dry hot spell, the accumulation of low, smeary stratocumulus. The sunset was too beautiful, bloodred and blazing. You had noticed how the air turned, the breeze bloated and chilled. You watched it happen in the car, you felt it as you hugged Tag. But it was far-off, literally on the horizon. You thought it was normal. You thought it was fine. Mostly, you didn't think about it at all.

There were times at the desk when you and Phil were so certain in your predictions, he'd quiz you. He'd roll his chair up next to yours and lean in, close enough for you to smell his floral fabric softener, telling you to pull up the latest report draft in your inbox, please. "Heavy fall rain, an advancing pressure system with freezing temps, and squeezed reserves," he recited, finger following each of his data points. You'd ask which crop while noting a missing period. "Ukrainian rapeseed and wheat." You'd scroll to the average area temperature and precipitation models, pretending to scan them, while he'd look at you, waiting. "Bull," you'd say. "Bull," he'd agree with a nod, satisfied. He'd scoot back to his monitors, you'd add the period, fix a few typos, and then send the forecast to the desk. And it'd be right: widespread winterkill, skyrocketing food prices, entire continents scrambling for reserves, Midwestern farmers lining their pockets. The firm earned thousands, their clients even more. Phil thanked you for editing, the traders thanked Phil. You'd treat yourself to an extra Diet Coke, nothing too crazy, because the forecast wasn't crazy, it was simple and straightforward, so much so you could do it in your sleep, and you periodically did. Dreams of drought and die-off and jet streams and typhoons, so mundane you'd wake bored and rested.

Easy to think when none of it was real. Millions—billions—of dollars predicated on futures that a few hundred overstimulated blue bloods have decided will happen. Sure, the conclusions were material: flying cross-country gets a little cheaper, bacon becomes shockingly pricey, and no one in Europe will want a Japanese car. But storing excess barrels of crude oil, cremating millions of mysteriously sick piglets, or piloting container ships through hundred-foot waves around the Cape? Not your problem. Your problem was the future, and the future never came, not really, because by the time Aug hedges arrived, you were already looking to Dec of next year, to the next play, the next trade.

It wasn't like you didn't think about it. You thought about it all the time. The rank subway platform humidity of summer, the umbrella-less downpours of spring, the stupid leafy sunshine of fall, the filthy, endless slush of winter. But at the office, the weather was a supporting character. Which made you and Phil the same, a role that weird, quiet Phil was more than happy to fill. You, too, but only to a point, and we already discussed that. The thing was, the derecho was supposed to be no more real to you than those barrels or piglets or ships. A distant data point in a constellation of models and algorithms and spreadsheets. Get the math right, get the numbers right, and you'll always be good, right?

Wrong.

Everything was different and you should've known. The springs had become streams, swollen with runoff and mud, the ground wrinkled in parabolic layers of silt and trash. There was no aspen, gone downstream forever, the juniper bush you planted it near also gone. You were lost, disoriented. Even the smell had changed, the sulfur undercut with something saltier and sharper that made your eyes water and sting. There were logs and gnarled branches looming around, a couple tires, a ripped tent, a slide from a child's play set, but it was the truck that made your heart jolt. Black and battered, its hood pointed to the sky, jutting upward like a breaching whale, its bed ripped away, gone. You walked toward it. There was no one in the cab, only a thick, dark layer of clay. Maybe the flood pushed it here, maybe it was already abandoned, but the engine was hot and clicking. You made your way around, your mother asking what you were doing, and you weren't sure, but you couldn't stop.

It wasn't until you were behind the truck, scanning the horizon, that you saw it. It was a couple dozen yards away, dark and curled, as if cowering. You shouted out to it, but only your mother replied. She didn't think this was a good idea. She didn't think you should go any farther. "I think we should leave it alone," she said, following behind you. "It might be a cow or deer or something."

But it wasn't a cow. It wasn't a deer. It was an animal, though. The closer you got, the more the night dissipated and the clearer it became, the matted fur, the quivering haunches. You took another few steps until the dog looked up at you, its black eyes wide and wet. It whined weakly and began to pant, its tongue a long pink petal. You crouched down and began to whisper the first things that came to mind, like, it's going to be okay, and why did I wear sandals, and holy shit. Your mother, meanwhile, yelled at you to get away from it. The dog gingerly tried to stand up, but its back paw was bent at an awkward angle, and it stumbled and fell. It cried. You got closer, your mother told you not to, it might bite, she yelled, but you held out your hand, its nose stretching toward your fingertips. You moved closer and it licked your hand, tail thumping against the mud.

It could've ended there. It should've ended there, but it didn't. It never does.

This is how it happens: There is a cheap orange collar but no tags. The dog is relieved, happy, shoving its snout into your belly. You let it lick your face. It shoves its snout into you again. It whines. Your mother says the aspen is probably gone. You ask the dog what, what is it? It looks behind, beyond, and cries. Your mother joins you. You follow the dog's gaze, eyes adjusting to the murk. You don't see it at first, but then. A single bare foot, a clenched hand. Your brain goes blank, and all you can feel is how small and knobby your mother's fingers are as they grip your shoulder, how warm your mother's breath is against your neck, and then, as she looks where you're looking, you feel how loudly, how deeply she screams. You do not scream. You do not blink. The soaked jeans, the battered skull, the torn flannel. The neck twisted back onto itself, the vacant, yellowed eyes. The mustache still, impossibly, curled. The mouth opened, but only slightly, as if he were deep in thought, deciding. You recognize him in a slow tide, his name surrounding you slowly and then all at once, and then the world goes tilted, your mother still screaming, screaming: Bob.

His name was Clayton Woods. The boy. They never found him. His wallet was inside the cab of the destroyed truck, but there was no other trace of him, no social media accounts or credit cards. The police said without a body, it was an open case. "His name is on the news," they said. "If someone knows he's all right, hopefully they'll reach out. Or he might himself. We just don't know." He could be gone, he could be anywhere. A mother across the country hung up when called, saying he was no son of hers. No record of a father. The driver's license had an address for a Lizard Lick Road in Zebulon, North Carolina; the internet revealed it to be a high-fenced property next to a Dollar General. Mail went unanswered. Messaging him on the Conversation was out of the question, the NCGuy account long banned, and no account reappeared with quite the same bravado. Tag called the dog Woody out of respect, though in the years to come they'd say they named her after Guthrie.

To everyone's surprise, Bob had a wife and twin daughters. They came to Mercy in the days afterward, a seemingly prim, redheaded hydra that nonetheless demonstrated a vehement group passion for karaoke, primarily Shania Twain, which they sang with a surprising tenderness, dedicating their performances to Bob. They didn't stay in town for long, just enough to identify the body and stand in the background during a press conference. Christy couldn't help but introduce herself as an internet friend of Bob's to his wife, Maxine, whom she found charming despite herself. Maxine admitted to a deep expertise in herbal dyes and gave Christy a lovely lavender-gray silk scarf. As she handed it over, she motioned at Christy's bruised face. "It'll draw attention away," she said stiffly. Christy told everyone she couldn't think of a nicer gift, but no one believed her.

Bob's funeral was held in Reno, and even though Hank offered to drive, none of them ultimately made it out. Bea became haunted by this choice, convinced for years that going would have relieved the ongoing nightmares of discovering his body, but at the time it seemed respectful to keep a distance. Better to remain the one who called and not explain the rest.

Christy didn't feel any guilt about not going to Bob's funeral. She figured there was no need to embarrass Maxine, the woman having chosen to believe Christy when Christy said she was just another believer on the treasure forum. Instead, Christy eulogized the man the best way she knew how: in a post on the Conversation. She announced Bob's passing a week after the storm, how he died doing what he loved best, that officials believed it had been a swift and merciful death, likely a heart attack. She did not mention how she found the body, or where it was found. She did not mention the boy or the lighter, the lighter that's still in her purse, the lighter she hopes to give back one day. Instead, she mentioned how Bob loved a good steak and a cold beer and an excellent hunt. He was known to be smart and fair on the Conversation. She knew he loved the desert. She knew he'd be missed. She knew he'd want them to remember him as the passionate hunter he was, and she knew he wouldn't be forgotten. After all, he was the Conversation's first death-by-hunt.

The response was immediate. People gave the anodyne respects, the so sorry to hears and the RIPs, but they also expressed shock. *Died?* While treasure hunting? Surely the Poet wouldn't hide the treasure somewhere that dangerous. Surely he would never mean for someone to hurt themselves. Cal1993 once fractured an ankle on a hunt, and there was the infamous time NoBoneJones slipped down a ravine trying to dodge a black bear and lived to tell the tale, but those were all part of the lore of the wilderness. Can't hunt without getting a little dirty. Still, no one attempted a solve without doing their homework or consulting the Conversation first. They prided themselves on being meticulous, not reckless. The thread bulged with anxious explanations and justifications, each one more ridiculous than the next. One commenter asked, not unseriously, does that mean dying is the most amateur move of them all? Amateur! Bob! Never! There was cursing and insults, threats of revealing true identities, but no mention of NCGuy. After less than a day, MadMax locked the thread, OUT OF RESPECT FOR BOB.

Christy claimed she saw none of it. A week after the flood, Christy still didn't have a phone or tablet, so Bea let Christy use hers. Christy published the post and then logged out, wiping her hands clean of it all. With Bob and the map gone, the claws of the hunt were no longer in her. Her brain was lighter and looser than it'd been in a long time, longer than she could remember, which meant not much past Gertie's death. There was space for something else.

She wasn't worried about much, not even how many times her landlord had called Bea's phone that day when he couldn't reach Christy, how he left a voicemail saying they had twenty-four hours to clear out the house in Salt Lake, threatening to trash anything they left behind. He had many nephews, he kept saying, and they all played college baseball. Athletes, he said.

In the meantime, Christy was busy realizing Hank's father had qualities that redeemed his pancake-making abilities. Jim loved jazz piano, but only knew how to play the ukulele. He and Hank's mother had gone to Hawaii for their honeymoon, he explained sheepishly, and he brought one back to Utah with him. He drank beer at all hours and didn't own nail clippers, but he said Christy could stay with him for as long as she needed. For the past week, he had slept on the couch. She slept in his bed, which smelled like ashy sweat.

She was intrigued. She deleted the landlord's voicemails and told herself she'd mention them to her daughter later.

They all reconvened at the grill the day Christy made her post, Bea taking her phone back from her mother to read it. Bea found it overly sentimental and complimentary, but she kept that to herself. There was no good way to explain how the old guy you found mud-mangled in a ditch was, at his core, an asshole. In any case, there was a more interesting link that caught her eye. "The Poet wrote about Bob," she announced to the table.

The Poet was equally glorifying and dismissive of Bob, how he was one of the first accounts on the Conversation, how the Poet always enjoyed Bob's theories, how Bob was always insightful and canny about the "ways of the wild." "And it was the wild, in the end, that decided to take him home," Bea read aloud. "He died doing what he loved, where he loved. May we all remember him with respect, though also with caution. The wild is wild for a reason, the desert more wild than most. Though is there a more beautiful resting place? Thank you for letting the community know, ChristineM. The hunt goes on."

"But Bob's buried in Reno," Hank said flatly. It was early, just before the dinner rush. Bea and Christy and Jim were huddled in a booth, eating burgers. Hank refilled their waters. "Christy listed details about the funeral in her post."

Christy shoved a few fries into her mouth. "The Poet doesn't read the Conversation."

"He thanked you by name," Bea said, showing her the screen. "You're famous."

"Username," Christy corrected. "Jim, could you pass the ketchup, please?" Hank's father handed over the Heinz.

"Do you think the Poet went to the funeral?" Hank asked.

"I mean, Bob died looking for his money," Bea said. "Feels only right."

Christy sniffed, annoyed. "I don't think there's any point talking about it. I'm no longer part of the Conversation." Bea watched as her mother squeezed a heaping, spiraling pile of ketchup directly over her fries, an exact mirror of Jim's plate. Christy began to ask Jim about his various arm tattoos. Was the mermaid from the Hawaii honeymoon, too?

"This one?" Jim asked, pulling up his shirtsleeve.

"Oh, I haven't seen that one yet," Christy cooed. Bea pulled up her texts. ETA? she sent.

Tag responded immediately. about to leave st george. already has a buyer in mind, some big luxury developer who saw the bob stuff on the news. going to be $$$$

wow! would you still be a manager?

not sure, but they liked how i knew the area.
has woody gone out?

yup

thx. i'll be back in a few hours.

meet me at the springs?

where else

Bea smiled despite herself. She responded with drive safe, which felt reasonable, but once the text delivered, read as dumb and needy. Bea chose and then deleted multiple emojis before putting her phone down. It'd been too easy, too quick: how comfortable she'd gotten drinking Tag's weak instant coffee, how happy she was taking the dog on long walks, how satisfying it was to easily open the trailer's sticky door. It'd only been a week. She couldn't trust it, she thought. It couldn't be sustainable. They had until that weekend to clear out the house in Salt Lake. The recruiter had stopped sending confused emails asking if she wanted to reschedule the interview. Her subletter posted a photo of her old bedroom, now unrecognizable, its walls painted a pink-and-green checkerboard, her dresser a fluorescent yellow: *living life in FULL COLOR!!!!!* There was nothing new posted from Grant or Carolyn or Martha, though Bea wouldn't know, having blocked them on all her social media feeds. None of it seemed to matter anymore. She'd wake up with Tag and Woody curled up on either side of her, warm and heavy and snoring, and she'd carefully pick her way out of bed, ducking under the trailer's upper cabinets and starting a pot of hot water on the two-burner, the light pinking, hot air already seeping in from the window's weak seal, and she'd think of everything she left behind in New York and Salt Lake and how she'd eventually need to deal with it all, the credit cards and the leases, but she'd gaze out across the junipers and sagebrush and think: Not yet.

Tag, Bea, and Hank had spent every day since the storm at the springs, clearing out the debris and trash. It'd been dry and sunny since the flood, the piles of thorny scrub and gnarled logs becoming brittle. Tag hired a tow to handle the largest items, including the mangled pickup truck. It had become cemented into the hardened mud, its twisted back bumper submerged in a small hot spring. No amount of pulling from the tow would dislodge it. "Got to wait until the next rain," Hank said, shrugging. The desert had quickly, hurriedly burst into color since the storm, speckled with bright green and yellow and purple and red. Shrubs became impassable with leafy growth, the ground littered with tiny, delicate blooms. Bea found a clump of tall, spiked red flowers near the bluff where the aspen was. She picked a few stalks and tucked them under the truck's windshield wipers.

The morning after the flood, a local news cameraman shot B-roll of the pickup until Tag came over and told him to stop. Disrespectful, he said. The cameraman scoffed, said it was the best shot. The sheriff agreed. Have to show people how powerful these storms can be, he said. They placed the newscaster in front of the truck. Even Maxine was cheerfully apathetic about it. The sheriff would know best, she said. The day after the news segment ran, Vera called Tag. She wanted everything out of the area. Get the springs exactly like they were before, she demanded. Tag didn't question her, he wanted the same thing, but they'd never be the same as they were. They had shifted, smeared outside their previous footprints into steaming, unfamiliar eddies. Some had become long, skinny pools, while others had disappeared completely, soft divots among the trash and dirt. "Unrecognizable," Tag said, which Bea believed, because when it was time to go home, she and Woody would search for him in the dark and find him staring at a random patch of ground, face blank and still.

Hank was creeped out by the area. "Bad vibes," he said as they bagged trash and loaded it onto Tag's truck. Tag would remind him that the coroner believed Bob drowned miles upstream, and in any case, it was Bea who found the guy, and she's fine. "I'm fine," Bea would echo. But Hank couldn't be convinced. "Bad, bad vibes." After the area was mostly cleaned up, Hank started making excuses. Tired from work. Jim needed him at home. Sore shoulder. Most nights, Tag and Bea were alone as they cleared the remaining pools, bagging garbage and clearing debris. There weren't many actual pools left, the flood smearing most beyond their bounds, but Tag piled rocks around one of the deeper springs to define it. He dug a shallow drain off to the side. "To let the bad stuff run off," he explained, though Bea hadn't asked. For her, the work itself was what helped the bad stuff—the hand, the screams, the eyes—drain out of her mind. She couldn't help the dreams, but spending the days cleaning with Tag gave her an unquestionable sense of purpose. More than anything, she looked forward to when she'd sit with Tag on the edge of the pools they made and they'd soak their feet together. Even when the sunset was weak and quick, even when Woody hunted a jackrabbit, the poor thing screaming in the dog's mouth, Tag would say something about how it was one of the best weeks he'd had in a long time. "This?" Bea would ask, almost laughing, and Tag would lightly touch Bea's thigh and say, what else.

Jim paid for their burgers. Christy, seeing the check, gave him a disgusted look, but Jim shrugged. "No rent means no tip," he said. Christy scoffed. She pulled a ten-dollar bill out of her wallet and waved Hank over. "What are you doing?" Jim asked.

"What you won't." Christy handed Hank the money. "Here you go, hon."

Hank hesitated. "Take it," Christy insisted. He did.

"When's Tag back?" Hank asked Bea, avoiding his father's glare.

"Not for another couple of hours, but I'm meeting him at the springs. Want to come?"

"Nope," Hank said.

"You know what, I'd like to go to the hot springs," Christy said. "I haven't been since—" She paused. "I'd like to see what you've done with the place."

"There's not much to see," Bea said.

"I won't know until I go," she said.

Jim pulled himself out of the booth and held out a hand to Christy. "We got plans, missy. I rented us *Mission: Impossible*. Bought us fancy popcorn, too. Stovetop."

"Not tonight, Jim," Christy said, a hand lightly on his arm. He looked at the hand, and after a quiet moment, said he'd leave the front door open for her. Christy gave him a small nod and he left.

Bea said she'd have to go grab the Chrysler keys from the trailer, but her mother said not to bother. "We'll walk."

"It's boiling out."

"You're not used to it already?"

They crossed the parking lot and Bea immediately began to sweat. "You really want to walk?" Bea asked. Christy held up a paper bag and pulled out two beer cans. "Hank snuck me something to keep us cool," she said, cracking one. Bea hesitated, glancing at the passing cars. "Oh, c'mon. Jim's cousin is the sheriff." Christy held out a can.

It'd been a long, hot day, and though it was beginning its slow downward crawl, the sun was still strong. Bea and Christy made their way down the road. The cold beer tasted, admittedly, glorious.

The dirt road was more pronounced now, tire tracks deep and obvious from her and Tag's daily visits. Vera installed a bigger, more fortified fence. Tag bought NO TRESPASSING signs but hadn't hung them yet. Christy paused next to the fencing and knelt down, elbows on her knees. "We waited for the police here, didn't we?" They had. The flashback of those horrible minutes, how quiet her mother had been, the dog frantically panting at their feet, when Bea couldn't stop saying how it must've been an accident, how it was going to be okay, but her mother didn't respond, merely stood next to Bea in the dark, Christy's face bruised and bloodied, vacant and pale, for a haunted, desperate moment, it felt like time had inverted, that this wasn't her mother but some terrible ghost. The memory froze Bea in place, gripping her by the throat, but Christy was unfazed. Her mother walked through the fence and over to the closest pool. "Looks great," Christy said over her shoulder. A pause, and then she motioned toward the truck. "Was that his?"

"Yeah," Bea said, coming back to herself. "The guy's. Clayton's."

Christy nodded. Her mother's face was better, healing, though she still had deep purple rings under each eye. Christy pointed toward the distant bluff. "We found him out over there?"

"Do you want to go over?" Bea asked gently.

"No need," Christy said. She sipped her beer. "You know, the rumor of hot springs was always one of the main reasons Bob and I wanted to come to Mercy. I wasn't sure where they were, only knew they were around." Her mother knelt and reached out a hand toward the closest stream, stopping just before her fingertips went in. "You swim in them?"

Bea paused. "No, not since the flood. Tag and I sit on the edge of that one over there, but only to soak our feet."

"This one?" Christy walked over and dropped her bag. She was pulling her shirt off when Bea asked what she was doing. Her mother laughed. "What does it look like?"

"There might be things still in there, trash and things, I don't know if it's safe."

"Suit yourself." Christy unhooked her bra, pulled off her shorts, and got into the water. "Feels great," she sighed.

There was no one else but her and her mother. Why not?

Bea got into the water. The water was like the night with Tag, the warmth and the smell, but the daylight made it clearer, less surreal. Things had changed, sure, but they always did. Bea lifted her beer. "To Bob," she said solemnly. And then, because she felt like she should, she added, "He was a good guy."

Christy snorted. "No, he wasn't." Christy raised her beer. "To family. To Gertie."

They cheered. They drank. The sun went behind a thin cloud, enough that the water dulled its glittering. They floated for a few minutes, the water gurgling. Bea closed her eyes. Her legs buoyed, hand cold against the can, the other hand light and fluttering against the current. The sun came back out, but Bea didn't squint.

"What are you thinking?" her mother asked.

"How we need to get back to Salt Lake," Bea said. "All our stuff is there."

"It is."

"We should leave first thing in the morning."

"We could."

"We should."

"We don't have to."

Bea snorted. "What about your plants?"

Christy's open palm pushed the water around in small, tight circles. "I'll tell the landlord to give them to the Zs. I think their fake snakes would like them. Anyway, I like it here."

"Jim?"

"He's kind."

"And doesn't charge rent."

"Neither does Tag," Christy said, and Bea smiled in spite of herself. "Jim knows the people who own the grocery store. I always liked bagging things. It's real life Tetris. Plus, you know I'd be great at keeping an eye out for any sticky fingers. And Hank said I could work a few bartender shifts. Forget Salt Lake. That landlord's going to keep the security deposit no matter what we do. The chef is trying out the new special tomorrow night. Green chile enchiladas. I'm not missing that."

Bea looked over at her mother. Christy's curls hung heavy around her face, a face that was soft and wrinkled and a little bit serious. Bea took her mother's hand and went for a hug, but as she pulled Christy toward her, they slipped on the rocks and mud, one of the cans falling into the water, the other still aloft, both women splashing and kicking, the air thick with sulfur and clay and sage and shrieks and laughs, the sun weaving in and out of the steam, more laughing, loud enough for a lizard to skitter out from the edge of the pool and hop off into the scrub, both beer cans bobbing in the muddied water, hot and bubbling, their fingers pushing hair out of their faces, water dribbling from their mouths. You all right? I'm all right. Did you feel that? What? There was something down there, something metal, I stubbed my toe against it. Where? Down at the bottom. It's probably trash. You sure? Maybe not. It was pretty big. Here, hold me while I reach for it.

Acknowledgments

The book's epigraph is from *The Quick and the Dead* by Joy Williams; Part One's epigraph is from *The Last Cheater's Waltz: Beauty and Violence in the Desert Southwest* by Ellen Meloy; and Part Three's epigraph is from *The Best of Edward Abbey*, edited by the man himself. The book Tag reads on the beach is inspired by a biography of Everett Ruess, long out of print.

Mercy is a fictional town, drawn from my experiences in and around the Grand Staircase-Escalante National Monument. Any errors regarding meteorology, desert geology, and commodities trading are for the sake of the story.

This book wouldn't exist without the archives of the Salt Lake City Library and Park City Library, as well as the rigorous journalism of *High Country News* and *The Salt Lake Tribune*. I'm also indebted to all the activists working to protect Utah public lands, particularly the Southern Utah Wilderness Alliance. The work of these local institutions and organizations is more essential than ever.

Thank you to Forrest Fenn, whose treasure hunt I discovered during an insomnia-induced internet search in 2017, and who inspired me to write my own. Though there are some broad similarities between the two hunts, the Poet and Conversation are fictional. Nonetheless, I hope this book inspires readers to appreciate and explore the wilds of the American West, just as Fenn's did.

Unending thanks to Meredith Kaffel Simonoff, whose brilliance guided me through multiple drafts and timelines, and who championed this book with such tremendous enthusiasm and grace. It is a gift of a lifetime to work with you, and I am so grateful. And to everyone at Gernert, especially Nora Gonzalez, Rebecca Gardner, and Will Roberts, for their tireless support.

To Allie Merola, whose genius and patience was a godsend. Thank you for the rambling phone calls, the laughter, and the insights. The book and I are both better because of you. Thank you, too, to Sonia Gadre for all your help. I'm sorry I send so many emails. Thank you to Elizabeth Yaffe for the dazzling cover. And to Emily Fishman and Anna Brill and everyone at Viking: It's been a dream.

To the Lighthouse Writers Workshop, most especially Andrea Dupree and Paula Younger and Alexander Lumans, where I first dared to write fiction seriously and, in turn, was taken seriously. Thank you for fostering such an inclusive and invaluable community.

To everyone at Louisiana State University, where the earliest glimmers of this book began. Thank you to Laura and Dana, for being a home away from home. To Jennifer S. Davis, for your tireless advocacy for me and the program. To Emily Nemens, for being such a generous mentor and friend. To MK Brake, my ride-or-die: Look at us now. And to Alicia Diaz Dennis and Mary Pappalardo: Here's to all the late nights, all the music, all the laughter. You two were the first to believe in this book, and I wouldn't have kept going without you.

To my past colleagues at Catapult/Counterpoint Press/Soft Skull

Press and all the authors and booksellers I worked with along the way: Thank you for the all the inspiring work you do for the writing and reading communities. To Jenn Kovitz and Dory Athey and Dustin Kurtz, for taking a chance on me. And to Colin Drohan, for your early reads, and for all the jokes.

To Allie Diehl, Peter McCormack, Denali Johnson, Nikki Pond, Paige Cross, and Olivia Boone: Thank you for everything, always and forever.

To Juniper, whose walks solved some of this book's trickiest problems. You're my best girl.

To Mom and Dad: Thank you for instilling a lifelong love of reading and the outdoors, and for supporting all of my wild treasure hunts with such deep love and patience. And to Meg and Brian: Thank you for being my first and favorite friends, and for always keeping me laughing and humbled.

To Peter, my greatest treasure. You came into this world at the same time as this book, twin dreams come true. Being your mother is the happiest adventure of my life.

Finally, to Brett. Thank you for giving me the support and space I need to write. Thank you for being my heart and my home. With you, the hunt ended. I love you.